Never Seen the Stars

Never Seen the Stars

KATE KORSH

SCHOLASTIC PRESS / NEW YORK

Library of Congress Cataloging-in-Publication Data available

ISBN 978-1-5461-3164-9

10 9 8 7 6 5 4 3 2 1 25 26 27 28 29
Printed in Italy 208

First edition, November 2025
Book design by Cassy Price

For the boys our little town lost too soon: Pete V., James, and Jason

CHAPTER 1

I've changed my mind about going to Mason's funeral, switched my mental RSVP from "yes" to "I'd rather chew glass." Now that the day has arrived and I'm sitting in the passenger seat next to my mom on the way to the church, going through the awkward and depressing motions of it all feels impossible. I don't trust myself not to underreact or overreact or both, since I know nothing about funerals except what I've seen on TV.

And who cares if I skip it? Not Mason. He'll never know the difference if I'm there or not. That's the worst part. This whole thing isn't even for him. It's for all of us ridiculous humans left behind, for us to have a *shared experience* (I just threw up a little in my mouth), or, more likely, just to prove to each other that we're not so self-centered that we would skip a friend's funeral.

So I can't really pretend I don't know who cares if I show my face. Asha cares, and the rest of our friends care, and Mason's family double extra cares with a cherry on top. Shit. I'm going to have to see Mason's family. I can't.

But it's too late. Maybe I could have pulled the rip cord back at the house, but I didn't, and so here we are, pulling into the church parking lot. Any change in itinerary now would strike my mom as *abnormal* and require being peppered with questions. Even hanging in the car for a few more minutes, listening to the radio and feeling regular instead of severe and silent, would earn me a question storm from her. One of my friends has died. Mom's going to have a magnifying glass on me pretty much forever.

"Here we are," she says. I push myself from the car like I'm attached to a bungee cord and I'm jumping off a bridge, like maybe I'll survive but everything under my skin will be jerked so hard it'll get rearranged. We join the flow of people walking in the crisp fall sunshine toward the front door, our footsteps crunching on leaves scattered across the sidewalk. St. Brigit's is as imposing as ever, as massive as a cathedral, with three high spires of white, sparkly stone. In our rural town filled with one- and two-story buildings, the church feels out of place, like someone wearing a prom dress to the drugstore. I like it, though. Everything about church is boring; might as well give us some interesting architecture to look at to pass the time.

I always used to forget that Mason was part of our congregation, because he never went to Mass. No idea how he got away with that. At the time, my only reaction was to be envious of his ability to be so persuasive with his parents. But now I realize I could have asked him to come with me. Sundays would have been so much more tolerable if we could have sat together, wordlessly sizing up the weird sweaters that the cantor always wore, Mason's signature raised eyebrow saying paragraphs. But would my mom have even let me sit with him? Even if she didn't, just having him in the pew across the aisle would have improved the whole church experience by several stars. How simple and solved everything would be if I could just see him in that pew right now.

But he won't be anywhere in the church, even though this whole thing is for him. He's skipping his own funeral. How fully textbook Mason. An unexpected chuckle bubbles out of me, and my mom gives me a sharp look. I meet her eyes with an innocent smile as we approach the entrance. Magnifying glass.

I hang back in the vestibule because the light is so low I'm afraid I might step on someone's foot in the middle of their grieving. That would be bad form. It seems darker than usual. Can't they turn the dimmer switches up a little? This is a funeral, for chrissake, not a haunted house.

Inching forward, I almost collide with the marble basin full of holy water, so I stall there to let my eyes adjust more, blessing myself repeatedly to buy time. The air in the vestibule is warm and thick with incense. It's weird to me that church smells the same as the backpack of that kid at school who always has a knit pouch full of weed around his neck. What do they call that when things don't match up in your head? Cognitive dissonance? Whatever it is, it's happening to me a lot today.

My mom gets impatient and takes my arm, pulling me inside the church itself. Down the long aisle, the coffin sits prominently on the altar, which is as bright as the beach compared to the rest of the church, and there are two ostentatious flower arrangements on either side of the wooden box. God, Mason would hate those flowers. He would hate it all. He'd smirk his sarcastic smile that basically never left his face and roll his eyes. But again, it doesn't matter. Coffin's empty. He's not here.

Mason drowned. He shouldn't have been kayaking by himself, especially not at night with no life jacket, and *especially* because he had epilepsy, but Mason did a lot of things you shouldn't do with epilepsy, like skip his medication, drink beer, stay up all night, etc. Maybe that's why he had been having more seizures. His "fuck it" attitude resulted in him really truly fucking it.

The day it happened, his parents came back to their lake house after an evening out and couldn't find him. He wasn't in his usual place in front of his computer. He wasn't anywhere in the house. Set on a steep wooded slope next to Seneca Lake, upstate New York's deepest and coldest Finger Lake, the house wasn't within walking distance of anything. So they called all his friends, who knew nothing. Well, I shouldn't say *all* his friends. They didn't call me. Thinking about it irks me all over again, because my brain can somehow manage to be petty in the most inappropriate of situations. Did they think we weren't close enough for me to have maybe known where he was? I mean, I didn't know where he was. But still, they should have called me. I deserved to be in that first handful of people who knew there was a problem. But by the time his mom called Jeff and Lucia and Asha, his dad had gone out to the water. Mason's phone, shoes, a beer, and the life jacket he was too cool to wear were all clustered together at the end of the dock. And I don't know if he's tangled up in a mess of sunken branches or what, but the search teams never found his body.

I see Lucia, Asha, and Jeff now, sitting with Nolan toward the front of the church on the left. I turn to my mom. "I'm going to go sit with my friends," I say as the priest intones a welcome to the congregation. And I start to move to make it clear that I mean, *Without you.*

She opens her mouth to speak, then sighs and turns to find a spot closer to the back. I'm her ticket to a front-and-center seat, but now her weird sense of propriety dictates that she leave those spaces for people who knew him better.

"What's up, Beavers," I loud whisper as I slide in next to Asha. Mason started calling us the Beaver Bunch after Lucia and Jeff took to wearing sweatshirts from Roots. It's basically a Canadian version of the Gap, and they put their logo on every shirt, sweater, and pair of underwear they sell. Said logo is a beaver holding a branch. It's *so* Canadian.

The nickname seemed innocent enough, until Lucia and Jeff got tired of wearing the sweatshirts but the name was still there. As it dawned on Asha, Lucia, and me that *beaver* was also slang for *vagina*, the name started to seem super awkward. But Asha, in her wisdom, decided it was too late to back away from the nickname without opening ourselves up to ridicule. The smartest path was to lean in. So we did.

Asha Chawla looks gorgeous as usual, her wavy dark hair shining lustrous blue when the light strikes it, and her eyelashes sweeping so long it's like she's wearing falsies even though she's not. Her frame is delicate and refined, from her slender wrists to her smooth collarbone, everything except her intimidating breasts. I honestly am surprised she doesn't tip over sometimes; she seems to defy physics the same way a Barbie doll does. She's the kind of girl it would be easy for me to hate for her unfair portion of physical gifts, if she wasn't so freaking funny.

"You're late, bitch," she loud whispers back, grinning. Asha's voice is like a Long Island sorority girl and a hokey country singer had a baby, nasally and twangy. She plays it up because she knows how surprising it sounds coming out of her elegant mouth. It's part of her comedy. The other part is mostly swearing. She leans into the hard consonants of those words, bending them to her will. *Bitch, beaver* . . . soon she will own them all.

An older couple who've been together long enough to look and dress exactly alike turn around in the pew in front of us and give her an icy glare. Asha turns around, too, as if searching for who said the profanity, and then shakes her head at the couple like the three of them are all on the morality police force together. The couple face front again, seeming vaguely confused.

"Christ, Ash, you're going to get us kicked out of Mason's funeral," I say under my breath.

She shrugs. "He would love that. What a tribute."

She's right about that. Anything against the grain—he was all for it.

Nolan Drake is sitting next to Asha. He has his money clip out and is absently pulling the cash out, then snapping the clip back on again, over and over. The money clip is one of his many little affectations that he takes on to seem—what—older? Cooler? Less pimply? I can see the chain for his pocket watch hanging out of his pants. If he came to school with a monocle and a top hat like Mr. Peanut one day, I wouldn't be surprised.

He has a big stack in that clip, so it must be all ones.

"What you got there, big spender?" I ask quietly. "Fourteen dollars?" Asha grins and nudges me with her elbow to show she approves.

Nolan fans the money like a deck of cards. "Enough," he says, trying to sound like he's got swagger.

"Enough for what?" Asha asks. "A new outfit for your avatar?"

"Shhhh!" hisses the woman in front of us. We cast our eyes to the floor, but our shoulders are shaking with silent laughter. This isn't as bad as I thought it was going to be.

Then Sarah, Mason's sister, gets up to do the eulogy. Before this, it's been church readings, droning passages about everlasting heaven with archaic syntax. Stuff that seemed irrelevant to Mason or his life. But Sarah is as real and relevant as my pulse, which I am suddenly aware of in my neck.

She starts out talking about cute things she remembers him doing as a baby, like when he fell asleep at the table with his face on a waffle and when he woke up, he just took another bite and said, "Nap waffle!" The air in the church is relaxed; people are laughing.

But then she shifts to talking about the recent Mason, as he was just a few weeks ago, and my skin feels like it's tightening on my frame, like it's constricting my rib cage.

"He could be kind of a jerk," Sarah says into the microphone, the last word echoing off the stone walls. "But I think that was because he didn't know what to do with how smart he was. I loved him anyway. And I always, always knew that he loved me."

I feel the lump building in my throat, but I am absolutely not going to let myself cry. I have no right. I was his friend, that's all. That was our official status, and just because I occasionally let my thoughts wander over the contours of something more, so what? That's standard daydreaming and gives me zero special consideration because there was exactly zero reality to it. So shut up and sit quietly, Hattie, like all the other "just friends" here. It would be so freaking selfish for me to start blubbering while his own parents are dry-eyed in the front row. His mother never liked me, and I can almost hear what she would whisper: *She's clearly looking for attention.* It's just that . . . I thought I'd have more time.

My eyes swimming, I try to distract myself by looking around the church. The most eye-catching elements of St. Brigit's are the huge stained glass windows that rise above us on either side. I often stare at the one to the right, which is of Jesus confronting the devil. It depicts the devil as a human figure, sneering, with horns and red skin and the whole thing. It's so over the top that it always makes me snort. I feel the lump dissolve. Close call.

I tap my foot rhythmically against the kneeling bench on the floor in front of me until I feel soothed. Sarah is still talking as I tune back in. "What's sad," she says, "is that he was just sort of figuring himself out. Getting comfortable. He had started working on his graphic novels more, and was talking about applying to art school. It seemed like he could finally just . . . be." Sarah looks out to the side, like she's talking to herself. "I wish he could have had time to enjoy that. But I guess I'm glad he got to that place at all before he was gone."

A small sob breaks the hush. It's only after several people turn around in their seats that I realize the sob came from me. Tears are escaping. I press at the corners of my eyes with the crook of my finger and push out of the pew, padding quickly down the aisle. I force a smile and shake my head at my mom to make her stay in her seat as I pass her. Eyes from all around the church bore holes into my back. I lean into the massive wooden door.

I knew I shouldn't have come. What are they thinking now, all those eyes? That I'm some kind of drama queen? An attention seeker? Just plain unstable? There are so many labels for this behavior, for drawing focus from what's important, for making everything all about you. I have no right.

As I enter through the vestibule again, the space is still dim, but this time I can see something I didn't before, off to one side. My brain tries to make sense of what it is. It looks like a life-sized cardboard cutout of Mason, like they make of athletes to sell stuff at the mall. I stare, struck by the rendering but also amazed that the adults in charge of this shindig would cook up something in such bad taste. The likeness to Mason is unnerving, adorable freckles and strong jawline and all, seemingly in 4D. And now I get why everyone goes so wild over the

Mona Lisa, because the fact that the eyes seem to be zeroing in on me is making me lose feeling in my legs. I stare so intently my head hurts, trying to get clarity on what I am actually seeing, when suddenly, the figure *blows me a kiss*. I stop breathing, more than a little terrified, but also not wanting to push past this moment that seems to have nothing to do with normal time and space. Am I hallucinating? I'm pretty sure I haven't blinked once since I entered the vestibule, and now my focus starts to blur. I blink several times, and when my vision is clear again, the person is *moving toward me*. It's too much. I gasp and stumble backward, bursting through the door into the cold sunshine outside. Mixed into the creaking of the large wooden door, I think I hear the sound of laughter.

At the bottom of the stairs, I sneak a look behind me to see if I'm being followed. The stairs are empty. I slow down. Holy crap, I'm more upset than I thought if I'm hallucinating shit like that. I try to remember how to do the calming breaths thing we learned during our yoga unit in PE, but it feels more like hyperventilating than meditating. I start to get lightheaded, so I quit. I should walk home, but I don't want to freak out my mom. I've already bolted outside; disappearing entirely would be pushing it. Instead, I sit in the grass, feeling the realness of the moisture from the cool, damp earth seeping through the back of my dress. I knew I'd be bad at this funeral thing. Maybe it's more than just missing Mason. Sarah's words ring in my ears. The idea that anyone could "just be" in life is so tantalizing and out of reach that I physically can't bear it.

I'm pulling apart orange maple leaves, calming myself by stripping the flesh from each leaf along the lines of its veins, when clumps of people start shuffling out to the wide front steps of the church. Their murmuring turns to talking as they move away from the doors, shaking off the formality still hanging inside. Then they all turn to face the church, and I can't help imagining Mason's family running out holding hands and jumping into a limo with tin cans attached to the bumper and the words *Just Died* written on it in shaving cream, while we all throw rose petals or something. It isn't just the stained glass devil that's ridiculous. The empty box, the rituals, the sheer fact that a guy can't even float on a lake without dying, it's all absurd. And me, of course. I'm the most ridiculous of all.

Over by the sidewalk, I see some tenth graders offering tissues to a girl with a pixie cut. What is *she* crying about? Who was Mason to her—a random boy in her precalc class? Then I reflexively scold myself for being critical. But this is exactly why I fear others' judgment, because judgment fills every cell in my body. And if I wasn't justified, she definitely isn't.

The Beaver Bunch is coming down the steps now, headed toward me. Just seeing them makes the world around me feel more grounded. I get ready for one of them to tease me about my sobisode, but they don't. Lucia squeezes my elbow while Asha playfully hip checks me from the other side. Teasing would be better. As it is, the more they smile, the more breakable I feel. The boys look uncomfortable. Their lips are pressed thin as their eyes dart around, as if there might be a sheet of instructions somewhere for how they should conduct themselves. Mason would have teased me.

Asha does a little wiggle dance. "Where's the bathroom?" she asks Lucia. "I have to pee."

"Don't ask me, I don't know," Lucia says.

"What? I thought you were a good little church girl. I thought that was what explained your . . . questionable fashion choices," says Asha, eyebrows arched in a lighthearted challenge as she continues to jump around.

"I go to St. Anthony's. Italian," Lucia replies, indicating herself with a little curtsy flourish. "This is the Irish church." She says it matter-of-factly, pointing at me. The whole town was sort of split down the middle 150 years ago, and if you take last names and match them up to addresses, you can still find evidence of the divide.

"Oh, you mean you don't go to the white church but instead you go to the white church?" Asha puts one hand on her hip. As the only Indian American kid in a town with a population as pale as the milk in the surrounding dairy farms, she has no patience for white people's claims of ethnicity.

"Pretty much," says Lucia. She shrugs, absently twisting her long brown hair up into a perfectly messy topknot and plucking out tendrils.

"It's in the basement," I say. "The stairs are to the left."

"Thank you, darling," Asha says, dancing away.

"Wait, I'll go with you," calls Lucia cheerfully. Lucia never takes anything personally. She has the best self-esteem of anyone I've ever met. "You can give me another talking-to about cultural sensitivity or whatever."

"Good, you need it." Asha turns back, links her arm through Lucia's, and starts dragging her up the stairs. "For starters, I prefer *awareness. Sensitivity* sounds like you can't have gluten."

I watch them disappear into the building. If I leave now, I can skip the emotional goodbyes that might restart my waterworks or hallucinating or some new nonsense. I turn to the boys. Even though they're the same age, Jeff Dean is at least a half foot taller than Nolan, and now he's bent over him awkwardly like my little reading lamp that I clip onto my books at night. They're both engrossed in some sports highlight reel on Nolan's phone. Every twenty seconds or so, without looking up from the screen, they softly bump fists and mumble "epic" in unison.

"All right, guys, see you tomorrow," I say quickly. My mom is standing a few feet away, talking with the choir director and the lady who sets up the doughnut table after Mass. I catch Mom's eye and point to the car, and she follows me to the parking lot.

"How was it?" she asks innocently as she unlocks the doors. Please.

"You were there," I say. I'm not sure when it started, but this is our pattern now. The more questions she asks me, the less I want to answer her. Which just makes her ask more questions. I've even taken to sometimes pretending I haven't heard her, which I'm sure she finds incredibly childish and selfish and probably a lot of other *-ishes*. It's like I'm hoarding all the information, information she's starving for, and I won't give her a crumb. But what am I supposed to do? She's insatiable. Whenever I ease up and let her in a little, she just wants more.

"I thought the service was lovely," she says, as if responding to a question I haven't asked.

"I'm sure the Learys were glad to see all his friends there," she tries again, turning on the ignition and checking her mirrors.

Maybe I could get this all out of the way at the same time. I unbuckle my seat belt and take a deep breath. The car starts beeping in protest. I let it finish, then say, "Look, Mom, I know you're concerned about me, but I'm really fine. The grief counselors at the school said that everybody processes grief in different ways, and I guess my grief processing style is, well, uneven, but it is mostly very private." Oh yeah, I can tell by the wrinkle in between her eyebrows that mentioning the counselors is having its desired effect. Now she's going to have to take whatever else I say super seriously. I pile it on, saying stuff I've seen on social media from the families of celebrities who've died. "So I would appreciate some time and space to process in this difficult time. Okay?"

"Of course, sweetie," she says, so serious I have to look away so she won't see me cringe. I'm exploiting a friend's death just to get a little peace from my overly involved mother.

She presses my hand with hers in a meaningful way that I have to sit and tolerate. Then, thankfully, she puts the car in gear. I lean my head back against the seat rest. I'm about to close my eyes and be numb for a while, but as we approach the front of the church I catch a glimpse of someone still outside. A lanky kid, loose in the joints, ambling down the steps, lost in thought. It looks like, no, it *feels* like Mason. He looks up and waves as we pass. Rolling down the window, I whip around in my seat, craning my neck. But he's gone. No one is on the steps, alive or dead. There are only autumn leaves making their own gentle cyclone, spinning up and up toward the sky, until they finally break free from the invisible forces holding them together and float away.

CHAPTER 2

Arriving home is like going from the depression frying pan into the depression fire.

"We're home!" I yell, banging the screen door as I come in. Dad is in his usual place in the living room, slouchy in his big armchair, some awful talk radio station in his headphones. He doesn't greet us. It's not clear whether he can hear me or not. I think he likes it that way.

My mom walks into the living room and touches his knee. "Dave?" she asks. "I thought the plan was you were going to make dinner today."

Dad pulls one earbud out. "It's on the stove," he says, and goes back to the radio.

"The funeral was great, Dad, and I'm feeling super mentally healthy, thanks for keeping tabs," I mutter under my breath on my way to the kitchen.

On the stove sits a pan of pierogies, a pot of steamed cauliflower, and some sort of whitefish I don't love the smell of that already looks cold. White and white with a side of white. Dad wasn't always this way. And our dinners definitely weren't. I was sort of ready for the moodiness and withdrawal, but the color palette of our meals has been one of the unexpected casualties of him going blind this year. That's not right, exactly. He's actually been going blind my whole life, but it's like his eyes have been headed toward Blind Town and this year they finally pulled up at the station. Like now I don't need to say "going" anymore, I can just say "is." He is blind.

He's got retinitis pigmentosa, RP for those of us in the know. He's got a cane now and everything. I'm not sure what the point of the cane is, though. He doesn't really seem to be applying himself in learning how to use it. I think he just carries it so that when we sit down at a table at Denny's the server is less likely to try to hand him a menu. Although usually they still do. People do all sorts of ignorant things, like hold out their hand for him to shake or silently change positions while he's talking to them so he looks like he's talking to empty air. But the most infuriatingly reliable thing people do when they see his cane is just talk to him a lot louder, like deaf and blind are interchangeable. And every time, I think about yelling right back at them. But of course, I never do.

I scoop a big helping of pierogies into a shallow bowl. Avoiding the fish, I pick up two florets of cauliflower with my fingers and put them on the side to meet my mom's healthy quotient. Then I grab some shredded Parmesan from the fridge and sprinkle it over the whole thing. This is usually how I save my supper from the brink of gross. A large quantity of shredded cheese.

I sit at the tiny table in our tinier kitchen and eat. When Dad isn't at dinner, we can usually skip saying grace and dig right in. I keep my eyes on my food as a way of transmitting "I need time and space" to my mom. Fortunately, my brother,

Nate, comes to the table and starts absorbing all my mom's attention. He's six years younger than me, so he's almost ten now. He's definitely at an age where he still wants to tell her everything he did in a day. Which she loves, and it takes the pressure off me.

Every once in a while, not here in our town but when we're on vacation in a big city like Philadelphia or somewhere, I'll see someone blind out in the world with their cane by themselves, and it seems more terrifying to me than parachuting out of an airplane. I can't imagine blindfolding myself and then just heading out the door, which is basically what they're doing. Tapping around in front of you can keep you from falling down a hole, I guess, but that's about it. What about what's to the side of you, like a speeding car? What about what's coming up behind you? I'm gonna go ahead and guess that blind people get mugged a lot.

So when Dad first got a cane, I registered my opposition. Vociferously (vocab points). I told him he should get a guide dog. Because a dog would know when a speeding car was approaching on the right. And a dog would sure as hell know when an ax murderer was sneaking up behind you. And then he could bite the ax murderer's murdering butt.

I told him all about how a dog would provide full-service protection, and that, added bonus, then he wouldn't have to be so pathetically dependent on my mom. I didn't use those exact words, but it may have been implied. My dad replied that he didn't need to be cleaning up feces on top of everything else, and that he knew what I was up to, that I was just trying to get a pet. That's how selfish my dad thinks I am.

I didn't just want a pet. But people are on the lookout for you to be selfish when you're almost sixteen. Although when I heard there were actually *miniature guide ponies*, I did circle back around and give it another whack. And here's the kicker about guide ponies: Horse hooves are too slippery to walk on tile or hardwood floors, so the handlers have them *wear sneakers*. Who wouldn't want the dedicated assistance of a miniature pony in a set of sneakers? My dad, that's who.

"And in the third book you find out that the bad guy is actually the main character's uncle!" Nate is obsessed with this book series that somehow creates suspense by putting every fairy-tale character ever together in the same story. "So he's trying to get the potion from the fairy godmother, and—"

"Did you get enough to eat?" I've pushed back from the table and cleared my place, which has grabbed my mom's attention. She always asks me this, which strikes me as a strange habit. I definitely don't look like I'm wasting away. I'm medium-sized, small on top but with strong legs and a butt that might be my best feature. I've gotten enough to eat every meal for my entire existence.

"Yep. And I've got a lot of homework, so . . ." I put my bowl in the sink.

"Okay, well, don't work too hard. Today was a big day. Give yourself a break." My mom smiles briefly at me and then turns back to Nate's excited blow-by-blow summary.

I pass my dad on the way to the stairs. He hasn't moved. I go in and sit near his feet, and put my hand up on his arm. I went to a funeral today, after all. Maybe the darkness in him and the darkness in me can somehow connect. "Hey," I say.

He takes his earbuds out. "How was the eulogy?" he asks. My dad teaches public speaking at the local community college. He always wants to know about the speeches.

"Really good," I say. "Mason's sister spoke. Very specific. It was a little too good, actually."

He doesn't ask me what I mean by that. "Well, you know what John Donne said about death. *Death, be not proud, though some have called thee mighty* . . ." He continues quoting some ancient poem, his reliance on other people's words extinguishing my hopes for a connection. I'm not sure what John Donne meant, but I know it doesn't have anything to do with me.

"I'll mull that over," I say as I stand up.

I try to picture a guide pony standing there next to his armchair, maybe with a bucket of oats around its neck, stomping its sneakers every once in a while. Yeah, there is no way in hell my dad would ever get a guide pony.

Maybe I will, though, because no matter how much I try to pretend it away, I'm going blind, too.

Right now, no one else in the world knows this about me. After all, most of the clues can easily be explained with simpler excuses. The fact that my shins are covered with bruises and scrapes from bumping into edges of low coffee tables and protruding chairs?

I'm accident-prone. Always losing things? Absent-minded. And when I don't see my friends frantically waving at me? I'm just lost in thought.

I know these reasons are convincing because I've convinced myself with them for years. Denial ain't just a river in Egypt, haha. But things are becoming undeniable.

Undeniable. I open my AP Bio text and turn to the chapter about respiration. When I signed up for AP Bio, I thought it would be like zoology, lots of in-depth information about the habits and family groupings of monkeys in Tibet, or videos about octopuses and how their colors can reflect their emotions. But AP Bio is more chemistry than anything. The chemical equations squat on the page in front of me. One undeniable thing is how slowly I have to read because there are so many little fuzzy obstacles in the way. I can't take in a whole sentence at the same time. Instead, I have to concentrate on each word, one by one. I lose my train of thought again. I end up reading the paragraph three times and retaining none of it.

The most undeniable thing happened right before school started this year, when the whole Beaver Bunch went camping the last weekend of summer. It was supposed to be girls in one tent and boys in the other to appease our parents, but since Jeff and Lucia were now a couple, they immediately commandeered the smaller tent. That left the four of us in the other one, which felt totally normal. With the level of trust we all had for each other, we were more wholesome than a veggie bowl. Which I think is ultimately why my parents let me go.

My mom had made us a big bag of trail mix. It was a little corny, but I couldn't be mad about it because trail mix is delicious. While Asha and I did all the work putting up the tent, Nolan and Mason sat on a wide tree stump and went through the bag, picking out all the M&M's.

"Guys, it's bad enough you're not helping, but now you're pawing through the snacks?" Asha was inching a pole through the gathered fabric loops of the tent. "It's supposed to be salty and sweet together. Now it'll just be salty."

"You're sweet enough to make it work." Nolan blinked and smiled an innocent smile, revealing chocolatey front teeth. "Okay, now I'm thirsty. You think the campground vending machine has milk?" He stood up and jogged toward the entrance.

"Flattery is not going to get this tent built," Asha called after him, wiping her hands on her jeans. "Hattie, pull on the other end. This fucking thing is stuck."

Together, we managed to force the end of the pole into its little pocket. But the next pole was even harder. Asha and I were both sweating. Mason was laughing.

"Mason, stop scarfing sugar and get your butt over here."

"Hey, hey. I am not scarfing. Nolan's the scarfer. I am carefully selecting the green ones to build my manly stamina. Then I will come help you ladies with all of my testosterone."

"Oh my God. Never mind," I said.

"Gross," said Asha.

Mason stood up and walked toward Asha. "All right, stop begging. The reinforcements have arrived."

"Just like a boy to do the exact same thing the girl has already been doing but make it like he's some knight in shining armor," Asha said, smirking at Mason.

"You're welcome," Mason said, stepping into her spot.

He and I moved in sync then, wordlessly navigating around each other to apply pressure where it was needed, bending the arc of the tent until each piece settled into place. Then he unzipped the front flap with a flourish and Asha unfurled the sleeping bags. We collapsed on the soft fleece inside, congratulating each other.

"I'm actually pretty proud of us," I said.

"We have a promising future of successfully assembling IKEA furniture," Mason agreed.

Later, we forced Nolan to build the fire while we ate the trail mix nuts, leaving just the sad little raisins in the bag. *This is it*, I remember thinking. *We're independent. We're practically adults.*

The feeling carried me through the evening, the six of us sitting around the fire, each face lit by the warm glow of the flames, looking like a commercial for an expensive SUV that could take us on adventures just like this. We stayed up late, talking about our favorite music and whether female vocalists could capture emotion that male singers couldn't (Asha thought so). Finally, we tumbled into the tent without brushing our teeth, crawling into our sleeping bags still dressed, succumbing to the deep untroubled sleep of summertime with no homework or obligations.

At some point in the night, I woke up needing to pee. I tried desperately to tell my bladder not now and go back to sleep. I tried lying on my side, my back, curled up in a ball. There was no avoiding it.

I crawled over the snoring lump next to me and felt for my flashlight in the mesh pocket that hung from the wall of the tent. Clicking it on, I slipped my feet into flip-flops by the door, unzipped the flap, and stepped out into the night chill. The dew was so heavy that it felt like it had been raining. I shivered and hugged myself. I wanted to get this over with as fast as possible and get back to the cocooned coziness of my sleeping bag.

The bathroom looked like a lighthouse, bright fluorescents beckoning across the gravel loop of the campground. Inside, it was the same dank mess I remembered from earlier in the day, trash on the floor and water from the showers creating suspicious puddles all over. I wondered if it ever dried out in here. In the humidity, I could hear mosquitoes buzzing, so I crouched over the toilet without touching the seat, peed, washed my hands, and hurried out of there.

I stepped from the thousand-watt bathroom into complete darkness. Before I had gone into the light I had been able to see vague shapes around me, the dark mounds of tents up and down the loop, the outlines of shadowy trees against a clouded sky. Now, after all that brightness in my eyes, I saw none of that. It was flat black, like someone had thrown a hood over my head. It made me nervous. I clicked on my flashlight. A tiny circle of light appeared in front of me on the ground, revealing gravel pebbles and weeds. I inched forward, the bobbing circle in front of me showing more of the same, gravel and weeds, gravel and weeds. I lifted my head. Just black. Where was the tent? Shit.

After what seemed like an eternity, I looked behind me. I was much farther away from the bathroom now, but was I going in the right direction? I tried to remember the angle by which I had approached the building just a minute or two before, but I had been concentrating on not wetting my pants so I hadn't really clocked what I was doing. I should have counted my damn footsteps or something. Too late for that now.

I considered the possibility that I would just have to sit down and wait until dawn, but I wasn't sure what time it was. That could be hours. Maybe I should give it another try. I headed back to the bathroom and started again, a little more to the right this time, pushing down the panic that was rising in my throat. *You're just cold, Hattie. You're not going to die.*

Finally, something appeared in my little circle other than ground. It was the corner of a tent, but there was a pickup truck next to it. It was not our tent. Still, it was a glimmer of hope. I had not been magically transported to the surface of the moon. Maybe I could follow the line of tents to our tent. I moved down the row, past three more unfamiliar tents, then five. Now I once again felt too far away from the bathroom. Shit shit.

I kept shaking my head and blinking my eyes, trying to force more of the world to come into focus. The tree shapes were visible above me again, but now they seemed menacing, like *Wizard of Oz* trees. Even more menacing was the awareness that this was not normal. Something was very wrong with me.

I felt like I couldn't get a good breath in all of a sudden. I was nowhere, and the distance between me and my parents seemed vast. I was not an adult at all. I was an immature child. I squeezed my eyes shut and tried to feel my body at home in my own comfy bed, tried to will myself there. I opened my eyes. I was still cold.

It was completely silent, that hushed time when even the night birds have dozed off, like the world had powered down. Breaking that silence felt like breaking glass, but my fear was calling the shots now. "Asha!" I whispered as loudly as I could. "Asha! I need you!"

I waited and listened. Nothing. I whispered again. Then a zipper ran along its teeth close by. Please God let that be her. Biting my lip, I clicked my flashlight off. Now I heard gravel footsteps.

"Just when I think you can't be any weirder." An amused voice came from right behind me. Mason. "What the hell are you doing?"

I shrugged and tried not to look terrified. "My flashlight died when I went to the bathroom," I lied, holding the dark flashlight up. "I was having trouble finding you guys." I never knew exactly why I lied about not being able to see. Somehow the truth seemed more unbelievable than the lie.

I felt him take the flashlight from my hand. He clicked it on. I winced.

"Um, you know how flashlights work, right, Murph?" he

said. Everyone else called me Hattie or Hatts, but Mason always called me Murph. And even though last names are supposedly more formal, the way Mason said it felt like the opposite. I could hear that signature smirk.

"Uh, yeah, Mason. It must have just been loose or something."

"All right, little girl, let's go tuck you in." I grabbed his elbow and he put his hand over my hand. "And if you wake up Daddy again you're going to get a time-out." He was still teasing me, but his hand was warm and his voice soft around the edges.

"I wasn't trying to wake you up," I said, mock offended. "I was calling for Asha. It's not my fault you came when I called like a puppy."

"Asha is snoring like a lumberjack," he said. He stopped for a minute, and we listened. He was right: I could definitely hear some heavy-duty snoring.

When we were at our tent, I hung back.

"I'm never going to get back to sleep now," I said. I felt like I had just had a big cup of caffeine—probably from the adrenaline still coursing through my veins, but maybe also a little bit from feeling suddenly like Mason and I were the only two people in the world right now. "I don't want to go lie in there, wide awake, and have to be quiet. Let's just stay out here."

"Seriously? It's freezing." He was still for a second. Then he said, "Hold on a sec."

He detached himself from my hand and went into the tent, which I could just see the outline of. He came back with both our sleeping bags seconds later. I followed him a few feet to a picnic table and he unzipped them, laying his on the bench and pulling mine over us against the chill as we scooted together.

"Check it out," he said. "Goodbye, stars; hello, huge ball of flame."

The sunrise had been sneaking up on us. Half the sky faded from black to a soft gray. Just moments later, it was all of the sky. The clouds were visible again, wispy and white. Already the gray was taking on more blue.

"Sweet," Mason said. "I don't think I've ever seen the sun rise before. Looks like not all of your ideas are bad, Murph." He slung his arm around me and held my shoulder.

The gesture made me feel cozier than the sleeping bags did. But then that warmth gave me a pang, made me think of something. "Remember when we first met? In fourth grade?"

"We knew each other before that," he objected.

"No, we didn't. I was at St. Brigit's before that. I moved to Fillmore in fourth grade. That's when we met. In Miss Davis's class."

"Oh. I thought you were there from the beginning." He shrugged.

"Nope. Started with Miss Davis. Remember how she let us have free reading time after lunch and you could sit anywhere? How we used to climb on top of the cupboards and sit near the ceiling to read?"

"Ha, yeah. We were so psyched for reading time, just 'cause we got to climb."

"I never understood you then. Not that I understand you

now. But you were a real mystery." I hadn't planned to rehash elementary school with him, but out it came. It was clear I thought about it more than he did. Even now, I was looking for clues to how Mason ticked.

"A mystery? Like a 'how could a boy be so handsome and so smart at the same time' kind of mystery?"

I pinched his leg. "No, you dope. Seriously, you were kind of . . . a flip-flopper. Half friend and half enemy."

I felt the energy change in his limbs. There was a tension, like he was struggling between the urge to make a snappy comeback and genuine curiosity. He landed somewhere in the middle.

"Murphy, I barely even remember fourth grade. And I definitely don't remember being enemies. Not with anyone. So what are you talking about?"

"Do you remember how we were always next to each other in line, 'cause of our last names? We would talk in the hall on the way to math class."

"Sort of. I remember math class. I hated Mr. Harding. Yep, you got me. I take back what I said about no enemies. I was enemies with Mr. Harding."

"Yeah, me too." I pushed on. "So, we'd usually joke around, but a few times, when I was walking in front of you, you did that thing where you reach out your foot and hook the ankle of the person in front of you. One time I fell pretty hard. My books went all over the hall. The whole class laughed. You don't remember?"

"Well, you've always been klutzy, Murphy—"

I sighed. I felt the snark wall going up. "Whatever. Never mind." I waved my hand a little bit, erasing the attempt to cut through to something real. My body involuntarily inched away a little, but Mason grabbed me and pulled.

"Hey now. Hey. Don't be like that." I could hear the half-joking pout of his lip. "I mean, I don't remember that, but it sounds like me, as in, a dick."

I shrugged.

"I'm sorry, okay?" he said. He turned toward me. "I really am. I'm sorry to fourth-grade you."

I laughed then. It was silly, after all. I'd been holding this against him all this time, a mental photograph of me splayed across the elementary school hallway rising in my mind like a barrier between us. "It was a long time ago."

He turned back toward the brightening sky, satisfied. The sun's rays hadn't broken the horizon yet, but you could tell the sun was sitting just beyond the curvature of the earth because it was already turning the fluffy clouds a Hello Kitty pink.

"Whoa. Look at that," Mason said. We huddled together, watching. I was not used to him being so serious, so quiet. "Well, we're not half enemies now, right?"

"No."

"Okay, good."

"We're one hundred percent friends now." It felt corny as soon as it came out of my mouth.

"Let's not get carried away," he said, predictably. I knew he wouldn't let me get away with that much earnestness. I smiled and shook my head. He had apologized to me, pretty sincerely, so that was something. I would hold on to that.

That trip was only a month before Mason died, but it feels so long ago now that it might as well have been someone else's life altogether. I have to stand up and shake out my limbs to stop feeling like I'm caving in. At the time I had thought, *Wow, maybe this is the beginning of something different,* but now I know that it was really the end. And it was such a missed opportunity. I could have told him my secrets then. What was so hard about that? I could have told him that I couldn't see in the dark, that I wasn't sure what was wrong with me but I had some ideas, that I was afraid of ending up like my dad, defective and trapped, utterly dependent on other people, ultimately alone. Then it wouldn't be a secret. Someone else would know.

Maybe it would have changed everything. Changed things enough so that maybe I would have been with him that night on the dock. And he would be alive now.

I'm used to feeling regret about stupid things I say, impulsive things. But this regret for all I didn't say is new, and it stings.

CHAPTER 3

Forty-eight hours have passed since the funeral, but I still feel like a wet dog who needs a full-body shake to get off all the unsettling residue. I arrive at play rehearsal twenty minutes late. It doesn't matter because this is one of my "observing" nights. When casting *Camelot*, our drama teacher, like a big baby, had been unable to decide whether to cast me or Amanda Drinan as Guenevere. So he cast us both. We're going to alternate performances, Mr. Price explained to us after he posted the bonkers cast list on the stage door. He said it like that was something totally normal that happened all the time, even though it totally isn't. Even worse, there are only going to be three performances: Friday night, Saturday night, and the Sunday matinee.

Apparently, Mr. Price chose drama because he's shitbad at math, since it didn't occur to him that two people cannot split three performances evenly. Instead, he pretended he planned it that way on purpose, because Saturday was the "big" performance, so the person doing Saturday, which turned out to be me, would be satisfied by the sexy Saturday glamour of it all, while the other person (Amanda) would get two doses of slightly less "big" fun on Friday and Sunday. In reality, I think Amanda feels shafted because I get the high-profile night, and I feel shafted because she gets to perform twice as many times as me, and all the other girls in the show feel shafted because they didn't get the lead at all. An epic fail any way you look at it. I'm not really surprised, though. Mr. Price's backbone is made out of cafeteria pudding.

I realize he's waving at me from the stage even as I'm thinking rude thoughts about him. I give him a nod. In response, he flourishes an elaborate bow like he's at his own third curtain call. He might as well wear a T-shirt that reads, I WANTED TO STAR ON BROADWAY BUT ALL I GOT WAS THIS LOUSY TEACHING JOB.

I'm resisting openly cringing when I see Richard chatting with the accompanist at the piano. Tiny jolts of electricity explode in my rib cage. I'm suddenly aware of every element of my face—what my eyebrows are doing, the shape my mouth is making, even the creases in my forehead. I will it all to be still and passive, to obey my strict orders to not have a care in the world as I try to figure out where a person with zero cares would let their gaze rest. Richard is the Arthur to my Guenevere. Sounds like the most romantic love story ever, except today he is the Arthur to Amanda's Guenevere.

Am I actually blushing now? I dig in my backpack for my pen and notebook that I use to keep track of all the blocking. Tomorrow I'll need to move wherever Amanda moves today and I won't have any muscle memory to help me, so notes are key. When I come up from the bottom of my bag with my supplies, I almost yelp. Richard is sitting next to me. How did he even get over here so fast? Must be his swing dancer training.

Yep, that's right. He's a swing dancer. And a drama geek. He is tall and skinny and his retro hipster clothes look as loose as they would draped around an empty hanger. He even plays the French horn. All these things combined could easily make for enough total dorkage to repel any reasonable girl. But the poles of that magnet are flipped somehow, and I'm pulled toward him in a way that feels like fate.

I have no idea if he feels the pull of the magnet, though. He's fun and flirty with me, but he's sort of like that with everyone. I'm not complaining. I'll take what I can get.

What I'm getting right now is a big inhale of his laundry detergent/Old Spice deodorant/boy sweat. I want to let my eyelids droop to half-mast so I can really focus on its deliciousness, but that would look dopey. Instead, I whip myself to attention and raise one eyebrow at him.

"Your Majesty," he says, nodding his perfect cleft chin to me. Even though his hair is a deep brown, his eyes are steely blue, which makes them somehow harder to read, more mysterious.

"M'lord," I reply, feeling my pulse surge.

"I trust you will be critiquing my every move up there tonight. I expect a thorough evaluation afterward. Don't hold anything back."

"My notes will leave you vulnerable and exposed," I say. Going for simultaneously businesslike and sensual, I click my pen a couple times.

"Promises, promises," he murmurs, shaking his head. He reaches over and clicks my pen once, slowly. Weirdly sexy. Although he could probably pick a zit and I would think it was weirdly sexy. Could he be the one? I think he might be the one.

"Arthur! Your kingdom awaits!" Mr. Price calls from the pit and sweeps his hand from our seats up to center stage, where Amanda is waiting. Thanks a lot, Price.

"Remember. Exposed. Don't hold back," he calls over his shoulder as he heads up the aisle. I bite the tip of my pen in a kittenish way, but he doesn't see it.

Part of what is hard about this role sharing is that half the time I am peripheral, bored. I don't get to be up there, lost in the imaginary world of knights and royalty. Singing and dancing and moving and feeling in a space that is safe precisely because it is pretend, and none of the words are my own.

But the other part that's hard is sharing Richard.

Either Amanda is the best actress in the world (which she's not), or she has her own chemistry brewing with Richard. They block out their cozy little dance routine to "What Do the Simple Folk Do?" with obvious enjoyment, each misstep highlighted by Amanda's giggles. I can't really fault her. I would be doing the same thing. But I still want to gag.

I'm supposed to be taking notes, but this is killing me. I need a break from all the nothing I'm doing. I scoot down a side aisle and slip out of the auditorium. Even though it's almost seven, I can see Mr. Leary in the band room across the hall, stacking sheet music. Officially, he's head of the music department, but in reality, he just runs the jazz choir, because the teachers who run band and orchestra are both like dictators of tiny countries and don't take orders from anyone, especially Mr. Leary. He's too sweet, too soft. There's no reason he would need to be here now. He must be afraid to go home and see Mason's room, Mason's chair, Mason's toothbrush in a cup by the sink. My jaw clenches.

He catches me peering in from the hallway. He smiles and I force a smile back. I should go in, say something nice or comforting, but I don't. I hurry away like he's contagious.

I hide in the girls' bathroom, examining my face while imagining Amanda's. Is she cuter than me? Her boobs are certainly bigger, but everyone's boobs are bigger than mine, so I'm going to have to win this competition on other grounds. Amanda's features are small and sharp, defined. I'm pretty sure defined cheekbones are supposed to be a good thing. My face is rounder, more babyish, and my cheeks are always rosy like I have blush on. My mom says I have skin that glows. Oh God, now I'm resorting to mom compliments to bolster my self-esteem? Someone slap me. No, wait, don't. My cheeks can't afford to get any redder.

I head back to rehearsal, making a mental list of other ways I could win out in the Richard tournament I've concocted. I want to have more mystique, but I have absolutely no idea how to do that. I'm almost back at the auditorium when out of the corner of my eye I sense someone at the other end of the hall. The surface of my skin prickles. Every cell in my body is telling me to look, but I'm too afraid because I know it's Mason. It's my dead friend down there at the other end of the hall. Something tells me he's now moving toward me, but I still can't look for fear of what I will discover. I can't handle this right now. I try to tell myself it's a trick of the light, but then why is every hair on my neck standing on end? At the last second before I rejoin the cast, I give in to the urge to know and I turn my head.

There's nothing. Nothing, that is, except reeling pain as I walk smack into the metal dividing frame between the open double doors of the auditorium. My skull clunks against the hollow pole with a loud reverberation, like the pole is a xylophone key and my head is the mallet. Business inside the auditorium stops. Tears spring to my eyes, and I feel the heat of a rising goose egg on my forehead. Amanda runs over to me, looking genuinely concerned.

"Hattie! Are you okay?"

I hate that question so much. That one little question has the power to take all your squishy insides and put them out on display. I back up, putting my right hand to my forehead and waving her off with my left.

She won't be stopped. "Don't worry, Mark! I've got her," she says over her shoulder as she puts one arm around my waist and the other under my elbow. Calling Mr. Price "Mark" is quintessential Amanda.

"I'm fine. I just wasn't looking where I was going. I just . . . need a minute." Even though I'm dazed, I can't help turning once more to peer down the hallway. But whoever was there, if there even *was* anyone, is gone.

Amanda shepherds me into the band room. In the back right corner, particleboard walls give the cubicle of the band director's office semi-privacy, so she deposits me in the deep-cushioned armchair there. I only notice how shaky my legs are after I sit down. Is it because I hit my skull or because this may have been the third time I've seen a ghost? Mr. Leary pops his head in, his face open, looking hopeful he might have something else to think about other than his dead son. I wonder briefly if he could have seen Mason in the hallway as well, but he looks too calm.

"Oh, hi, Mr. Leary," Amanda says, seeming to enjoy her newest role as ER doctor. "Hattie just bumped her head. Do you have an ice pack, by chance?"

"Of course. BRB," he says with a wink, clearly trying out something he thinks might be cutting edge.

Amanda turns back to me, about to do some more mothering. I look at her, thinking about the tally I was keeping in the bathroom. I'm going to have to add "nurturing" to her column and "hot mess" to mine, which does not help my case at all. Before she can put my feet up or some shit, I stop her.

"Okay, thanks, Amanda, I'm good," I say. "I'm sure they're all waiting for you. You better get back in there."

She looks at me doubtfully. "You sure?" She is really milking this.

"Positive."

She and Mr. Leary pass each other outside the door. He hands me the ice pack and clucks. "That's a doozy."

I put the ice pack on the bump, more to cover up the evidence of my embarrassment than to bring down the swelling.

"Thanks for the help, Mr. L." I think about saying something real; I haven't said anything to Mr. Leary since before the funeral. But saying something about Mason seems inappropriate, and talking about anything else is absurd. "I'm going to pause here for a bit."

"Take your time," he says, smiling. He stands for one more beat, like he's also considering whether to talk about something bigger. But instead he settles on, "Just relax." Then he's gone.

Mr. Leary's voice is always so smooth, so even. I guess it's because he's a singer. I melt into the soft armchair, my head throbbing. Actually, maybe it has nothing to do with singing. Maybe Mr. Leary is calm because he's had so much practice handling intense shit like Mason's seizures. Because to me, if you can stay cool during one of those, you might as well get a job defusing bombs, deciding whether to clip the red wire or the blue wire.

The day that Mason's epilepsy became more to me than just a word they wrote on all his permission slips is still burned in my brain. We were talking on the phone, and Mason was hassling me, as usual. This time it was about Dan Ludwick, the senior who sat in front of me in precalc. Before class that day, Dan had inexplicably raised his shirt to expose his nipple to me while asking, "Jealous?" Jealous that he had a nipple? The moment had completely mystified me, so I had made the mistake of telling Mason. He hated dicks like Dan, and was relishing examining his idiocy from every angle, but for some reason it was starting to make *me* feel like the idiot.

"I think it was actually his way of proposing, Murph. Don't

dismiss it. You should consider building a life with someone with such superior nipples."

"He wishes," I said, trying to blow it off.

"I mean, he was literally baring his heart to you. Under the nipple, that is. Don't be so cold."

"If you say the word *nipple* one more time—"

"Face it, Nipple Ludwick is a catch. I mean, Dan Nipple."

There was no winning when he was like this. I tried to cut through it, to be straightforward. Sometimes that worked.

"I don't like this conversation anymore, Mason. Be nice or I'm hanging up."

"All right, all right, Hatts. Don't make me suffer the deprivation of your company."

That was better. "Just behave," I said.

"Yes, ma'am," he said. "So what do you want me to talk about then if I can't talk about the sexual politics of America's youth? The weather?"

"Are you going to go to Mia's party on Saturday? She's having it out in the big barn on their property. It sounds like she invited the whole grade. Asha said the last time Mia had a party her parents actually hired a guy to do a real fireworks show. We should definitely go."

He didn't respond. It sounded like he was rubbing his phone against his sweater. There were all these muffled bumping sounds.

"Mason, what the hell? Are you trying to pretend you're jacking off or some shit? Quit."

Nothing.

"Mason, seriously."

"Mason? Mason, are you there?"

Suddenly, Mrs. Leary's voice was on the line. "Mason can't talk now." Click. Something in his mom's voice made me not call back.

The next day he wasn't in school. Lucia told us that her parents had talked to his parents and it turned out that he'd had a seizure. He was fine, just tired and worn out.

It was awful. I couldn't believe I was so insensitive that I'd accused him of masturbating while he was having a seizure. Had he heard me? Had his mom heard me? I really hoped not. But when I'd called that afternoon because I wanted to, no, more than that, I *needed* to see him, his mom just said he couldn't have visitors that day. Not a good sign.

I must have been dozing through the memory, because now I reenter the world to hear everyone streaming out of the auditorium into the hallway. Rehearsal is over. Not surprisingly, adults in performing arts education aren't exactly EMTs, because they just let me take a nap after I hit my head. I guess we're assuming I don't have a concussion. My mother would throw a fit if she knew. But it appears the only damage done is a little drool on my shirt.

Speaking of my mom, I need to catch my ride. I return to the auditorium, carefully sidestepping that pole like it's white hot, and grab my jacket. I pull it on and am flipping my hair out of the collar when my fingers brush against a pair of hands coming to rest on my shoulders.

"How's our patient?" Richard says in my ear.

Wow. Unbelievably, he seems unfazed by my humiliation in the doorway. I try to summon whatever mysterious allure I have left after becoming a human hammer and then taking a nap with my mouth open.

"I might need some tending to," I say. "Maybe even a sponge bath." Yikes. I have a bad habit of going overboard when the flirting has a time clock like this.

He turns me toward him and holds me at arm's length, lips pursed, assessing me. "Yes, you're definitely dirty." Then he grins, and my breath catches.

Amanda appears, looking windblown from outside. "R-dubya, you want a ride or not?" She spins her key chain on the end of her finger.

"Yes, please, Miss Mandy." He salutes and starts jogging in her direction.

She has a car now? And she's driving him home? And they have nicknames for each other? This is entirely too much information to discover at once. I think for the millionth time how my sixteenth birthday can't come fast enough and how the second I have my license I'm going to get a key chain that I can start spinning on the end of my finger.

But no matter how hard I want it, all my car dreams are still weeks away and I've got to do something about this situation right now. I've got to log some hours with Richard, solidify our relationship before it's too late and he has kids and a dog and a picket fence with—barf—Mandy.

"Richard?" I blurt. "Want to come by my house Thursday? Help me with the blocking I missed tonight?"

He stops on a dime, turns, and bows. "It would be my pleasure." And they're gone.

I can't believe it. The moment I have been daydreaming about to the detriment of my class participation grades is actually going to happen. An opportunity to be completely alone with Richard. For, like, *hours*. We'll move past the flimsy flirty stuff and talk for real, and we'll find out how overlapping our hopes and dreams are, how we understand each other on a level of the soul. And then I'll fall into his arms, and it won't be forced at all, it will be totally natural because it's meant to be. *God, deep breaths. Don't get ahead of yourself, Hattie.* What are the chances this giant bump on my head will be gone by Thursday?

CHAPTER 4

I plop my tray onto the lunch table in my usual spot between Asha and Lucia. Asha eyes my lunch choices and I know what's coming next. I smack her hand away before it can get to my plate.

"Hey!" She rubs her hand and pouts. "But you have an extra!" she says, pointing to a glistening pair of garlic breadsticks.

"Correction," I say. "I have two breadsticks. No extra. These are both essential to my well-being." I take one in each hand and start alternating bites to rub it in. Ever since Ruth the lunch lady's son took my dad's course at community college, she's been giving me little bonuses at lunch. One of the few perks of living in a small town where everyone knows everyone.

"Look, I was attempting to save you from an inevitable carb coma, but you do you, my double-fisting friend." She flips her hair. "And as the natural-born lady that I am, I won't even comment on the phallic spectacle that is happening right now."

"Mmmmmm, phallus," I say. I caress a breadstick.

"You are disgusting," Asha says, delighted. Then she knits her brow as she looks at me more closely. "Disgusting *and* injured. Hatts, what the hell happened to your head?"

I touch my forehead where the still-prominent bump is. "Ugh, it is a story simultaneously embarrassing and boring, and I will give you the rest of this breadstick if you don't make me tell it."

"Deal!" Asha says. She plucks the breadstick out of my hand and takes a large bite off the end.

Lucia is rolling her eyes on the other side of me. She has no patience for Asha's and my antics. She reaches into her backpack and pulls out a stack of flyers. "Hey, can you two help me pass these out after class today?"

Before I can answer, Nolan and Jeff sit down with their trays, debating loudly as usual. From the sound of it, Nolan is once again trying to convince Jeff that the country should more fully embrace soccer because it's the most exciting sport and Americans are missing out.

"Nothing that ends with a score of zero-zero most of the time is exciting!" Jeff says, throwing his arms out for emphasis. He has room to do it because Jeff and Nolan have seated themselves one seat apart from each other out of habit. The seat in the middle, the seat directly across from me, is Mason's.

I pick up the top flyer on the stack. It's an invitation to a 5K to benefit the Epilepsy Foundation, and the back is printed with a sign-up form for pledges. This is Lucia's way of coping. She's not student council president for nothing. Her default stance is action.

Asha is looking over my shoulder at the flyer. "Did you talk to Mason's family about this?" she asks Lucia when the boys have both taken a pause from their debate to chew. "Maybe they don't want a spotlight on the whole thing."

Lucia gives her a "Don't you know me at all?" sort of look. "Of course I did. I asked his mom when I brought her all the stuff from Mason's locker."

Wait, his locker? How did she get in his locker? Did she have the combination? Or maybe the janitor let her in. This is a lot to take in. I wish I had gotten to clean out his locker. Did she find the Post-its?

The first day of school this year, I found a Post-it slipped through the crack in my locker. It read, *Sloths are three times stronger than humans.* Sloths are my favorite animal, so of course I already knew that fact. There was no identifying information on the note, but I could recognize Mason's handwriting anywhere. The next day I went to his locker and popped in a Post-it of my own, with the fact about sloths that had originally sparked my interest in them: *Sloths are blind.* Since then, Post-its had been going back and forth every morning—looking forward to the next one had been helping me get out of bed more than my alarm clock. *Sloths can fall 100 feet without hurting themselves. It takes sloths a month to digest a leaf. No one knows how long sloths live.* Until that night at the lake, of course. Then the notes stopped.

I want to ask Lucia about the Post-its, but I can't figure out a way to know if she saw them without drawing attention to them, so I stay quiet.

"I'm just surprised," Asha is saying. "Because when I talked to Mason's mom, she seemed pretty, um, denial-y about it. *Very* chipper."

"Uh-huh," Nolan agrees. "I went over there with some tuna debacle my mom made, and his mom's always been a little . . . intense, but that day if you'd told me she'd had eight Red Bulls I would've been like, *yeah, I'm seeing that.*"

So everybody's been over there. To pay their respects, to do the ritual. Except me. I picture myself standing on their doorstep and Mrs. Leary slamming the door in my face. Or worse, inviting me in to explain in detail why she's never liked me and how her son was always too good to even be seen with me.

"Yeah." Asha is nodding. "She's brittle. So, Lu, I don't know, maybe wait a while?"

"I mean, I want to be respectful," Lucia says, sounding like we just accused her of being the opposite, "but can't we be respectful and do something? This sitting around and doing nothing is making me spin out. He's slipping away. Don't you feel that? Every day it's harder to remember what he looked like in my mind. What he sounded like. I don't want to forget." She's suddenly on the edge of tears, like she's been holding it together but the slightest breeze might split the seams of her composure wide open. It scares me a little.

But Asha thrives in the real. She often refers to herself as "the provocateur," and she does have a tendency to get people to emotional places. So she also gets a lot of practice with the calming back down part. She touches my arm and gives me a look, and I immediately switch seats with her. Then she takes both of Lucia's hands in hers and brings them up close to her face. Lucia's eyes are brimming.

"We are never going to forget him. You hear me?" This is a rhetorical question, because even though it is hushed, the conviction in her voice gives each syllable diamond clarity. It feels like the rest of the cafeteria, the rest of the world, has fallen away as we huddle together in this intensity bubble of Asha's. "Never ever. Not for one second."

"Okay," Lucia whispers. "Good."

"He's still ours. He'll always be a member of the Beaver Bunch." Then Asha relaxes her hypnotizing posture a bit. We all exhale.

"Yes. He's ours," Lucia says. She clears her throat. Then she reaches into her incredibly well-organized bag and produces a pack of travel tissues. She pulls one out for herself, and passes the rest of the pack across the table to Jeff. He blows his nose hard. This is a perfect example of what I love about their coupleness. Lucia's pain makes Jeff cry, and in return she is there ready with a tissue for him before a single tear has a chance to fall.

This is the first I've seen of my friends' sensitive underbellies about Mason. We've all been brave-facing it alone, even though we're basically going through the same thing. Does it make me feel better or worse now to know that they're suffering, too? A little of both, I think.

"Where do you think he is now?" I ask suddenly. Part of my solitary denial has been to studiously not think too much about the Mason encounters I've been having except when I'm actually having them, but if one of my friends saw him, too? That would mean he was real and I'm not mentally unraveling.

I realize how badly I want him to be real, to just have a little bit more of him.

"Like, are you asking if we believe in an afterlife?" Nolan responds, his mouth now full of spaghetti.

"I guess."

Nolan swallows, eager. He's clearly been giving it some thought. "If you subscribe to the idea of a multiverse, then when we die we just go to a different dimensional reality for ourselves. As in, Mason could be eating lunch right here in another dimension." He runs his fingers through his curly blond mop of hair as he talks and it gets even wilder. The resulting mad scientist look seems to lend legitimacy to his theory.

"I can't tell if that's comforting or creepy," says Lucia, the color in her face returning to normal.

"Kudos, Nolan. Not everyone can find their spiritual path in a comic book movie," says Asha, smiling.

"Multiple comic book movies," says Nolan, pointing a correcting finger at her. Oh man, he sounds just like my brother.

"I'm going with reincarnation," Jeff says now, like we get to order our eternal destination from a menu. "It's almost like being a shape-shifter. I bet Mason got reborn as a baby shark."

Asha tilts her head. "Could be. Who knows how his energy persists." I scan the others for any sign that they've had a similar experience to mine, but it seems like to them this is all theoretical.

Then Asha pulls one knee up under her chin and hugs it, considering. "Maybe we should have a séance."

The idea of Mason being controlled in some sort of occult ceremony makes me shiver. "Ew, gross," I say, scrambling in my head for a way to change the subject so Asha doesn't get too enthusiastic about this.

"C'mon. It would be just like in the movies! Worst-case scenario we have a fun night of eerie mystery, but best case? Best case we actually get some sort of message from him."

"That would be so freaking cool." Jeff looks entranced.

"No, people, no way are we doing that. Mason would not be about that sort of thing. Plus—" I know this is a little risky in terms of revealing my odd close encounters, but I say it anyway. "If Mason is still around, I would want him to visit on his own terms. I wouldn't want to force it. Maybe he can come to us organically if we let him, if we pay attention." The faces looking back at me have confused eyebrows. I try to cover. "You know, like in our hearts and thoughts."

Lucia reaches across the table and touches my hand. "I get it," she says. "He lives on through us."

Maybe more than you realize, I think. Who knows, he might be here at school somewhere right now. Maybe he'll sit down in his seat in a second. But out loud I just say, "Yeah."

Lucia looks hopeful again. "And if he's okay, then we can be okay, too."

I'm not sure how big an "if" that is.

"We're so okay that we're going to run a 5K for the Epilepsy Foundation," says Asha now. "We'll let the adults take care of their own business. Give me some flyers for this excellent cause.

I don't know why I wasn't more supportive from the start. You're an inspiration, Miss Lucia Spataro."

"I know," says Lucia, showing a little attitude because she knows Asha will appreciate it. "And I'm not even done. Next on my list is a boating safety drive."

"How about starting a Doofus Foundation?" says Jeff now. "'Cause one thing's for sure. He was a total and complete doofus." We all smile and nod like that was the most reverent and loving thing Jeff could have said. And it sort of was.

I stretch out my legs and touch Mason's seat with my toe.

CHAPTER 5

When I step outside of school after lunch, a couple drops of icy drizzle land right down the back of my neck. My mom is waiting at the curb, engine idling. I hustle into the front seat and arrange my backpack at my feet as the car pulls away. I know most people love getting to miss school, but whenever my mom comes to pick me up early, it always seems to be for something even more unpleasant than the excruciating boredom of health class. Like getting an HPV vaccine, or passport photos, or, in this case, for an ophthalmologist appointment. Mr. Price was leaning in through my mom's passenger-side window the other night after rehearsal, reliving my mortifying moment in detail, and I guess it was alarming enough that my mom decided to take action.

"But, Mom, it's not that I didn't see the pole," I say again, making one more attempt to get out of this unnecessary ordeal. "I just wasn't looking where I was going,"

"We're going to get you checked out," she says firmly.

"But, Mom, I swear, I was just . . . distracted." The bulk of my ponytail is uncomfortable against the car's headrest. I pull out the rubber band and start winding a low braid, taking my frustration out on each section of hair as I yank it tight.

"Henrietta, please. With your father's history? Frankly, we're overdue on this."

She clearly wants to have this appointment to rule out the

possibility of blindness. But she doesn't have all the data points I do, experiences that suggest this appointment might do the exact opposite. It might rule it *in*. One thing she doesn't know, for example, is that when I go to the movies with my friends I always make sure to get there early, because if the lights are already dimmed I'll get stranded in the aisle while the people I'm with evaporate. Then I'll have to start fumbling around for armrests until one of my friends finally notices and grabs me, jokingly asking if I'm drunk. I'm so familiar with that feeling, the one where I'm the biggest dork in the world, and I definitely do not want some doctor to tell me that soon I'm going to feel that way all the time.

Because there was a chance of a thunderstorm, Mom picked me up thirty minutes earlier than she needed to, and now we're almost forty-five minutes early to my appointment. Apparently, according to my mom, this doctor is at the forefront of retinal diseases, and so we drove the fifty miles to Upstate Medical Center to see her. We walk in the office, and everyone else in the waiting room is about two hundred years old. I can't possibly belong here, can I? One of the ancient ladies looks up at me sort of shocked, clearly thinking the same thing, like I must be there to cause trouble or walk on her flower bed or something. I stifle an urge to give her the finger. In fact, I want to give the whole office the finger. The very best possible outcome of this appointment is that we're here for no reason, which is preferable, but also dumb.

When my mom planned this lovely early arrival, she was

definitely not factoring in how much time it would leave for panicking. I sit there with my Global Studies book open, not reading it, not even really thinking, just sort of clenching my whole body. I try to think about my upcoming night with Richard, what I will wear and what the first thing I say should be, but the reality of my surroundings makes it impossible. My heart feels like it's bracing itself for an oncoming blow. Every five minutes or so, a nurse appears at the door with a clipboard and calls out a name that isn't mine. Then one of my waiting room companions, decrepit and crumbling, starts the process of gathering up their purse and sweater and scarf and mittens and entire wardrobe that they have piled on the chair next to them, double-checking for their purse, and then shuffling inch by inch across the waiting room carpet. It's like a performance art piece to show what forever looks like.

Finally, the clipboard has my name on it. I slip my book in my backpack, zip it, and stand up. I've kept my jacket on, even though I realize now that I've been hot this whole time.

"Should I come with you?" My mom moves to get out of her chair.

"No," I say, without turning my head toward her. Let's get this over with.

They take me back to a low-lit room with a contraption that looks like a bowl suspended on its side. In front of the bowl is a little chin rest lined with clean gauze, a flat bar several inches above to lean your forehead into, and a chair. Your standard torture device.

I hear clicking and make out a technician sitting in the corner on a computer, inputting data or something. He's big, with massive legs and shoulders, like his only other activity besides checking eyes is pumping iron, like he might even be scary if he didn't have scrubs on. I cough.

The technician looks up. "Henrietta?" he asks in a deep voice that goes with his frame. I hate it when people call me by my full name, but that's what's on every official form in the world, so if they don't know me personally, that's what they call me.

I give a smile that doesn't turn up at the corners. "Here," I say.

"Have a seat. We're going to do a periphery test before we dilate your eyes. It's sort of a game." He hands me a plastic joystick attached to a cord. "Go ahead and relax onto the chin rest and stare directly at the red dot in the middle of the field."

I follow directions and suppress a snort at the idea that anything about this could be relaxing.

"Okay," he continues, "you are going to focus directly on the dot for the duration of the test. Don't let your gaze wander. Whenever you see a point of light enter your field of vision, click the button."

"Well, I usually prefer a virtual reality headset, but I'll give it a try," I say, attempting to be cute, but I get no response. The bowl starts to hum. In a second I see what looks like a laser pointer light out of the corner of my eye. It's hard not to look directly at it, to keep focused on the center dot. I click. A few seconds later another light comes wandering down from the top. I click again.

The clicking goes on for another ten minutes. I forget that

this is a diagnostic test to get an accurate understanding of my vision. The overachiever in me takes over. I just want to do well. I want to catch all the little lights as soon as possible, which makes it hard not to look around, so every few seconds, I have to rededicate myself to the center dot.

In the middle of the test, the timing changes. There are a few long stretches where I don't see any lights. I get the distinct impression that the technician is holding his breath. I decide to click anyway, even though I can't see anything, because there is definitely something out there that I'm missing. I know I'm messing up the results, but I can't help myself.

Whatever cheating I did doesn't help, though, because when the technician walks me out of the room, his face looks forced, like he's making an effort to be neutral. I failed that shit so hard.

We go into a bright little room and I'm left with a new babysitter.

"I'm going to put two sets of drops in your eyes now," she says through smacks of gum. "The first set is to numb your eyes so the dilation drops don't sting." Turns out both sets of drops sting, so thanks for nothing. Then she deposits me in yet another, smaller waiting room for people already dilated. The lights are off here, which I appreciate, because I can already feel how sensitive my eyes are getting.

I mentally dub this place "The Holding Cell of Pathetic Blobs" because our eyes are all out of focus and we can't really do anything that a person would normally do in a waiting room—can't read, can't look at our phones. Even looking at the

TV mounted near the ceiling gives me a headache. My brain is trying hard to adjust pupils that are now completely out of its control. I feel nauseous. I look around to see how the other pathetic blobs are feeling. There's an old man with a cane between his knees that he taps on the floor whenever he clears his throat, which is often. The slowest purse gatherer from the outer waiting room is here, too, wearing dark glasses and sitting motionless with her hands folded in her lap.

Now the purse lady hasn't moved in the last five minutes. *I wouldn't be surprised if she's dead,* I think, then feel bad for it. We, the dilated, are silently bonded in our uncomfortable prison. We should be on the same pathetic team. I almost reach out to touch her hand. I want my mom like I'm five years old. But she's still out front, where I told her to stay.

And where is Richard right now? When I left the first waiting room it was already after two, so the dismissal bell probably just rang. He might be hanging by his locker, loitering until the river of pimply humans eases up at the front entrance. Or he might be climbing onto the bus, doling out smiles to all the girls already in their seats. Or—I can't even—Amanda might be giving him a ride home again. The helplessness that overwhelms me makes me stand up. But there's nowhere to go, so I sit back down again. The other blobs don't seem to notice.

Another person in scrubs calls my name. We recently watched *A Clockwork Orange* in my film criticism elective, and as I follow her to a third exam room, I wonder if this is when they'll pin my eyes open with claw clips. But this room is the mildest yet. I've been wearing glasses or contacts since third grade, so I recognize the equipment as the same as at the optometrist's office. It looks like the coin-operated telescopes they have at Niagara Falls, except you can look in both sides. An energetic lady with a bouncy bob and a white coat comes in, pumps the hand sanitizer, and smiles at me while she rubs it in between her fingers.

"I'm Dr. Porter," she says. She picks up a tablet off the counter and scrolls a few times. "How are you today, Henrietta?"

"It's Hattie," I say. "I'm fine, I guess. A little blurry."

"Oh, I know. Dilation drops are the worst, aren't they?" She sits opposite me. "But hopefully they've done their job, and I can get a really good look in there. Lean forward and put your chin on the pad and let's see what we see."

She leans forward, too. "Look straight ahead." A painfully bright vertical line of light passes over my eye. I succeed in not blinking. "Look left." Again with the light. "Look right. Now down." This doesn't seem healthy. If I'm not already going blind, I will be by the time she finishes examining me.

Finally, she sits back. "I am seeing some sunburst patterns," she says, half to herself. "Your dad has RP?" she asks me, picking up the tablet again.

I swallow and nod.

"So you're probably pretty savvy about these things, hmm? You know how it works?"

"Uh, well, I don't really know the science," I admit. "I just know the results." Did my dad never tell me or did I never ask? Does it seem like I was too busy doing my nails to care?

"You're here with someone?" she asks. I nod again.

"My mom," I say, almost a whisper.

Dr. Porter stands up and steps into the hall, stopping the first person who passes by. "Can you bring in Henrietta—Hattie—Murphy's mom from the waiting room?" Then she turns back to me and smiles again, hands in her coat pockets, and starts asking me about my classes at school.

Oh God. This is not good. All of a sudden I feel like I'm in trouble, like my mom is coming back so that the doctor can tattle on me. *She totally failed her peripheral vision test. It's like she wasn't even trying.* Or maybe they just need my mom to blow my nose when I burst into tears.

My mom appears, face drawn tight, her hands strangling her purse strap, her lips pressed thin. She tries to smile at the doctor as she sits on the only other seat, a small black stool. It looks like she is baring her teeth.

"Hi, Mom, thanks for joining us," Dr. Porter says. "I wanted you to be here while we talk, just so we're all on the same page."

"Of course," my mom says, but it sounds like, *Hurry up and say it.*

"Now, I know a little about Dad's eyes. Do you have vision loss on your side of the family?"

"No, I mean, I wear glasses, but that's it." Everything my mom says sounds like something else to me, like I have a mom translator implanted in my skull. This particular statement sounds like, *No, thank God, he's dirty and defective, but I'm clean.* I look away.

"Hmm, well, RP is usually recessive and therefore when it's expressed, it's carried by both sides of the family. But not always, not if it's the autosomal dominant type, which could be what we're seeing here. I'll want to do a blood test today, too, if that's all right," she says to me.

"So—I have it?" I croak. Why am I asking?! There's no taking it back once she says it. Once she puts the words into the air, that's it. It will be true forever, and any chance of everything turning out fine for me will be gone.

"I am seeing some physical signs inside the retina, yes. And the imaging we've done backs that up."

I must look like she slapped me, because she backs away from the diagnosis and into an anatomy lesson. "Your retina is made up of rods and cones." She gestures to a big eyeball diagram on the wall behind her. "Rods tend to break down first with RP, and they're the ones that are responsible for seeing in low light. They also tend to be more concentrated on the edge of your retina, with more cones in the center. That's why the peripheral vision suffers. Later the cones get involved, too, but we're a long way away from that."

I stare at her. My brain is stalled. I can't move past this moment, and I don't want to. I want to go backward, to yesterday, when I was still telling myself that I was normal, or to years ago, when I still *was* normal. Dr. Porter seems to be waiting for something. I open my mouth and close it.

"It's a difficult thing. I wish I had better news," she says. Her smile is full of tsking sympathy now.

“What’s, I’m sorry, what’s her prognosis?” my mom asks. “I mean, how will this progress?”

“It’s hard to say. She’s doing great now, and we’ll meet with her once a year to track it. And also to keep you up to date on any advancements. Currently, there isn’t a cure, but a lot of exciting research is coming down the pike. Clinical trials in the works. Really groundbreaking stuff.” Her voice sparkles when she says this, as if she’s talking about a new roller coaster at Six Flags.

“So I have RP, and there’s no cure, and I have to come back every year just, what? Just to remind everyone how it’s getting worse?” I’m angry now, angry at the other two people in the room who get to have a regular conversation while my life is falling apart, angry at the powerlessness filling my limbs.

Dr. Porter doesn’t flinch at my tone. Clearly, she’s been through this before. “This is a lot to take in, I know, but there’s no reason to think you don’t have many years of functional vision in front of you.” Functional vision? What the hell does that even mean?

As if reading my mind, Dr. Porter adds, “The only major impact right now, unfortunately, is that I’m afraid you won’t be eligible for a driver’s license.”

Whatever hope I had left falls right through the floor.

“Even Dad got to drive for a few years. Even *Dad*.” We’re back in the car and all I can think of is how I’m sentenced to the passenger seat forever.

"Oh, honey," my mom says, plaintive, almost whining. She's not equipped to handle me when I'm this upset. She puts her hand on mine. I push it away.

"Hatts," she continues, trying a different angle, "after hearing what the doctor said, about how you don't always know what you're not seeing, how your brain will just fill in the gaps, do you even *want* to drive? Do you realize what could happen?"

She's sniffed out the selfish. How can I think about putting others at risk? But it's not fair. "I just want to be regular and do regular things." I slump down low and put my feet up on the dash, even though I know my mom hates that. To get words out at this angle, I have to practically spit them.

"Guess that frees up the money I've been saving for a car. Maybe I'll go blow it all on a bunch of canes. So everyone can see what's wrong with me. Except for me, of course. Ha."

"I'm so sorry," Mom says. "I wanted a normal life for you, too. I didn't know the doctor was going to say that. I really didn't."

She wants me to let her off the hook, but I don't. I just sit there.

Then she says, "Sometimes, I think about how I should have known better. About what effect your father's vision would have on you—on our children." She squints through the swishing wiper blades as rain pounds on the windshield. "Sometimes I think I shouldn't have married him."

The car is suffocating. It reeks of old road trip snacks ground into the seat cushions. I crack my window and let the coolness of stray raindrops hit my face. "Great, Mom. Thanks for the heads-up. Now I'll know why no one wants to marry me when I'm older."

"Oh, no, Hattie, that's not what I meant. Of course people will want to marry you!"

"Whatever. What do you expect me to do with all of that? I mean, Nate and I wouldn't even *exist* if you hadn't married Dad. So you're basically saying you regret my existence." I want to scream at her, *I'm the one going blind! This isn't about YOU!*

But Mom is crying. I should lighten up, apologize, show how accepting I'm going to be, how well I can cope, but I can't talk anymore. I threw up all my bad feelings on her and now I'm numb. I stare out the window, not really seeing anything, my eyes still dilated. The world is green-and-gray fuzz.

By the time we pull into the driveway, the storm has passed and the dilation drops are finally wearing off. Instead of following my mom up the front walk to the house, I go in the opposite direction, back toward the road.

"Where are you going?" she calls after me, sounding tired.

"For a walk." I say it mildly, like it's no big deal, like we haven't said things to each other that can't be unsaid.

"Why don't you come in and talk to your father first? I'm sure he's anxious to hear what happened. Maybe he'll have some insights."

There's no way in hell I'm going to watch my dad detach

from reality by quoting another dead white guy to me. Not today.

"Later," I say over my shoulder, starting to jog.

When I hit the end of the driveway, I break into a sprint. I'm going to run until I forget about this day, or who I am, or both.

CHAPTER 6

I head downhill so that my feet can be on autopilot, the rhythm of my pace beating in my ears like a train clicking along a track. Our street is on the edge of town, just one super long block lined with houses, but at each end it meets country highways that lead to other small rural towns. There are no sidewalks, but the shoulders are wide and covered with gravel that spews out behind me. At the corner, the houses give way to the first farm as I turn left. In the summer, this stretch is like running through a green tunnel, with cornstalks rising high on either side to give shade, but now the corn has all been harvested and the fields leveled, brown and barren. With the dark storm clouds still rolling in the sky, the place looks like some dystopian postapocalypse.

Past the next cornfield is a stand of trees with a creek winding its way among them. The wire fence that sits between the fields and the road is sagged and broken here, which to the neighborhood kids is the equivalent of a formal invitation to come in and explore. The creek is often little more than a trickle, but today the rain has made it loud and ambitious, and it rushes past my feet on its way to the drainage tunnel under the road. I break a big stick into bits, tossing them in and watching them swirl away like so many plans.

Even Dad got to drive. The very last time my dad drove a car is etched in bold in my memory, like my brain outlined it with a Sharpie and then put three big exclamation points afterward. I was twelve, which means my brother was only six, and we were all headed downstate to visit my grandma in north Jersey. I was sitting in the very back of our minivan in my usual spot, doing my best to ignore my brother, who was telling me knock-knock jokes that he improvised on the fly and that therefore made zero sense. The fact that I had not said, "Who's there?" even once had not slowed him down in the slightest. He simply whispered the responses to himself to keep his rhythm. In fact, the only way I knew I was involved in the game at all is that he was completely turned around in his seat, his head hanging over into my space, his bright eyes examining me intently for any sign of amusement after each pathetic punch line. I tried to rat him out to my parents for his technically unsafe position in his booster seat, but that had only succeeded in straightening him out for about thirty seconds, then he was back in my face.

As he was giggling at his own hilarity, I stared intently out the window into the woods lining the highway. The embankment leading up to the tree line was overflowing with electric green—ferns and wildflowers and weeds bursting with the kind of life plants only get in places where it rains every freaking day. I had been trying to imagine I was out there in the forest, to escape the monotony of our ancient, stale-smelling car, when my parents' conversation unexpectedly intruded into my thoughts.

"I'm serious, Dave. I think it's a nerve thing." My mom's voice was loud, not loud enough to be considered yelling, but loud enough to easily reach me in the back. "The pain is shooting right down my leg."

"It just strikes me as interesting that this always happens when we're on our way to see *my* mom, and never when we're going to see *your* mom," my dad said, his tone faux detached, as if he were comparing the migrating habits of two species of butterflies.

"I hope you're not suggesting I'm manufacturing it," she said. He wasn't wrong about the timing of these attacks, but still, calling it out like that was pretty harsh. I tensed my jaw. My parents always claimed they didn't fight, they "had discussions," but some of their so-called discussions would make a five-hundred-pound gorilla back quietly out of the room.

Even so, I was not prepared for where this one would go. All of a sudden, as if it were no big deal and he wasn't the person who constantly had a twisted ankle from falling off curbs or missing that last step, my dad said, "How about I drive?" My dad had not driven the car in months, presumably because his vision had declined to the point that it was impossible, so this was an alarming offer.

He must be joking. And even if he wasn't, Mom would refuse, right? Wrong. In an impressive display of how immature two mature adults can be, my mom pulled over like she was going to prove a point by having him kill us all in a fiery crash, and my dad was too proud or too delusional to back down. Without either of them looking back at or consulting with their precious children for a hot second, the switch was done. And at first it seemed like I was the one being silly, because it was actually fine. We were in the right lane, maybe going a little slower than usual, a little under the speed limit, but that was no big deal. For a few minutes it seemed like a real victory, that he could see a lot more than I had imagined. I almost felt a little tricked, like he'd been hiding this secret ability.

Then the diamond-shaped orange signs with a silhouette of a man digging started appearing every twenty feet or so. We were approaching a construction zone. The left lane disappeared, blocked by a string of orange barrels. The air seemed to drain out of the inside of the minivan, but we wouldn't have needed it anyway because all four of us were now holding our breath. Next, the shoulder to our right disappeared, replaced by a long, semipermanent cement barrier.

"Uh-oh," my mom finally said, but I don't think she knew she said it out loud.

Our speed dropped to about twenty miles an hour, which still felt impossibly fast with that cement wall looming on our right. I willed the cars behind us not to honk, not to pressure us into going faster; the tensed tendons on Dad's neck seemed to be all that was keeping us from pinging around inside the lane like we were in bumper cars. There was nowhere to pull over, no way to cry uncle, no room for error. Then my mom, in a hoarse whisper, started giving instructions. "A little to the left. Good. Hold there. Curve to the left coming. A little more. No, more. Okay, good." Oh my God. It was like they were playing Hot and Cold like we used to do during Easter egg hunts.

Speaking of God, I hadn't really prayed since first communion, but now I was silently praying a furious mantra: *please God don't let us die please God don't let us die please God.* My brother had silently situated himself back in the correct position in his booster seat. I was glad he couldn't see my face because he probably would have burst into tears.

Finally, the cement wall ended. My dad didn't wait for an exit, just said, "Can I pull over here?" and when my mom gave the all clear, he pulled just out of the lane and stopped, so he had to hug close to the door when he got out in order to not be flattened by the impatient caravan of cars that now accelerated past. When he got to the passenger side, he took out one of the tissues he always kept in his pocket, wiped his forehead, and blew his nose. Then he said something under his breath and my mom laughed. Pretty soon they were both cracking each other up.

Looking back on it, they had both just been relieved, the pent-up energy of adrenaline and fear coming out as laughter. But at the time, I had been so angry, and the anger still crackled around the memory. How could they think it was funny? He almost killed us; we almost died. All so he could be the big man. They were the parents—they were supposed to be responsible.

I will never drive. In a way, that will make me more responsible than my own father. And more powerless.

I reach into the water now to pull out a handful of pebbles and hurl them into the stream as hard as I can. The roundness of the plunking sounds they make as they break the surface is strangely satisfying. It releases a valve inside me, and the tears start to stream down my face, mixing with the sweat from running and landing double salty on my lips. I'm about to grab more rocks when I see someone standing on the bank out of the corner of my eye. I am not alone.

A startled sound escapes my mouth as I quickly wipe my face with my sleeve and turn, almost falling into the freezing water. Nothing. There's no one there. I'm positive someone had been standing just behind me to my right, but there are only scrubby bushes and maple saplings. I sit down, take a deep breath, try to steady myself.

The idea that the RP could be responsible for these visual hallucinations I've been having occurs to me for the first time. The doctor mentioned floaters as one of the RP side effects, and I thought I knew what she meant. Sometimes it looked like translucent caterpillars were wiggling midair in front of me. It felt weird to admit that I had experienced floaters to Dr. Porter. I'd never even admitted it to myself before. I'd written them off as dust until she gave them a name. Could these visions of Mason just be giant floaters?

As if to answer the question, the figure appears again, looking very un-caterpillar-like. If it's a floater, it's a floater doing an excellent Mason impression. He walks down the bank, crunching through the leaves, and stops next to me.

"Hey, Murphy, long time. I'd hug you but you look really sweaty. Like, you-might-want-to-be-checked-for-a-gland-condition level sweaty."

My eyes get wide. Floaters don't talk. And visual hallucinations are just that—visual. This . . . whatever this is . . . is the whole package.

"Hello?" he says. "What's this, the silent treatment? What'd I do now?"

I take a deep breath. Mason looks the same as he always did, all elbows and limbs, piercing gray-green eyes, and freckles on his earlobes, except for one thing. He seems to be ever so slightly illuminated from the inside, like those glow sticks that make a crackling sound when you bend them.

"Mason?" I finally manage.

"Christ, it took you long enough."

"What . . . what the actual fuck?"

"What the actual fuck what?"

Where to begin with this question. "What . . . what are you doing here?"

"Well, the angels said I had to save the person in my life who had wandered the farthest off her fated path, and then I could get my wings."

I swallow. Holy shit. "Really?"

"No, you twit! Murph, could you at least try not to be so gullible?"

This is definitely Mason. I'm still waiting for an answer. "Well, then . . . ?"

There's a pause, then a shrug. "I'm here to see you," he says finally, sitting down on a rock next to me.

He's here to see me. Electricity runs along my skin, and the other goose bump moments from the last few days flash in my mind. "Were you at the funeral?"

"Are you kidding? Wouldn't you want to go to your own funeral, see who would come? What everyone thought of you? Of course I was there! And I'll tell you a secret. I discovered something important."

Revelations from beyond the grave. I inhale sharply. "What?"

"I should have hooked up with Becca Reardon when I had the chance. She was verifiably heartbroken at the church!" Oh yeah, Becca. That was the name of the girl with the pixie cut faking status she didn't have.

"Mason, jeez! Can you be serious for one second?" I turn to where he's sitting, but there's nothing there. Shit, shit, shit. Did I make him disappear? I sit as still and as quietly as I can. I concentrate on my breath, lungs filling up, chest expanding, lungs emptying out, belly button in. Please come back. Please come back. Pl—

"I also might have noticed that Becca wasn't the only one feeling a little weepy." He's back, sitting on the other side of me now. Smirking, as usual.

I smile. *Stay awhile.* My limbs loosen. "Oh, you mean me?" I say. "I was just filled with emotion about mortality in general. Life and its meaning. You know, existential crap." I untangle my braid and start weaving it again, trying to look nonchalant the way I always have when I'm with Mason. But my insides are doing somersaults and cartwheels and backflips. What is going on? This can't be! But it feels realer than anything else that's happened in weeks.

"Sure you were. Like, 'life is meaningless without Mason' kind of existential crap, amirite?" He smiles, too. I go to give him a little shove, but my hand just moves through open air. So that's an added wrinkle. I guess feeling real and being tangible are not the same thing.

"Whoa. Why can't I touch you?" I ask.

"I'm dead, dummy."

"I got that. But you look totally three-dimensional. And . . . the leaves crunched under your feet before!"

"How should I know? I've only been dead for like three weeks. I'm not exactly an expert." He lifts his hands and drops them, and they seem longer and thinner than ever. I have an urge to hold them, then shiver at how futile that would be.

"Fair point," I say. I guess we're both a bit clueless about what's happening, which is surprising. Not just because he's dead, but because I've always sort of thought of Mason as having more definitive answers than me.

"Besides, you should count yourself lucky," Mason says. "I tried to hang with my mom—I practically swung from the chandelier in our living room—and she never even twitched. It sucks, 'cause I really wanted to tell her some stuff. But nope. Looks like you get me all to yourself."

I wonder in that moment how he feels about being dead. Is he sad? Is it a relief? I think about asking, but I don't.

It's almost like he can read my mind. "But enough about me.

That's boring. How are you, Hattie? You seemed a little unstable there for a second, with all the rock throwing and the sniffling. More of grieving yours truly, I assume?"

I feel guilty as I realize I wasn't sad about Mason at all in that moment, that what made me saddest was exclusively about me.

"I'm good. I'm fine," I say, trying to gloss over the truth.

"You sure? Don't want you getting all desperate on my account. Don't isolate, Murph. I eavesdropped on several sessions with the grief counselor about me, and that was the main takeaway."

"Yeah, I'm fine." I hug my knees. "I'm actually doing okay." He looks doubtful, so I add, "I might even have a date tomorrow."

Mason pounces on this information in a way that makes me instantly regret it. "Oh, really? Well, that's a very modern interpretation of grieving. Not the same as wearing black every day, is it? But no, seriously. I like it, Murph. You should escape a little. Who's the lucky guy?"

I try to backtrack. Oof, how can I still feel so self-conscious in front of someone who's dead? "It doesn't matter. It might be nothing. I'm not even positive it's a date."

A car goes by on the bridge over the creek and it brings me back to reality. I wonder if the driver can see me. More importantly, can they see Mason? Or does it look like I'm talking to myself?

"Nope. You have to tell me. No one needs to live vicariously more than me."

"Fine. Richard Walker."

"Little Dicky? Did not see that coming. You are full of surprises."

"Oh, for Christ's sake." I run my hand over my face.

Mason is enjoying himself far too much. "I get it, I mean, a girl needs Dick every now and then. Needs to go on a little Dick date." He seems to ripple with silent laughter.

"Mason!" I'm agitated. Am I embarrassed because I realize I'm actually looking for approval from a dead person or because it's clear I don't have it? "What's wrong with Richard Walker?"

I can tell he's about to come out with another double entendre, so I cut him off. "And no more dick jokes."

He gasps. "Who, me? I would never."

I snort. "Right. So what's your problem with Richard? Out with it."

"No, nothing, nothing at all. Except—well, doesn't he sort of seem like not a real person? Like he's an imitation of a person? He's human aspartame."

"That's big talk from someone who is literally a phantom. And I think he seems like an excellent person."

I hate it when I get huffy like this. This is quintessential Mason, though, so clever and quick that you can't help sort of crushing on him. Until he turns his critical laser in your direction, and it suddenly seems ridiculous that you could have entertained the idea that he could see you as more than a friend. Or that you would even want that.

The thought of more than a friend gives me an idea, though.

An angle for distraction. "Anyways, it sounds like someone might just be jealous."

"Jealous?" He leans in closer to me, like he's intrigued. "You mean me?"

"That's right," I say, doubling down even though I'm already feeling stupid that I came out and suggested he would want me like I'm some hot shit or something.

He stands up and kicks at a rock at his feet. Then he shakes his head and says, "I didn't want to admit it, Murph. But it's the truth. I am jealous."

My stomach starts feeling twisty and weird, like it's trying to fold itself up with my lungs the way you pair freshly laundered socks. I can't breathe. Is he actually saying this? Without thinking, I reach toward him. "Mason—" I start, but he interrupts me.

"I am so jealous of you. Because I want a little of that sweet Splenda Dick, toooooooo." He howls the last word to the sky.

I groan. I should have known. This is our familiar pattern, but the sting still feels brand-new. I'm out of my depth. I start toward the road.

"I've got to get home. My mom will be freaking by now."

"Okay, Murph." The air changes and suddenly feels empty, the way a house feels when you walk in and no one is home. I shudder. I got rid of him. Why did I do that? Being with him felt uncomfortable, but being without him feels worse, especially since I don't know if I'll ever see him again. Well, I'm not going to let that happen, because right now, I need him. I need to see him, and maybe more than that, I need someone to see me.

CHAPTER 7

By the time I get back to the house, I've convinced myself that I should confess to my parents that I have become completely unhinged, that I am having full-blown multisensory hallucinations and have lost touch with reality. But then I cross paths with the delivery guy from Pontillo's Pizza getting into his Civic, and suddenly everything feels so . . . normal. I had forgotten it was Wednesday, which in our house means Pizza Day. At last, something not shitty is happening. I decide to go with it, as I am a firm believer that cheese cures most things. I make a quick stop in the bathroom to wash my hands and get rid of any tear streaks on my face and then slip into my seat in the kitchen. My dad is already at the table, waiting for buffalo wings. Mom is bustling around the island with the to-go containers. She's busy and energetic all of a sudden. She clearly has an agenda.

"Nate and I have decided to watch that new superhero movie—I think it's the Avengers team up with Batman?" she says, utterly failing at seeming spontaneous. "Why don't you keep your dad company in here, Hatts?"

Before I can respond, Nate appears in the doorway, remote still in hand. "Mom!" he says, outraged. "How many times have I told you that you can't mix the Marvel and DC universes?"

"I don't know, I just can't keep them straight," she says, putting the plate of pizza, wings, and blue cheese next to my dad's left hand. "Wings at nine o'clock, babe, pizza at three." The clock system is how we let Dad know where the location of each food item is. I've always relished its efficiency. "Now I've got to go watch Batman fight Iron Man or whatever." She laughs as my brother puts his hands over his ears like he's hearing a deafening screech, and the two of them disappear into the den. My brother makes my mom endlessly happy, with his simple needs and perfect vision.

It's going to be all giggles and rainbows in the den, but the mood in the kitchen is severe. I take a deep breath. We are clearly supposed to have "a talk," though I'm not sure if Dad is in on the planning of this or not. We each eat a whole pepperoni slice in silence, as if we're hoping the grease will provide wisdom.

Just get it over with. "So I guess you heard," I say.

"Yes," he gets out, licking oil off his fingers and then wiping his hands on a paper towel. Now he's ready, I guess. "I'm sorry, Hattie. It wasn't a surprise to me, though. Since you were a little girl, we suspected something was wrong. You couldn't see the stars."

The basic truth of this sentence almost knocks me off my chair. He's right, of course. I'm flooded with my earliest memories of hearing nursery rhymes all about "star light, star bright" and flipping through picture books filled with sparkling illustrations of star-studded skies and wondering where those wonderful skies were. Because when I looked up into the dark, even on our rural property untouched by light pollution, all I could make out was the moon. At some point, I decided that the notion of stars in the sky was as made up as unicorns or the Tooth Fairy. And even though by now I knew that stars were technically real, I hadn't ever revised that comforting default belief in my mind.

"Did Mom know, too?" I ask.

"Well, you know I can't speak for your mother. But I will tell you that I have a theory."

"Uh-huh." The word *theory* already has me inwardly groaning.

"I've thought a lot about this, Hattie, and I've found this helpful. I hope it might help you, too."

"Uh-huh."

He's leaning forward, and I can tell he wants to make an impact on me. But his gaze is missing the mark; he's looking about two feet to the right of where I'm actually sitting. I'm used to that—he's guessing based on the location of my voice—but for the first time it sinks in that I'm going to do the exact same thing someday. And all my friends will feel sorry for me as I look at empty air instead of at them.

"You and I are exemplary in a lot of ways. We are imbued with gifts." My dad always talks like this. Not special—*exemplary*. Not filled—*imbued*. It's like living with a Scrabble board.

"Okay."

"So our diagnosis is here to keep us humble and human. It's a blessing from God."

I'm thrown. My family is a model Catholic family, so we never talk about God or spirituality at home. That is saved for

Sundays, at church. Talking about God at home feels about as appropriate as talking about your period during English class.

"I don't know, Dad. Feels like the opposite of a blessing from God to me." Not that I'm even sure I believe in God, but I'm not going to say that to my dad. This conversation is uncomfortable enough.

"The good news is you are doing much better than I was at your age." Then he launches into a story I've heard before that he always relishes, how he used to play baseball with his friends on summer nights at the park, how he couldn't see the ball when it was pitched, so he would just swing at every pitch and would still get a hit every so often, and one time he got a grand slam. I think he thinks the story highlights how athletic he was, but it makes me sad.

When he's done, I clear the plates and excuse myself. He doesn't protest, so I guess our big talk with all his great insight is over. He's not surprised I have RP? Well, I'm not surprised he can't make me feel better. So there.

In my room, safe from fake silver linings, I scroll through music to find just the right thing. Something that knows how stupid life is and how clueless people are. Billie Eilish. Overplayed, but in this sitch, perfect.

I dim the lights, make a nest out of pillows, and snuggle down. But instead of thinking about my depleted future and the canceled dreams that will go with RP, all I can think about is Mason. What really happened at the creek today, anyway?

I try to be analytical about it. It seems to me there are only three possible explanations. The loudest one reverberating around my skull is that I have made contact with a legitimate ghost, that somehow Mason's spirit is not yet at rest and is instead wandering our town, eerie but seemingly harmless. That I can't see what most people see, but instead I can see ghosts, or at least this ghost.

Now that I'm thinking about it, I can actually eliminate the second explanation. I had been considering the possibility that he wasn't actually dead, that he staged his own death so that he could run away and now he is trying to suss out if I am a safe ally while officially still keeping his undeadness a secret. But that wouldn't explain that weird inner glow, or how he could disappear and reappear somewhere else. He was on the cross-country team, and he was fast, but he wasn't that fast.

The last possibility is one that I really don't want to consider but is definitely the most likely. And that is that I am messed up in the head. That I'm spinning out over my friend dying or my eyesight or both and it's causing me to hallucinate. Maybe I've always been mentally unwell, and the grief just woke it up. I don't feel crazy, but isn't that exactly what crazy people say?

"Hey," Mason's voice says in the dark. "Is this okay? I know I was a lot before."

I take that back. At this exact moment, I feel completely bat-shit crazy. Because right now, I am filled with relief that I get to make up with a ghost. I am so glad he's here.

"Hey, yeah," I say.

"Good. Billie Eilish? Jesus. Why don't you just put on Rick

Astley while you're at it?" Mason took (takes?) his music very seriously, to the point that he was sort of a music snob. If more than three people on earth had heard of a band, that was too mainstream for him.

I turn the music down and the lights up a bit so I can focus on him in the corner of my room. He's perched on top of my desk with his feet on my desk chair. It's maddening how he manages to look extra attractive when he's giving me a hard time.

"You showed up to mock me?"

"Never."

"Then why *are* you here?"

"Why are *you* asking so many questions?"

"I'm sorry, I just . . . Indulge me?"

"Hmmph. Proceed." He sweeps his hand out in front of him in an official sort of way to show that I have his full attention.

Now that I have permission, I'm not sure where to start. I try to organize my thoughts, going back over my possible explanations. "Are you really dead?"

"Yes."

"Are you really here?"

"I mean, look, philosophically speaking, you could just be a brain in a vat with electrodes sticking out and nothing you experience is really there."

"How about not philosophically speaking?"

"Then yes."

"Do you think being able to see you makes me crazy?"

"Philosophically speak–"

"Don't make me actually put on Rick Astley."

"Ha!" A laugh escapes from him. He shakes his head. Then he says, "Murph, you might be the only one out there who's not crazy."

The statement rolls over me like a wave of oxygen. I feel reassured, and my muscles untense for the first time in many hours. I inhale. "Thanks, man."

"I just call 'em like I see 'em," he says. "Keep going."

"Can you see the stars?" I hadn't planned to ask him that, but what my dad said earlier is nagging at me.

"You mean, like, have I gone to heaven? Been one with the celestial bodies?"

Now I laugh. I can never anticipate what's going to come out of his mouth. "No, no, I mean, like, can you see the stars in the regular way. Like when you were alive. Did you look at the stars ever? Go stargazing? That whole thing?"

"Uh, okay. Yeah, sure, sometimes. The lake house was good for that." The mention of the lake house makes us both quiet for a minute. "Why do you ask?"

The safest person to confide in is probably a dead person. Still, I hesitate. "'Cause I can't see them, and I was just wondering what the big deal was."

"You can't see the stars?" His voice is mild, conversational, but I think I might hear a hint of concern underneath.

"Nope."

"Huh. Well, they're not really a big deal for me, honestly. I don't know, there's a lot of them? People like things that twinkle?" He starts to pick up speed. "They're these little points of light in the sky that look totally still, but you can also sort of feel them moving. Gets a person thinking, I guess."

"Are you going to keep hanging out with me?"

"Even though you can't see stars?"

"Even though you're dead."

"I suppose we'll see." The weight of the unknown hangs in the room, the awareness on both our parts that every word between us might be our last. It sparks something urgent in me.

"Okay, I only have one more question, but you might not like it."

"Fire away."

"Why didn't you wear a life jacket in the boat?" Saying these words out loud is precarious; I don't want him to feel like I'm blaming him for what happened. But I can't help running through the events of that day over and over in my mind, wishing that something, anything, had happened differently to change the terrible result. It just doesn't make sense that a couple of random details could create such a massively awful outcome.

He fills his cheeks with air, then blows it out with force. Finally, he says, "Because I'm a dipshit."

"That's not an answer."

"Well, then I'll have to mull that one over." He's not ready to tell me, I guess. Maybe I'm not ready to hear it.

But a whole new set of questions begins to form in my head from his response. *Where will you do this mulling? Where are you when you're not with me? Are you even experiencing, I don't know, linear time?*

But I said that would be the last question, and I don't want to scare him away again. Instead, I look through my phone for a musical choice that might pass muster with Mason. Funk would be good, but that's not the vibe here in the late-night quiet. Ooh, here we go. It's a throwback, but for Mason the older the better. The sound of Simon & Garfunkel has an immediate hypnotic effect.

Mason slides into the desk chair and slumps low, his legs kicked out in front of him, his signature winter flip-flops splaying out at the sides. I settle back into my nest, and we let the music fill up the room and the air between us.

At some point, I fall asleep. I wake up hours later, close to dawn, and Paul Simon is still singing, still soothing, even though I definitely did not put that song on repeat.

CHAPTER 8

The day I've been waiting for has arrived. Unfortunately, the bump is not only still there, but it has also now decorated itself with a rainbow of colors. I spend an extra half hour in front of the bathroom mirror after dinner to get my hair to swoop over it, so now I'm not sure whether I'm more mock-worthy because I have a huge bump on my forehead or because I look like I think today's Halloween and I'm going as a 1920s flapper.

The doorbell rings, and Richard is standing at my front door in his standard striped Oxford button-down, hands in his pockets. He's framed by the setting sun behind him, making his skin look even more perfect than usual. His hair wings out around his ears for a completely adorable effect, and something about the way he always tilts his head to the side to look at me makes me shiver in the best way. He's doing it now.

"Hi," I say, a little too loud. My hand reflexively checks on the bump to make sure it's covered. It still feels huge.

"Hi," he says, relaxed.

"Hi," I repeat, realizing I forgot to come up with a mystique-filled first line. "Um, come in."

He glides inside. All his movements are like choreography. He's like a character from some old movie where the women pluck loose each finger of a pair of satin gloves, pull them off, and tuck them away in a clutch without missing a beat of conversation. I'd probably have to break out the scissors if I wore those gloves. Currently, I'm just trying not to trip over my own feet.

I lead him downstairs to our rec room. I don't pause at the living room to introduce him to my dad, even though I might get a lecture for that later. Avoiding the awkwardness seems worth it, though. I don't want to put Richard through any sort of gauntlet. And anyway, technically I'm allowed to have boys in the house as long as I leave the door to the room we're in open.

Our basement is "finished," but it was done so long ago that the definition of *finished* in this case means "washed-up and ready to be retired." The wallpaper is meant to resemble a vintage newspaper, covered in sketches of ladies with bustles trying on hats and ads for blacksmith tools. The flooring is thin carpet directly on top of cold cement, so it always feels damp, and the drop ceiling is made of those institutional Styrofoamy tiles that pop into a metal frame. It's as ugly as a room can get, but it has a pool table, a flat-screen, and most importantly, some privacy.

I'm used to seeing Richard in public, in large spaces like the auditorium and the band room. Being here at home with him, alone, feels vulnerable and invigorating all at once. It's like I can sense electrons jumping off him and careening from air molecule to air molecule until they collide with my skin.

Say something. "So, what do you want to do? Should we run that scene?" That was why I said I wanted him to come over, after all. Figure I should stick to the script.

"Do we need to? You're such a quick study," he says.

"Flattery will get you everywhere." I swing into flirt mode, and he raises an eyebrow.

"How about we watch a movie? I want to show you *Doctor Zhivago*. Omar Sharif is so good. He's my inspiration for our show." Richard is a boy born a century too late. But I'm happy to agree. Sitting and watching other people talk rather than coming up with all the conversation ourselves is a relief. We pull up the movie and I purchase it, again skipping the part where I check with my parents.

As the strange chords of the balalaika fill the basement, I click off the overhead lights to stop the glare on the screen, leaving only the lamp on the end table providing a soft glow. The fact that the romantic quotient in the room just went to an eleven embarrasses me. I wasn't sure whether he knew I wanted this to be a date when I asked him, but suddenly it seems like we both know exactly what this is. He's spread his lanky limbs over the entire couch and is reclining sideways, his elbow bent and his head propped up in his hand to face the screen. He looks supremely comfortable, like this is his own couch at his own house.

I sit on the edge of the couch in front of his legs, tentative. I try to pay attention to the actors, to figure out the jumping around of time and place in the first scenes of the movie. But his electrons make the air alive around me.

"Come down here," he says, like of course the next logical step is to just lie down next to a classmate. I bring my feet up and slide down in front of him. I can't believe we're spooning. I think of the moments he's touched my hand before, how overwhelming that felt, and now here we are, pressed together along the entire length of our bodies. I lie stock-still, like if I move a muscle, this whole fantasy will evaporate. If I got an itch in this moment, I would just have to let it itch.

At first, I don't even think I'm breathing, but then realize I am because our inhales and exhales have become synchronized. I take in his amazing smell. Is he wearing cologne? Does he own cologne or is it his dad's? Then his arm reaches around me. He interlaces his fingers with mine and pulls me closer. Wow. I try to stop my brain from wondering what this means and what our relationship status is now. I try to relax into the warmth.

It's too late for me to figure out the plot, so I let the movie wash over me, all snowy rooftops and fur hats and significant looks. We are watching a great love story. Maybe *we* are a great love story. At play rehearsal, I'm always scrabbling for Richard's attention, a stray smile, a few exchanged sentences. But here I have him all to myself for the length of an epic film. I lie in front of him, a barrier between Richard and the rest of the world. It reminds me of how people say, "To get to him, you'll have to get through me first." Good luck getting him now, Amanda. He's mine. Honestly, I can't believe my luck. I can't help it, I finally move. I turn to look at him, and he kisses me.

This isn't my first kiss. I made out with a boy at overnight camp last summer while we were at a dance in the dining hall. But that was different. The boy at camp was all tongue, his mouth open so wide that it was like he was trying to swallow my face. I had liked that he liked me, liked that he was hard for me under his jeans when we danced, but while we were kissing I found myself mostly just getting through it and wondering when it would be over.

With Richard, the kissing is everything. His mouth is pressed against mine, like we might be sealed together, and then he pulls back a bit. His tongue flits in, gentle. He nips at my lips with his teeth, which for some reason makes me think about my own mouth differently, makes my lips feel very full and luscious. This dance between urgent pressure and playfulness makes me forget where I am, who I am. My hands clutch at him, one on his back and one in his hair, pulling him closer even though he's already as close as he can get. He still seems relaxed somehow, almost amused. I, on the other hand, am in full swoon. I can't keep track of his whole body at the same time, and my attention is bouncing around, to his lips, to his hand on my waist, to my fingers on his scalp, then back to his lips.

"You've been keeping a secret from me," he murmurs.

Oh, crap. What does he know? Reality threatens at the edges of my pleasure.

"What do you mean?" I say, trying to also murmur.

"You didn't tell me you were a world-class kisser." I can't respond for a minute because he starts kissing me again, hard.

When he pulls back for a breath, I'm ready. "Only when I'm inspired," I say.

He rolls on top of me, and the weight of him pressing down

on me makes my body arch up to press back. I start to wrap my arms around him but he catches one of my hands and presses it down above my head, like he's captured me. Where did he learn that move? I can't help it, I love it. It makes me feel like I've bewitched him with my sheer sexiness, like he's beside himself with desire. Maybe he is.

His pelvis presses against mine and a rhythm starts between us, and now the feeling has shifted from simple enjoyment to being more goal oriented. Each rub of his jeans against mine takes me farther down the path, good feeling piling on top of good feeling. What do they call this—dry humping? That sounds so gross, but this isn't gross at all. I always thought that having an orgasm with someone else would be more difficult than what I can accomplish in my own room by myself, but this is easy, natural. I feel his knees pushing into the couch on either side of me as the energy between us becomes so intense that every muscle in my body is contracting simultaneously. As long as he doesn't stop.

Suddenly, I hear a voice behind me.

"Hattie?" It's my dad. Richard's eyes fly open. We both freeze.

I manage to pull my mouth away without making any smacking, kissy sounds. I look at Richard fiercely, trying to transmit a message. *Don't panic and everything will be fine.*

I reach above my head to the armrest and press pause.

"Yeah, Dad?" I say breezily. Looks like I'm getting some acting practice after all.

My dad is halfway down the basement stairs. Of course he

can't see us, but it feels like we're standing on a tightwire in a high wind. One false move and this could be messy.

"Your mother and I are going to our appointment." Oh, right, it's therapy night. No wonder he doesn't have time to worry about his daughter and what she's doing with some stranger in the basement.

"Okay. We're just going to finish up this movie."

"What are you watching?"

"*Doctor Zhivago.* One of your favorites, right, Dad?" That could have been an error. He might want to stay for a beat and quote some of his favorite lines now.

But no, we're safe. All he says is, "Yes. Great film. Mom has her phone if you need us." And he feels his way back up the stairs.

I stand up, my hands over my mouth in disbelief at what has just happened. Richard groans and rolls onto the floor, making like a dead body.

"You know my dad's blind, right?" I say.

He grimaces with his eyes closed. "I fucking do now!"

Richard always looks calm, cool, and collected, but he doesn't look that way currently. He looks disheveled and traumatized, like he went through a cycle in the dryer. I start laughing. He looks at me, mock offended, but I can't stop. Life is too ridiculous. He starts laughing, too.

"Hey, wait," he finally says. "If your dad is blind, how does he have a favorite movie?"

My laughing almost shifts gears right into crying. I clear

my throat, try to sound objective about the whole thing. "He wasn't always this way. Plus, you know, there's a lot more to movies than what you see. There's the great dialogue, plus the score, the sound effects. He still watches movies, actually, even though he's not technically watching." I know I wanted to talk about deep stuff with Richard, but this is not the topic I would have picked.

"Ah. So was he in an accident? Traumatic brain injury?" Richard runs his hand through his hair and it falls effortlessly into place, any hint of his recent dishevelment gone. He's all business now. I appreciate the respect he's giving this, but I'm not sure I want to do the whole genetics lesson. Especially if he makes the logical leap to my own hereditary situation.

"No, it just got worse over time. It's progressive," I say, plucking tiny nubs of lint off the throw pillow I've pulled into my lap. I look at the floor. I'm suddenly embarrassed, but what is there to be embarrassed about? It's just medical fact. But even worse than that, somewhere underneath that discomfort I'm ashamed. What's wrong with me that I can't be proud of my own father? And why not? Because he's a little bit outside the band of normal?

Richard drops onto his knees in front of me, and tips up my chin so our eyes are locked. "That must be really hard," he says, his voice soft.

I bite my lip. "Yeah, I think it is. He hasn't been handling it that well lately, to be honest. He might be in denial or depressed or something."

He closes his hands over both of mine. "I meant for you."

For me. I'm so stripped inside that I almost spill my guts all over the clammy basement carpet. Like, hey, Richard, you think that's bad? That's nothing. I'm going blind, too. Just enough that I see dead people—either that or I'm also going crazy. You wanna go back to making out?

Instead, I smile and smooth my 1920s hair swoop back behind my ear. "You're sweet," I say. "But I'm okay."

"If you say so, m'lady," he says, and slides back onto the couch to sit next to me. "Now, how about we get serious about this movie? I feel like you weren't even really paying attention before." He winks.

"I'll be more disciplined, I promise," I say.

So we start actually watching the movie. The energy in the room is different now, comfortable, almost *more* intimate. I suddenly don't regret the conversation. Some truths came out tonight. Not everything, but something, some actual unpleasantness, and he didn't scream and run away, so that's encouraging. Plus, now he's resting his arm in my lap like we've known each other for a hundred years. And this is just the beginning.

CHAPTER 9

The show is still over a week away, but after last year's *Little Shop of Horrors* debacle where the plant left her mic in the dressing room and Mr. Mushnik had a major wardrobe malfunction, Mr. Price has decided on double tech and dress rehearsals. Which I guess in this case works out, since he has two female leads.

My run-through is starting any moment now. I shift from foot to foot, fidgety energy tingling in my limbs, as Asha attempts to suit me up with a cordless mic. Asha is into all things audio. Usually that means she DJs the dances in the gym, which she asserts is the best way not to ever have to deal with the social-anxiety cesspool that is a school dance. This month, however, her talents have made her sound boss for the play.

"Ouch!" I yelp as I feel tiny peach fuzz hairs near my ear detach from my skin.

"Well, stop moving!"

"I will if you stop torturing me!"

She coos fake sympathy, peels the cordless mic off my cheek one more time, and retwists the wire. "So is Richard your boyfriend now or what?"

Asha is uncannily good at asking things that I'm afraid to ask myself. I attempt to deflect the question. "Asha, I love you, but you are a shit listener. I told you. I don't think there's going to be a label like that. I'm pretty sure that's not the way things are done anymore."

She frowns and makes an incredulous *phhht* sound. "Who told you that? Him?"

"Look, not all of us can get with college boys. Try not to judge the rest of us lowlies." Both of Asha's parents teach at Cornell, which is her stated preferred environment for looking for love. Although, from what I can tell, that's as far as she tends to get. Looking. Can't really blame her, though. There might not be a guy within a thousand miles actually good enough for Asha.

She leans in so that I can smell her cinnamon gum and hooks the wire back over my ear. "My sympathies," she says. She tears a strip of tape with her teeth and secures the mic again, while I try to ignore the follicles pulling at my temple. "Just don't forget to be the interviewer."

"What?"

"Don't you remember when we went to that thing on career day? The guy said, when you go to a job interview, they're interviewing you, but you're interviewing them, too. Like, do you even want this job?"

"Okay, so?"

"So, you got to do that with boys, too."

"Um, he's hired."

"All I'm going to say is, he's at all the dances. Occupied."

"Well, of course. He's a really good dancer," I say, defensive.

Asha puts a hand up, like, *no offense*. "All right, don't let me yuck your yum." She gives the mic one last tug, squints at me, and nods to herself. "Practically invisible." Then she tucks the other end of the wire under the tunic overlay on my costume. I wiggle around, letting gravity pull the wire straight.

"Great. Let's let my love life go for a hot second. New subject," I say.

"What did you think about what Nolan said the other day, about different dimensions?" she says without missing a beat.

One might assume I'd have a clear answer for her, since I've seen Mason—what—four times now? I could easily say, "Nope, he's still in this dimension, and he doesn't look like a baby shark. Although he seems to be glowing." But I have a reservation or ten about revealing to Asha that I might be a few French fries short of a Happy Meal in the sanity department.

"Oh, you know Nolan," I say. "His whole life is a response to whatever media he's absorbed in the last forty-eight hours. Remember when we watched that James Bond marathon? He thrifted a tuxedo and wore it to class for a week."

Asha seems dissatisfied with this answer. She hooks the controls to my waistband, plugs in the cord, and clicks on the volume. Then she sits down at the soundboard and throws on headphones. "Now talk."

"I was talking already," I point out. "You just didn't respond."

"All it takes is a mic and this girl goes straight diva. Say 'testing one, two,' please, Your Highness."

"Testing one, two. How's that, Headphones?"

"Perfect." She pulls the headphones off again, lays them

down, and exhales deeply, tapping freshly manicured nails on the soundboard.

“I don’t know,” she says finally. “I mean, I never thought I’d say this about Nolan, but maybe he’s got the right idea. Typical heaven doesn’t seem to make much sense, logically, you know? Like certainly nothing up in the clouds with wings and shit. But the thought that everything we are just disappears when we die doesn’t seem right, either. There’s got to be some sort of energy transfer.” She said that before, at the lunch table. Something about energy. But the particular phrase *energy transfer* makes the hair stand up on my arms. Is that what’s happening? I feel like I’m holding out on her, like I’m hogging Mason all to myself, but I don’t know how to get around it.

“I like this theory, that somehow our energy is forever,” I say.

“I have to think that way, ’cause otherwise I can’t stop imagining Mason at the bottom of the lake, all white and waterlogged and bloated.” She shudders.

“Oh my God.” I’m shocked.

“Sorry, overshare alert one sentence too late.”

I shake my head. “No, I hear you. Look, I never thought about death at all before and now I think about it all the time. So it makes sense that you’re focusing on what you need to in order to not completely wig out.” The creek flashes back to me, the unmistakable Mason I couldn’t quite grasp, who seems to be slipping in and out of my reality like a tide with a fierce rip current. Does that make me more okay? Or less?

The walkie-talkie next to Asha crackles to life. "Ten minutes, everyone. Ten minutes."

"Yikes, I'm behind," she says. "You're all set, Queenie. Can you go grab Lancelot and tell him to come get miked up?"

"Sure." I open the door and there's Richard, about to knock. He smiles.

This is the first time I've seen him since his tongue was in my mouth and the surprise almost makes my knees go out. I gasp, accidentally breathing in a little bit of my own spit. A coughing fit follows. It's all very sexy.

He seems not to notice. "Just the woman I was looking for," he says, pulling a blindfold out of his pocket. Asha raises an eyebrow at the blindfold, then looks at me. "Never mind, I'll radio for Lance. You look like you're going to be busy not getting labeled."

"Haha," I say over my shoulder as Richard pulls me down the steps while I try to suppress the continuing tickle in my throat. When we get to the hallway, he turns me away from him and ties the handkerchief snugly around my face. It sinks in that in this scenario, being blind is fun and romantic. How fucking ironic.

"Come with me," he says, taking my hand. I do, trying not to look helpless and stumbly.

"I'm entirely in your hands," I say, getting into it.

"As it should be, gorgeous."

Gorgeous. Am I gorgeous? I'm going to have to check a mirror ASAP to see if I had some sort of radical transformation.

I'm still trembling from this compliment when we stop and he pulls off the blindfold with a snap. We're by the front doors of the school, facing the wall. A large poster hangs in front of me.

"What am I looking at?" I ask.

Richard indicates the poster with a flourish. "Snowcap Mountain. The school ski trip. I go every year. And I"—he pauses for effect—"have signed you up."

Richard takes my hands and steps back from me to take me in, looking expectant. I would go just about anywhere with Richard right now. I would go into the janitor's closet next to his left elbow and make out with him in between the bottles of bleach if he was into it. So I want to give him the response he's looking for, of course I do, but—

"I don't know how to ski," I say, biting my lip. I've never been on a ski trip, so I'm not sure, but it seems like knowing how to ski might be a prereq. Visions of me splayed out on the snow like an awkward starfish come to mind. This might not create the romantic scenario he has in mind.

Richard squeezes my hands now in a celebratory way, like we've won something. "That's why you're going with *me*. I will teach you."

This interaction is making it crystal clear. I am officially bad at surprises. The risk of embarrassment is just too high. So the excuses keep dribbling out of my mouth. "Is it expensive? I'm not sure my parents will let me." *Jesus Christ, Hatts. So you're a paranoid toddler now? Remember mystique? Just bat your eyes seductively and say, "Let me check my calendar, darling."* Instead,

I say, "And what about rehearsal?" What a downer.

"You know what, Hattie? Sometimes you are too smart for your own good," he says. He's determined to get through to me. He comes close and puts both hands in my hair. He tips my face up and rests his forehead against mine.

"Don't worry about any of that. That stuff is easy. We are going to spend the whole weekend together. Just you"—he pulls back a bit and kisses my left cheek—"me"—he kisses my right cheek—"and the mountain." And he kisses me full on the lips, mouth open just enough to make us interlock perfectly. We're now kissing in public, on school grounds. Plus, we are going away on a trip together. Asha won't be able to argue with the official status of that.

"Okay," I breathe when he pulls back. I feel dizzy.

"Now come on, smartie, we're going to be late for our scene," he says, as if this whole thing was my idea. I float behind him back toward the auditorium, seeing myself for the first time through the filter of the Richard Effect: a girl with a hot romance, a girl entangled with her costar, a girl who will soon be hitting the slopes with that romantic entanglement, no less. It's so good, I want to take a screenshot of my brain so that I can always feel this way. But I can't think about it too much, the way you can't look directly into the sun. Acknowledging it makes me afraid of losing it, and fear and bliss don't mix. So don't think about it, Hattie. Just be that girl.

CHAPTER 10

There's nothing like a dress rehearsal. Before that, no matter how good you are, how talented, how serious, you're basically a bunch of kids playing pretend. Lancelot in a tennis visor is not romantic, and the battle scenes between him and the other knights are hard not to giggle at. It's just a bunch of boys I know dancing together. But once all the lights have color filters, the sound is amplified, and costumes are on, the drama of it all permeates, and it's possible to be transported.

The only hitch for me personally is that although my chemistry with Arthur in the first act is shooting sparks out into the audience, it also makes Guenevere's great love affair with Lancelot in the second act look a little limp. Our original Lancelot got mono, so Mr. Price tapped some guy from the community college who'd played the role before to come and fill in. Even though this guy, Carter, is only like three years older than me, he treats me like I'm in preschool, and he's constantly doing belly breath warm-ups backstage that make him sound like a pregnant lady in a rom-com about to give birth. The whole thing is the opposite of sexy. I'm hoping the boost of tech and costumes will help me set the second act on fire.

So far, so good. I fly offstage. I've got eight bars of music to do my quickest costume change—off with the peach tunic and on with the sky blue—and grab up a dozen flower garlands. I've done this transition plenty of times, but now that the stage lights are on, they've contracted my pupils into pinpricks, and backstage is a sea of black. I put my hands out into empty air, inching my way forward to where the props table ought to be, but my trajectory is off and the nothingness goes on indefinitely. I almost wipe out on some coiled cables. I stop.

Shit. More than my inability to see, I'm frustrated by my own incompetence. Why hadn't I anticipated this? I should have known, should have made a plan. When am I going to stop pretending to myself that I'm just like everybody else? I'm worse than my dad refusing a Seeing Eye dog.

My musical cue comes and goes. I hear the pit pause, then start up again eight bars earlier. They must think I'm spacing out back here, but we all have strict orders from Mr. Price to treat this like a performance and keep going no matter what. "Hello?" I whisper hoarsely. Where's the stage manager? Isn't there anyone back here to grab those garlands for me? If there is, they're sadistically witnessing me freeze up like a lawn ornament. The idea that I'm currently being observed is intolerable. I turn and look back at the tempting brightness of the stage. Missing that cue again will be mortifying. I guess I'll wing it.

I burst back onstage empty-handed and already singing, a little too forcefully, like if I sing loud enough I can muscle this scene into working. When the rest of the cast onstage sees me propless, surprise registers on their faces. All our choreography for this number involves the garlands—tossing the garlands, dancing in and out of the garlands, playing tug-of-war with the garlands, even pretending to knight the ladies-in-waiting with the garlands. Garlands I do not have. I sing the lyrics on autopilot as I try to improvise movements, most of which, weirdly, seem to end up being square dance moves. I do-si-do with ladies-in-waiting and promenade with knights, half of whom look pissed. The other half look baffled, like they just woke up on an iceberg and are now dancing with a penguin.

I grind my teeth. This is the real trouble with being double cast. It's not that I get half as much performance time. It's that I could be fired at any moment without a second thought. My replacement is prepared and ready. She's sitting in the auditorium right now, and she's probably enjoying the hell out of this. In fact, everything that is good in my life right now—this play and Richard—could be lost in a quick switcheroo. Amanda could slide right in without missing a beat.

The end of the song is the worst, because by this time I should have given away all the garlands, and the chorus members are supposed to attach them to a pole that is lowered from above and then weave them together in a climactic May Day dance. As it is, everybody is just sort of walking in a circle as a random bare pole descends. And all the while, their eyes are throwing daggers at me. Or at least it feels that way. Even the pit seems to be accelerating the tempo, as if the whole woodwind section has decided to get through this train wreck as fast as possible.

When the run-through is over and everyone is back in their street clothes, we all sit in the first couple of rows to get notes.

Mr. Price flips through pages on his clipboard and clears his throat. “Really nice work, everyone. Overall, I feel confident in saying that the magic is coming alive up there. Especially you knights. Thank you so much, boys, for learning your lines. You were supposed to be off book ten days ago, but better late than never. Arthur, make sure to hit all your marks in that first scene so the spot can pick you up, and Guenevere—” He looks up at me over the top of his reading glasses. “I’m almost afraid to ask. Where were you and what happened to the wonderful flowers?”

The heads in the row in front of me all turn in my direction. “It was really dark backstage,” I say. “I couldn’t find the props table.”

Mr. Price looks at me like this is the least believable performance I’ve given yet. “As the lead, my expectations for you are here,” he says, indicating the high bar with his hand. Apparently, there is something magical about expectations set at the left temple. “At this point in rehearsal, there should be no excuses. There’s no room for lapses.” Ouch. “And Sofi”—here he puts his arm around the stage manager’s shoulder as if to protect her from a nonexistent attack from me—“has done an excellent job of organizing the props so you will always know where they are. Garlands are where, Sofi?”

“All the way to the left,” she replies, looking bored.

Oh my God, am I going to have to explain my diagnosis right now? In front of the entire cast? I am not ready for today to be the day where everyone changes how they see me, where I become Hattie, the disabled girl, or worse, the differently-abled girl. Not for some trite May Day dance.

I'm stuck in suspended animation, still trying to decide what I can possibly say that won't make a bad situation into an annihilating one, when Richard speaks up from several rows behind me. "I'm not busy during that transition," he says. "I can hand them to Hattie if there's no time for her to get to the props table."

My hero. I turn to him and mouth, *Thank you*, my eyes burning in adoration with enough intensity to light a match.

His eyes twinkle back at me, and he lifts his chin in a reverse nod as if to say, *I got you.*

But Mr. Price is trolling for drama, and he seems somewhat disappointed to be moving on. He takes one more jab at me. "And I presume you will remember the real choreography once you have props in hand?"

The relief I'm feeling makes me goofy. I'm not getting fired. I don't have to quit. "Absolutely, Mr. Price. Real choreography. One hundred percent. Count on me."

He finally cracks a smile. "I do like enthusiasm," he says. "And that goes for everyone! T-minus six days to final dress, everyone! Get psyched!"

Oh, I'm psyched all right, Mr. Price. No thanks to you. I'm psyched to be the one making that twinkle happen in Richard's eyes.

CHAPTER 11

When my mom drops me at school Saturday at dawn, the bus is already there—not a school bus, but a real touring bus with sleek lines and tinted windows. Its engine is rumbling a deep impatience, and it's belching steam that surrounds the bus like a halo. Kids swarm around the bus, loaded down with every kind of ski equipment imaginable, much of it in fancy nylon cases with brand names I don't know how to pronounce splashed on the sides. I look down at my own small duffel at my feet. I'm going to have to rent everything but my clothes, which suddenly feels demeaning, like my house is filled with rent-to-own furniture or something. I wrinkle my nose at the thought of the ski pants and jacket sitting inside that duffel, borrowed from my mom from when she used to ski twenty years ago. The pants are navy and the jacket a royal blue, which seemed fine when Mom showed them to me because I like blue in all its forms. But everyone wearing their ski jacket here is in neon: oranges, pinks, and greens that make them look like a deluxe pack of highlighters. I've now lost count of the number of ways I'm going to stand out on this trip. *Go big or go home*, I think grimly.

Mom is watching me, frozen in the front seat, my hand on the door handle. "Hey," she says. "You don't have to go if you don't want to."

"No, I want to. I want to," I say again, convincing myself more than my mom. I gather up my stuff and open the door. The weather has fully cooperated with the plans of the school's ski club, and a biting blast of icy air hits my face.

"Okay, then, have fun and be safe," she says. "I love you. You're going to do great. Call me anytime." She's not always the worst.

"Thanks, Mom." I hitch my bag over my shoulder and walk lopsided to the bus.

Richard is loitering against the outer wall of the auditorium like it's a warm, breezy day in June. I wince as I see the person next to him. I already knew Amanda was coming on this trip, had made sure of it, in fact, because I couldn't leave her here with Mr. Price while I was off skiing and missing rehearsal. I would lose the part for sure. So in a way I'm glad she's here, but does she always have to be within three feet of Richard? I guess I thought that once Richard and I kissed, things would be different, but she seems more present than ever. Always beside him, usually laughing and jangling her keys. The constant need to stake my claim is exhausting. I wish I could make him wear an ugly Christmas sweater with a picture of my face on it. Of course, then I would have to look at my own face when I was with him. Not optimal. More brainstorming needed.

She sees me. "Hey, lady." She sort of gasps it, as if she has to catch her breath from the very excellent time she'd been having with my guy.

"What's up?" I say as I slide next to Richard. Can I grab his hand? Touch his arm? I can't bring myself to be that bold, so I just stand very, very close to him.

"We were waiting for you," Richard says, which reassures me. All is well. "Let's get on. It's freezing."

I still have to wait in line to load my bag in the luggage compartment underneath the bus, so I get on after them, praying that they're not sitting together. But no, they're across the aisle from each other and Richard waves me over. *Stop being paranoid*, I tell myself. *Enjoy this.*

Jeff is standing in the very back row, apparently waiting until the last minute to fold himself into a seat. "Hattie!" he says, surprised. I realize I didn't tell anyone in the Beaver Bunch I was going on the ski trip. I didn't really believe I was actually going myself until about thirty seconds ago. "Come on back!"

Hesitating, I glance at Richard. He is looking at me, amused. He extends his palm toward the seat next to him. An invitation.

"I'll be right back," I whisper, dropping my backpack into the space next to him to hold my spot, just in case Amanda gets any ideas about moving. Then I walk toward the back of the bus, already blushing at the thought of filling my friend in on my new . . . situation.

"Want window or aisle?" Jeff asks amiably. This is an overly generous offer, since Jeff's knees would be smashed against his chest if he tried to squeeze his basketball-player-sized frame in by the window. Actually, even though people always think he must play basketball, the closest he's ever come to playing on a team is when he's playing *Madden* on his game console. Nolan's the same, and so was Mason. That was probably part of how they originally started hanging out. Not that they're lazy or unathletic; Jeff's already got a ski pass for an additional ski resort hanging off his zipper. Just, I think, that they never really cozied up to the "organized" aspect of organized sports.

"Thanks, Jeff," I say, "but I think I'm going to sit up front. With Richard." I try to say it as casually as possible, but I see the possible implication dawning on Jeff as his eyebrows go up. At least Asha hasn't revealed this part of our conversation to the rest of the group. "We're . . . trying something." *Trying something? What the hell does that even mean?*

But Jeff, in typical form, gives me an out on any cringiness. "All right, all right," he says, nodding. "Cool, cool."

"I still love you, though," I say, breathing easier.

"What's not to love?" Jeff grins, turns his back to me, and pretends to make out with himself for a second. Then he immediately becomes engrossed with hassling the kid across the aisle. "Dude, you've got your shoes off already?! We haven't even left yet. Bro, your feet are rank. Who's got some Febreze?"

I return to my backpack and climb over Richard's lovely legs. No big deal, totally normal, just because the whole bus can now tell something is going on between us, that's no reason to shrivel into a tiny raisiny version of myself. I get situated for five hours of together time. My self-consciousness is neutralized by how glorious this is going to be. He's already got his AirPods out, and he hands one to me.

"This is my ski playlist," he says. "I have another one for

après-ski." He raises an eyebrow. I love how fancy and sexy this sounds, but I have no idea what it means. I nod knowingly.

We sit close together and listen. It's mostly jazz and big band music, stuff I normally hate. I like music with lyrics so you can sing along, so you know what the song's really about. But this morning, instruments-only is working for me, mostly because it was picked by Richard, but also because it's creating a mood. It's like a scrim onstage, in front of which Richard and I can improvise our own scene.

By the time we've listened to two tracks, we're already speeding down the highway. The countryside around us is desolate and brown. The autumn leaves have fallen and everywhere exposed branches crisscross like a scraggly bird's nest. The trees look lonely even as they cluster together. The only hint that we might actually be able to ski at the end of this ride is a handful of flurries blowing across the road, swirling but refusing to accumulate.

Richard reaches into his backpack and pulls out a fleece throw blanket. The tour bus is pumping heat on full blast and it's already pretty warm, so this choice is a mystery to me until it becomes clear that his goal is actually a privacy screen. He spreads it out over both our laps and pulls it up to his chin as he leans into me. He noses at my arm like a puppy and ducks his head when I lift my elbow so that my arm is now wrapped around his shoulders and his face is resting on my collarbone.

"Are you going down for a nap?" I ask, amused.

"Mmm, just getting comfy. Time for a little snuggle." He

scooches in even more and slides his arm across my lap so it rests on my thigh.

I tilt my head and rest my cheek on the top of his head, inhaling his hair. He smells like cedar today. I close my eyes and let myself float in his aura.

After a few minutes he tiptoes his hand off my leg to stroke the place on my wrist where my pulse is quickening. It feels just to the left of ticklish, giving me goose bumps. Then his hand wanders along the bottom hem of my shirt, his fingertips grazing the skin underneath.

The parts of me that were drowsy moments before are now wide awake, enlivened, my nerve endings tracking the touch of his fingers like a helicopter searchlight tracking a car chase.

All the while, he looks as unmoving as a dead body to anyone viewing us from outside our blanket retreat, his head so heavy and still on my chest that even I am having trouble believing that it's attached to the curious hand exploring my torso. His caress is fully under my shirt now, moving along the edge of my bra until he finds a gap. When he brushes my breast, I gasp audibly, then quickly cough in a pathetic attempt to cover it up. I look around, but no one seems to notice. Across the aisle, Amanda is fully engrossed in a movie on her phone, and the window seat next to her is empty. Periodically, a Nerf football launches over my head from the back of the bus to somewhere midway up the aisle and back again.

We are in a parallel universe, a bubble unto ourselves, able to observe the activity around us but somehow invisible. My eyes are resting on Amanda's placid face when Richard's fingers start to trace circles, and the opposing impact of my two senses makes my cheeks hot.

But why am I trying to hide my connection with Richard from Amanda, anyway? Maybe this is exactly what she needs to witness to brush her back, so she'll go and find herself a different boy to drive around and have cutesy nicknames with. When Richard starts to tease my skin, stroking and then stopping and then stroking again with more intensity, I allow myself to giggle audibly. "Richard!" I say in a perfect stop/don't stop sort of way. He looks up at me, grinning, then resumes his position. I sneak a look over at Amanda, but there's still no outward sign that she's paying attention to us. Man, she is like a Jedi or something. I decide to give up on my agenda with her for now, to put her out of my mind. I don't want anything to interfere with the deliciousness of this moment.

Richard has settled into a rhythm now; he's swirling his fingertips around and even throwing in a light pinch here and there. But it's when he pulls back and barely touches me that I wriggle with elation.

My other breast feels decidedly neglected; there's a strange desire for symmetry tugging at me, but the way our limbs are intertwined Richard would have to have an extra joint to reach it. Instead, his hand wanders from under my shirt to down between my legs. I'm sitting with my thighs pressed together, there's really nowhere for his hand to go, and it feels too embarrassingly obvious to just spread my legs. But his hand encourages me, pressing gently outward on one of my thighs until it slides to the side enough for his fingers to be able to trace all the way up the inner seam of my pants. At first, I'm not really sure how much he can accomplish with his hand when there is a layer of thick denim in between him and my skin, but everything has felt so good this far that I'm not about to discourage him. He seems to instinctively find the thinnest spot in the fabric right next to the seam. He leisurely rubs the spot with the tip of his fingernail. Somehow he's exactly on top of where I must have about a trillion and one nerve endings. My body recognizes this as a match that sparks a forest fire.

The striving nature of it fills my body, and I realize this is going to go all the way for me, right here on the bus, in a public place. If anyone noticed, it would be the most mortifying moment of my life, and yet I can't bear to stop it—I still want him to keep going. I also want to grab him, throw him on the ground, and tear his clothes off, but that is unfortunately off-limits with Amanda within arm's reach. I just have to keep my breathing nice and even, and keep the pleasure growl lurking at the back of my throat in check.

And then it happens. The feeling of perfection spreads outward from my core, followed by total contentment. Anything that was tense now relaxes. The change causes Richard to lift his head to look at me. I feel so good, and Richard looks so proud of himself, that I burst out laughing.

"You seem refreshed from our little nap," he says with a smile.

"So refreshed," I say. "Positively invigorated. I should make naps a part of my daily routine." I stand up to stretch and an arcing Nerf ball hits me on the back of the head. The universe never seems to skip an opportunity to keep me humble.

"I've got it!" I call, as if I haven't just had a revelatory sexual experience and was instead waiting around to be part of this fun travel game. I grab the ball from where it has tumbled by my feet. Jeff claps his hands and holds them up high to show he's ready, and I toss it to him at the back of the bus.

"Nice spiral, Hatts!" he says after he catches it, then immediately launches it again toward the front. I slide back into my seat.

"You're a woman of many talents," says Richard.

"I might say the same about you," I say, giggling, then, "I mean, except for the woman part."

"Such a talent," he repeats. "Although you do seem to get hit in the head a lot."

"That's my secret. It keeps the brain stimulated."

"Ah, so that's what I've been doing wrong. I have so much to learn from you," he murmurs, picking up my hand, kissing the center of my palm and locating nerve endings I was entirely unaware I had. For a moment, I think he's going to start round two of canoodling under the blanket, but instead he takes a 180-degree turn.

"And now, I believe it is time for snacks!" he announces. It seems like he's said it louder then he needed to until I realize he has not one or two bags of goodies in his backpack, but three. One for himself, one for me, and one for–sigh–Amanda. As I watch her find the gummy bears inside and hold them up like a trophy, I try to pep talk myself again. Better to share food than to share the kissing, right? My pretzels taste like sawdust. I want to snatch the bag away from her, to announce my unilateral decision that her bizarre privileged status with Richard has now been permanently suspended, and she should feel free to walk right off this bus and out of our lives forever. But that would make me look paranoid and insecure when how I want to look is like I've never had a petty thought in my whole life, and certainly not one about Amanda. Like she's barely on my radar.

"Want mine?" I say, reaching across Richard's lap to hold out the candy to her. You can have all the gummy bears, and I'll have the guy, sound fair?

"Seriously?" She takes the bag and holds it to her cheek like she's cuddling with it. "Don't you like them?"

"I do, I'm just in the mood for something else, I guess," I say, trying to catch Richard's eye. But he's looking at her.

"Remember that giant gummy bear you got at Six Flags?" he says to her.

She rolls her eyes. "I remember the vet bill when Archie ate half of it! Oh my God, my parents are still mad about that."

They keep reminiscing, which means there is precisely no place for me in the conversation. I look out the window, trying to act comfortable, like I want to be left alone with my own thoughts. Suddenly, I find myself imagining what this trip would have been like if Mason were still alive and sitting in the back seat with Jeff right now. Would I even be sitting with Richard then, or would I be in the back, too, laughing with the

Beaver Bunch boys? Richard and I wouldn't have fooled around, that's for sure, not where Mason could have witnessed it; he would have teased me endlessly. Which then makes me wonder—did Mason get to hook up with anyone before he died? Ever even kiss a girl?

I realize I'm imagining what kind of kisser Mason would be when Richard tucks his hand back into mine. He's still talking to Amanda while he touches me, which in this single isolated moment is a good thing because it means he doesn't notice my cheeks burning red as I quickly push the image of Mason's lips out of my mind. Where did that thought come from, anyway? Too many hormones running around inside me after that pleasure-fest, I guess. It's Richard I want. And I've got all weekend to prove that.

CHAPTER 12

Every so often you find out about entire other worlds, worlds you never knew existed but that have been bustling and thriving just beyond the perimeter of your awareness for your whole life. The skiing world is one of these for me. I knew that some people were skiers and I wasn't, but I had no idea how rounded out the culture was, complete with its own language, costumes, and rituals. And so, so many people.

Even though these people come from all over the state, all over the country even, they somehow all know each other. And they are so ecstatic to see each other that their greetings involve a lot of screaming and yelling, usually in the form of "Oh my God, hiiieeeeee!" or "Broooooooo!" That is, unless one of them is a skier and the other is a snowboarder. Then they are coolly suspicious of each other, because apparently these two tribes are at war. It feels like I should be taking notes, compiling audio accounts.

I am clearly an outsider in this world, but even witnessing it is exciting. Everyone has the air of a hero, either heading out on a journey with the fire of ambition lighting their eyes or returning from an adventure loaded down with bragging rights. For me, all it takes is managing to get my heels stuffed inside my boots and my boots clicked into my skis to feel a sense of accomplishment, of belonging.

Richard and I shuffle into line, and in the five minutes we wait to get to the chairlift, my toes turn into little toe-shaped ice cubes. There must be a trick to keeping warm that I don't know about, a special kind of socks or something, because no one else seems to be suffering. I daydream for a moment about a day when I'll know all the tricks, after Richard and I get married at a ski resort and spend our honeymoon flying down black diamond trails, the most famous skiing couple that also happens to have a show on Broadway. I return to reality as I'm prompted to step onto the painted line. The chairlift whisks us up and away with startling velocity. My feet feel like they're tied to cement blocks with the bulky weight of the skis, until I discover I can slip them on top of a short metal bar below my seat. A slim bar for your feet, a slim bar coming down over your head; it's as if the designers thought it was best to make any level of support or protection almost invisible, because clearly skiers love danger.

About halfway up the mountain, Richard points out a sign far below. It reads, THESE MOUNTAINS WILL BE AS COLD AND LONELY TONIGHT AS THEY WERE 200 YEARS AGO. DO NOT SKI ALONE. I shiver. Great. As if I wasn't already practically peeing my pants with nervousness.

"That's why you've got me." He nudges me, winking. I wink back, my stomach's butterflies quieting slightly. I've got the protection of his old pro status on the slopes.

The part I'm most worried about is managing to get off the chairlift before it starts heading back down the hill, but

Richard tells me to point my skis up and lean forward and then it's done. I don't even fall down! I'm a natural.

We start out on the bunny slope for my benefit. Richard is literally skiing backward down the hill in front of me, which is simultaneously humiliating and also fully dreamy. The air is so crisp and cold it feels like I've chugged an energy drink with each inhale; I'm extra awake and alive. I try to follow Richard's directions.

"We're going to start with the snowplow. Whenever you get into trouble, you can always get back to basics with a snowplow."

"Okay." I make the V shape with my skis just like the line of toddlers cruising down the hill next to me. I immediately slow down. This newfound power to control my speed makes me confident enough that my brain has space to wonder if I look cute in these snow pants. The fact that skiing is fun dawns on me. I start to play, pulling the backs of my skis together to speed up, pushing them out to slow. There are no brakes or gas pedals in my future, but this might be the next best thing. The melody from an electric guitar line that's been playing behind a lot of video shorts lately runs through my head, and I rock out a little bit, bouncing my bent knees as I go. I'm killing this.

Suddenly, as I push my heels out again, the curved tips of the skis cross and slide over each other. Instantly, my legs are crossed. What happens next feels like a denial of basic physics: my left and right sides switch places, up becomes down, and I am at the total whim of gravity. Then, just as I had imagined, I am splayed, a snowy starfish, a kindergartner attempting a snow angel. The shadow of Richard's head appearing above me allows me to open my eyes more than a squint.

"Falling is part of skiing," he says.

"Glad I'm getting the full experience, then," I say as he helps me back onto my feet.

Then he shows me how to turn by shifting my weight, toward the left to turn right, toward the right to turn left. It seems counterintuitive, but in minutes I'm doing it! In my mind's eye I see myself, like I'm a drone watching from above, as I cut back and forth across the hill, carving a clean white S trail into the snow.

I hear Richard behind me now. "Pop quiz!" he calls.

"What?"

Suddenly, he skis in front of me and stops. I'm barreling toward him. I don't want to break both his legs—that is definitely not part of the ski-couple fantasy—so I turn to the left. Now I'm hurtling toward a very lethal-looking tree trunk. I turn again, hard. I've ended up on a small side trail, with the trees looming tightly on either side. Somehow my speed has increased and I seem to have lost control of my limbs when Richard flies past me and gives my left shoulder a tap. I tip into a snowbank, breathless.

Richard backtracks and flops down behind me so we're almost spooning in the fluffy powder.

"You forgot to snowplow," he says into my hair, his skis intertwined with mine.

"I had a lot on my mind. I was busy not flattening you."

"I'm afraid you failed your quiz." I feel his hand on my waist as he leans in and gently nips the part of my earlobe peeking out from under my hat.

"Oh no, how can I possibly make it up? There must be some extra credit you can assign me."

I feel his tongue flick into my ear. If someone had told me before today how glorious a tongue in your ear could be, I never would have believed them. I've always had the firm conviction that wet ears are icky. But somehow, impossibly, this feels amazing.

"I've got a few ideas," he says. He growls, wolf-style, and squeezes my torso in both hands with considerable force, like it's taking all his self-control not to consume me right there.

I chuckle. "I'm sure you do."

A couple of snowboarders come down the trail, bringing us back to reality. Richard pulls himself away and stands, hand out. "Looks like we have to explore this new trail you've chosen."

"More like it chose me," I laugh. We start down the hill, side by side now. The sensation of being synchronized with him makes me bold, and soon we're at the bottom. Richard is flushed and bright-eyed, and I probably am, too, with the fun of it all.

"Want to go again?" he says.

"Absolutely."

I am athletic and clever, I am rocketing up the learning curve of this chic sport in a place that looks like a scenery postcard, and the boy I am currently lusting after is openly lusting after me back. My fantasy life and reality have never overlapped so much, not ever. The only thing that could tinge this perfection is my totally maladaptive tendency to be suspicious of things that seem too good to be true.

“Don’t think,” I say to myself. “Just ski.”

CHAPTER 13

1629. I look back at my hand, confirming the number Richard scrawled in ballpoint pen on my palm before we parted ways to shower and change. I get to the end of the hall and knock on his door, and then I shift from one foot to the other, trying to loosen up my legs a little, since they're screaming. I've just come from my room, which I'm sharing with Amanda. It was all I could do not to say, "And your enemies closer" when I found out the room assignments. I wonder how many guys are in Richard's room.

But when he answers, he's alone. He steps back so I can come in, then puts a sock on the outer doorknob, closes the door, and throws the bolt. He doesn't waste any time with our newfound privacy. He pulls me toward him and turns me so my back is against the door. Burying his hands in my hair, he gives me a long kiss. He runs one hand up and down the side of my body. It seems impossible how quickly he can wake up every nerve ending I have.

Richard's room is little more than a window dormer flanked by two twin beds. The ceilings are low and slanted with the roof. When we read *Crime and Punishment* in Enriched English last semester, the main character lived in a garret, and this is sort of what I imagined. Richard looks like a giant in it because he can only stand up straight right by the door; everywhere else he has to stoop to not hit his head. It makes for a perfectly reasonable explanation of why we have to kick off our shoes and stretch out on the bed. We're mirror images of each other, stretched out on our sides, hands holding up our heads, elbows propped on the pillow. He's looking at me intently; his eyes are an invitation. It makes me think about how many things I could tell him, how many things I haven't told him. The only thing that stops me from opening Pandora's box is I don't know how to start.

"What's going on in there?" he says, touching my temple. "I can see a lot of wheels turning."

I shrug. "Just catching my breath."

"I didn't know you were breathless."

I scooch closer to him. "A little."

He starts kissing me again, and it's just like on the bus. It feels like I'm drowning in it, no, swimming in it, NO, *floating*, like I'm weightless and surrounded by sheer yumminess. I let myself relax, and the places where our bodies are touching take turns being at the front of my consciousness—first our lips, our tongues, then my hand on his arm, then his hand on my waist, and then our two sets of socked feet intertwined.

Now he's working on the buttons of my shirt, and with one hand it's going pretty slowly. I realize I don't want him to get frustrated and give up, so I help him with the last few. The whole time that button business is happening, our mouths are crushed together with a four-alarm-fire level of intensity that makes me feel like a different person, not an anxious, self-conscious person but someone untamed, like I just emerged from the woods or something. Like I'm wild.

He sits up then and grabs the back of his collar, pulling his T-shirt over his head in one swift motion. I take the cue to do the same, but there's no way to get my bra unhooked and off without looking clumsy and awkward. Why didn't I wear my bra that hooks in the front?! I try to hold his eyes with mine and just get it off as fast as possible so it won't take up too many frames in the mental movie I'm hoping he'll play of this later.

Then we come together again, his arms encircling me. There's so much skin, all of it smooth. Richard only has a few chest hairs right at his sternum, downy and soft, which I like. I touch his nipples, and am surprised when they get hard the same as mine do. Apparently, we are both thinking about my breasts at the same time, because he rolls me onto my back and then moves down to put his mouth on each of them. I almost cry at how good it feels.

Suddenly, he's pulling away from me. He reaches over and tugs the curtains closed, so that there is only a long strip of light left on the opposite wall from the rays of the setting sun sneaking through the crack. Then he reaches down into his backpack sitting on the floor next to the bed. I hear the crinkle of plastic as he finds what he's looking for. He brings it up, holds it with both hands and tears the wrapper. It's a condom.

My body goes cold. I feel like he just skipped about ten steps.

"What's that for?" I ask, my voice flat. How did we get here?

He smiles at me, still playful. "You know what it's for."

I'm so confused. "But we only just started— I mean, this seems fast . . ."

"Why? I'm ready. You feel ready. What's holding us back?" The last question is muffled as he leans into me, kissing my neck.

But everything yummy has evaporated, and now I am acutely aware of the sticky wetness of his spit on my skin. The room smells stale and sweaty. I sit up quickly and almost crack my head on the ceiling, ducking at the last second and scooting down to the foot of the bed so I can put both feet on the floor. I grab my shirt and stuff my arms in the sleeves.

"Hey, where are you going?" He says it plaintively, like a little boy, pulling on my hand. "Come back."

I reclaim my hand and try to clear my head. Maybe I can save this. We're just having a misunderstanding.

"Look, Richard, I don't expect you to know this about me, 'cause we haven't really had a chance to talk about this yet, but I would only . . ." Only what? Go all the way? Make love? Fuck? "I can totally see myself having sex with you, I want to, but we would have to be in love first, you know?"

Immediately, he says, "Well, I love you."

A bark of a laugh jumps out of me at the ridiculousness of that statement. What the hell? "No. You don't. You barely know me." My body seems to be done with this whole scene before my brain can catch up. I'm surprised to find I'm already putting on my shoes and tying the laces. I stuff my bra into my pocket.

He looks unbothered by what I just said. "I think I do."

The calmer he is, the more out of control I feel. "No. I promise. You don't know me at all. And you definitely don't love me."

There's a minuscule shift in his gaze; his eyes get stony, as if he is looking at a stranger who may have stolen his bike. There is a hard edge to his composure. "You don't have to hold on to these old-fashioned ideas of what gives women value, Hattie. You'll be the same person afterward." What is he, a women's studies professor?

"That is not what I'm doing. Don't tell me what I'm doing." I'm stumbling over my words, I'm so agitated.

He props up a pillow and sits back, putting his hands behind his head. "I'm just saying. It doesn't need to be a big deal. Everything doesn't need to be a big deal."

The note of condescension curls my hands into fists.

"You can throw that condom away." I have to go. I feel like a failure even though I'm pretty sure he's the one fucking up. I open the door, then I pull the sock off the doorknob and toss it into the room before shutting it behind me. I'm moving on instinct now. In the hall, I turn toward my room. But halfway there, I spin around. What if Amanda is in there? I'm not ready to interact with her. I head outside and the inevitable cold hits me, shocking me with its impact. With no coat on, my teeth are chattering within seconds, but I want it. I want the punishment.

The regrets are ganging up on me, screaming in my ears. *Did you seriously just blow up this whole relationship? Walk away from the boy you've been obsessed with for months? And why? Because he said he loved you? You could still be kissing him right now if you weren't so melodramatic.*

But even as my guilty verdict is being prepared by my brain, some other, more visceral part of me is pulling up wordless images in my defense. That icy expression on Richard's face, the way he put his hands behind his head like he'd already lost interest, the gross smugness of it all. It was like he was trying to make me out as some sort of prude, which is completely unfair, because I'm not against sex, not at all. I'm not even afraid of it, really. None of that part of the Catholic Church ever rubbed off on me; it doesn't feel true in my body to think of sex as bad. I just want it to mean something. And I guess, yeah, that's especially true for my first time. But I could have seen us getting there in a few weeks or months, and doing a lot of amazing fooling around in the meantime. Fuck! Why did he have to push it? Why did it have to be today?

After I've circled the lodge three times, I'm too cold to be upset. I'm numb inside and out. All my nose hairs are frozen and the chill I felt in my limbs now feels like straight-up pain. I can't avoid my room anymore. I decide to pop in and grab my coat, act like I'm meeting Richard without saying that explicitly.

When I get there, Amanda is inside as expected, trying to do a French braid around the top of her head like a crown, but her hair is so silky and fine it keeps falling out. Fortunately, this appears to be taking up all her concentration, and she doesn't grill me on anything boy related. You would almost never know that she is seething with jealousy. She is a pro at hiding her feelings, which in this situation is fine by me.

"Shoot! I can't believe I have to start over again! My arms are going to fall off." She pulls out the braid and brushes her hair smooth. "Hattie, would you help me? I want to look Swiss, like I belong in a ski chalet with a big tray of beer steins."

She wants to look like a waitress? "I think steins are a German thing," I say, then feel cringy about correcting a factual technicality and go to help her. I take the brush and separate the hair by her left temple into three sections to start braiding. I notice that she's completing the look in a blouse with a bodice and ribbons and everything. Her boobs are pressed together for some impressive cleavage. Guys may come and go, but she'll have those babies for life. I wonder if my jealousy for her physical attributes is more obvious than her jealousy for what she thinks is my romantic situation.

"German, Swiss, whatever," she laughs, then looks determined. "I want to look like I'm in *The Sound of Music*." I almost blurt, "They were Austrian," but manage to stifle it in time. After all, who doesn't want to look like the Baroness in her gold lamé gown, or Liesl in the greenhouse in the pouring rain? Of course, they don't have braids, and Julie Andrews has no hairstyle at all in that movie, unless "chopped" is considered a hairstyle, but I get what she's driving at, and I'm definitely not going to correct her again.

I nod and keep braiding, soothed by the meditative quality of it, the ability to concentrate on something outside of my roiling thoughts. I get all the way across the top of her head and then stop, stuck. "Now what?" I ask.

She laughs again. "You know what, I have no fucking clue."

"Wait, let me try something." I start to grab strands behind the braid until I am braiding back in the opposite direction. After another full braid across the top of her head, I secure the rubber band low behind her ear and cover it up with the hair spilling down her back. I examine her in the mirror, proud of my work. As I do, I realize I'm admiring how my efforts have made my main competitor look more attractive. I snort at the irony.

"I know, I know, it's way over the top, but I'm into it," she says, misunderstanding my noise. "Okay, I'm off to après-ski!"

There's that phrase again. I make a mental note to look it up. I smile and make a thumbs-up, which I instantly regret. Something about Amanda's energy makes me my uncoolest self. She goes and I exhale into the quiet of the room.

I need a second opinion on the Richard situation. Was I overreacting? "Mason?" I ask softly, seeing if I can conjure him up at will. Nope. No Mason. Was there ever really? It's so hard to be sure. In any case, time to turn to the land of the living.

I pull my phone out of my bag and call Asha. She'll be able to break this down for me. If anything, she'll be harder on him, which I would appreciate, since the idea that this was somehow all my fault keeps creeping into my mind.

"You have not reached Asha," her familiar message tells me. "Guess she's too busy for you. But here comes a beep you can talk to. Go ahead. Talk to it." *Beep.*

Shit. I hang up and call my mom, not sure yet how much of the story I even want to tell her. It's more just to hear the voice of someone who is definitely on Team Hattie. My dad answers. I guess he counts?

"Hi, Dad."

"Well, my other child is in the house with me so I guess this must be Hattie!" he says, making an attempt at a dad joke.

"Ha, you got it. Why do you have Mom's phone?"

"Apparently she left it behind when she went off to book club." Ah, no wonder my dad sounds so jovial. He's probably having an extra beer without the tsking disapproval of his wife.

"Okay, well, I won't bother you." I don't feel like I can talk to him, but if he asks me what's going on, I might. Maybe this could be the start of us finally understanding each oth—

"I'll tell her you called," he says, like he's merely Mom's assistant and not also my parent. "We'll look forward to your triumphant return tomorrow." *Click.* God, he is so, so weird.

So this is the culmination of all the big "we need to talk" lectures my parents have foisted on me since before I was even getting my period. All the promises of "always being there for me" and "available whenever I want to talk" evaporated by a book club and an oblivious dad. Guess I'm on my own.

CHAPTER 14

Richard has appeared next to the lobby fireplace, where I'm reading a book in a rocking chair made entirely out of antlers.

"Hey, I've been looking for you," he says. "We're going night skiing. Come with."

I turn toward him and the chair pokes me hard in the ribs, like there's a dead deer teasing me for my absurdity from beyond the grave. I may or may not have been sitting in this incredibly uncomfortable chair for the last half hour with the hopes that I looked perfectly at one with ski lodge life to any onlookers. Particularly onlookers named Richard.

"Come with." That's how he says it, simple and easy, like we didn't just have a stand-off about meaningless sex in his tiny room. Like he hadn't implied that there was something wrong with me at a very basic level because I didn't want to lose my virginity to an acquaintance. After all, he'd gone to the care and preparation of putting a sock on the door.

And night skiing? To a total novice like me who doesn't do well in the dark, this sounds terrifying on several levels. At this point, I wouldn't be surprised if Richard approached me with, "Hey, Hatts. We're going skydiving. Oh, and we're going to be naked except for our parachutes. In fact, maybe we'll skip the parachutes. Come with."

But his eyes have lost their cold edge and regained their

twinkly playfulness. He seems human again, and so part of me wants to. Not the part that was in the bedroom a couple of hours ago, but the part that was on the bus with him, the part that is playing opposite him in the school musical, the part that watched *Doctor Zhivago* with him. That part wants to give him the benefit of the doubt, to wipe the slate clean and move forward. After all, he didn't force me to do anything I didn't want to. And have I mentioned how excruciatingly good he smells?

Still, at night? "That sounds so fun, but it's really dark out. I don't—well—I just don't see that great in the dark." Congratulations to Hattie Murphy on the Understatement of the Year Award.

He comes close to me and puts his hands on my cheeks, a move I've quickly grown to recognize as the "don't worry, I'll take care of everything" maneuver. It's a little hacky but supremely effective. "They light those trails up with a quadrillion watts," he says, then smirks and nods. "That's the official number."

The cuteness makes me give in. "I've got to get my gear. Wait for me by the chairlift?"

He winks, and I hurry off to suit up, feeling like I'm on a sugar high. What was I being so melodramatic for? We can work this out. So he wants to be physical. That's okay, I want to be physical, too. The only thing we disagree about is the timeline. *A little scheduling snafu, that's all this is,* I think as I pull on an extra pair of socks. And he seems to want to be a feminist, even if he was using it to get what he wanted. At least he's thinking about my rights.

Moments later, I glide up to him and the corners of his eyes crinkle in welcome. He points to my breath streaming out in front of me and says, "That's hot." I giggle and we scoot over to let the seat of the chairlift make contact. Richard nods in approval at how seamlessly it happens, and then begins discussing the pros and cons of the various trails that await us at the top. I can't take it in: I'm distracted by the pride that's filling my lungs. My mom always comments on how fast I pick things up, how I'm a quick learner, but she often pairs the comment with the criticism that I don't give things enough of a chance when I'm not immediately good at them, so that's the part I usually walk away with. But she's right, I am a quick learner. I'm rocking all this skiing stuff.

As we slow toward the top of the mountain, though, all my newfound pride drains away. I gaze at the skiers passing below us and realize something weird is happening with my eyes. Richard was right, there are a lot of lights, but it's like I didn't put my contacts in this morning. No, it's worse than that. Like I'm looking through a windshield in the pouring rain and there are no wipers. What the actual fuck?

Fear prickles on the back of my neck. Dr. Porter said that my declines would not be steady, that there would be long stable periods followed by steep dips, but I didn't expect to go blind all in one night. Is that what's happening?

"You ready?" Richard puts the bar up, and before I have time to gather my thoughts the ground rises up underneath our skis and we slide down off the chairlift. We stand at the top and I blink, my eyes trying ineffectually to focus, to cut through whatever thick acrylic sheeting has sprouted up between me and the rest of the world. I blink again and rub my eyes a little, but I don't dare do it too hard or my contacts will get all bunched up in one corner of my eye, or worse, pop out. Rubbing helps precisely zero percent.

I heard once that if you smell burning toast that could mean that you're having a stroke. Am I having a stroke in my eyes? Is that a thing? I can't spend too much time considering it, because I'm on top of an icy death trap in the middle of the night and I have to get to the bottom. How that is going to happen is, at the moment, more urgent and more bewildering.

"Um, Richard?" I say. I have to tell him. There's no way I can fake my way out of this. He's re-Velcroing his ski gloves and pulling his insulated buff up over his face to guard against the wind that has whipped up. "Something's wrong. I can't see."

"I know, you told me in the lodge," he says, stamping snow off each ski. "I get it. I'm blind as a bat without my contacts, too."

Blind as a bat. People seem to love making this claim, like somehow it makes them special or more likable. But not only does it not do either of those things, it is also always a lie. Needing glasses doesn't mean you're blind, for fuck's sake. Real blindness doesn't have a fix, a simple little accessory that erases the problem. I bristle but try to keep my voice even.

"No, this is different. I'm not talking about reading letters on a chart, I'm talking about light and dark. My eyes don't adjust. And there's something else happening, something extra. Like something's blocking my vision."

"Hattie, look out there! Look how bright it is. I told you the trails are like the surface of the sun." Other skiers glide past us on both sides, like they're the river and we're a couple of moss-covered rocks.

"It's not helping, Richard. I don't think I can do this."

This is the problem with living in the space between the fully sighted and the blind: a lot of times I can cope. I can hide the problem. So when I can't, it doesn't make sense. Richard clearly doesn't get it. He doesn't believe me.

He sidesteps toward me now. He puts both his poles in one hand and places the other gloved hand over mine. "That's your fear talking! Remember how great you did this afternoon? Channel that, okay? That's my girl." A patronizing forced patience drips off every syllable, and I don't know who I hate more in that moment, him or myself. I swallow hard on the bile at the back of my throat.

"Maybe we can flag down one of those dudes in a snowcat?" I'm begging, but there's no helping that. I know I saw some of those fancy snowmobiles patrolling the trails earlier today. There seemed to be so many of them. Now, though, there are none.

Richard glances around and notices this, too. The temperature is plummeting. It reminds me of a cartoon thermometer where the mercury drops through the bottom so hard it breaks the glass.

"Hattie, Hattie," he says, like he's talking to his senile

grandmother. "Hattie, this is not an emergency. It's not like you have to pick out every snowflake. We've got nothing but open trail in front of us. Just follow me. C'mon, let's go before we freeze."

"No, wait, just help me think a minute. What are the options? Can I maybe ride the chairlift back to the bottom?"

"No, you can't. Don't be dense." He faces away from me, as if he's mad that I made him insult me. He's actually huffing now. "God, just– This is getting ridiculous!"

Everything else is blurry, but Richard's whole scene is suddenly clear to me, as if he was wearing the costume of a good guy and has now ripped off his mask. He doesn't care about me, not really. I am only remotely interesting to him when I am convenient and offer the things he wants. The image of him earlier today telling me he loves me comes flooding back. What a joke. It's a good thing I have skis and poles weighing me down, 'cause otherwise I might actually punch him.

"Just go," I say. Knowing what I know now, being alone feels dangerous but being with Richard feels even riskier.

I hear that shift again in his voice, the shift I heard earlier today in his room when he was assessing me from his reclined position in the bed, where ice fills his words and he and I become strangers.

"You know, this is so stereotypical actress. I would think you would be more original," he says. With that, he pushes off with one foot and he's gone. The curve of the hill is so steep I can't see over the edge. He just disappears.

I can't think about whether I'm devastated or not. The cold keeps me in the urgency of the moment. I look around, my eyes trying so hard to compensate for all the junk that's in the way of a clear view that I'm getting a headache. My eye sockets ache, and every time I blink it's like a million flashbulbs pop. But I can still see the difference between the white snow and the dark trees. And that's going to have to be enough.

I'll just take my time. No rush. But even though I set off almost sideways, the incline of the mountain has other ideas for my speed. I sit down twice in about ninety seconds. I finally manage the first switchback, but heading out again across the trail makes panic fill the sides of my throat. I keep accelerating against my will, and my adrenaline is shaking my legs so badly it's hard to stay on my feet. If there's anything sticking up out of the snow, like a branch or a rock, I'm not going to be able to see it. And if another skier comes close, I won't see them in time, either. A crash is practically inevitable. It occurs to me that if my school ends up with two accidental student deaths in one month, it'll probably be national news. But there's only one way down. I keep going.

I've only crisscrossed twice and my thighs are burning from the tension. I make the turn and squint, trying to get a sense of whether there's anything in front of me. It's like there's a TV remote for the whole world and someone has turned the contrast way down. How can I go slower? I think about turning the points of my skis uphill, but can't figure out the physics of the consequences. I definitely don't want to end up skiing backward.

“Let me be the first to say that you were so right, Hattie. I was wrong. That Dick–uh–Richard Walker is a real gem.”

When Mason didn’t come to my call earlier, I sort of decided I could only see him in my town, in a place we both shared. So now, having him materialize on the mountain freaks me out all over again. His ability to be everywhere makes him less real, more like a dream. Yet there he is, at my right elbow, taunting me. Whether he’s also skiing or simply floating is somehow impossible to tell, since like everything else in my world right now, he is infuriatingly blurry.

“Jesus. Can you not right now? I’m trying to concentrate.” I press my lips together and will my legs to do what they’re supposed to do without overthinking it. The weight shifting for each turn happens faster than I can bear, so each time I feel like I might go spinning away, like a top off a string.

“Yes, of course, don’t let me bother you. I just wanted to compliment you on your judgment. I mean, what a keeper. Don’t let him get away from you.”

Just then an orange snowsuit flies past me, his proximity creating enough breeze to move the wispy hairs poking out of my helmet. I yelp and fall over. The feeling of the solid ground along my body is actually a relief. I scooch to the side until I’m off the hard-packed trail and into the soft powder among the trees. I lie still, my legs sideways to accommodate the skis. Maybe I’ll stay here forever.

“Graceful as ever, Miss Murphy.”

I’m angry now. “I don’t know why you persist in expecting

perfection from people, Mason, but it's pretty unfair. No wonder you were always disappointed by everything. You think I should be some great skier?! This is only my *second time*. You think I should have been able to read Richard's mind, see into the future, know what someone I don't really know is going to do?"

"Like I said, he's human aspartame," he says with a shrug.

I growl. "You are so. Damn. Infuriating!" I want to keep yelling at him, but I can't because I've started to sob. It's messy and loud, with lots of chokes and snorts. I don't even care that I'm making a fool of myself. "It's all falling apart! Everything. Everything is going to hell! And you're making it worse!" I feel splotchy and contorted.

Mason's presence starts skittering around me, hovering over me. "Hey, hey there," he says, sounding panicked. "I was only kidding. It was a joke. Fuck. Don't cry, Murph. It's not that bad."

"How would you know? You're not even really here." I let the vowels of *here* stretch out in a wail, like a preschool kid whose mom has just left on the first day of school. If he were really here, he could hold me while I cried, make me feel better and warmer. The strength of my wish for that makes my heart hurt. I close my eyes and try to stop existing. What have I been holding myself together for, anyway?

I can tell he's staring at me hard now. Assessing me. "Hey, Murphy, we've got to get you down this mountain. You are really cold. Like, hypothermically cold. Let's go somewhere warm."

"Nah," I say. All the crying has exhausted me. "I'm good here." I'm probably shivering too much to ski now anyway.

"Nope," he says, all business. "Up you go. Get up. Right now, Murphy. Let's move." Weirdly, it seems like he is becoming clearer and more solidly of this earth. Is that because he's so serious?

"Why should I listen to you? You don't even wear a freaking life jacket on a freaking lake." I am free to say anything I want now. My inhibitions are gone. I rest my head back in the snow and listen to the rhythmic whoosh of passing skiers, and somewhere in the distance, a generator. I'll take a nap here, and I'll feel more energized to ski when I'm rested.

Suddenly, something is pushing and pulling me at the same time, as if the snow below me is surging upward like a wave, like I'm a paper clip and there's a giant magnet in front of me. Without making the decision to, I'm standing.

"What did you learn to do when you started skiing earlier today?" Mason says.

"Keep my body weight forward?" I say.

"No. What do the little kids do?"

"Snowplow," I mumble.

"That's right! That's great, Murph. Let's see that snowplow." I start to inch out of the trees, the tips of my skis coming to a point. "There! That's great! You're great at this, Murphy. Stay right at the edge of the trail and keep that snowplow, just like a pizza slice, push the backs of those skis wider with your heels. You're in control now. You're doing it."

"I'll hit a tree," I protest.

"Nope. No way. I'll let you know before anything like that happens."

Somehow I'm moving again, concentrating on keeping the line of trees just to my right and not crossing my skis in the front. Mason is talking the whole time, cheering me on, occasionally giving directions. In fact, he won't shut up. It's weird to hear him so full of positivity.

"This peppy vibe is a new look for you," I get out between chattering teeth.

"Just high on life, I guess."

"You mean high on death."

"Semantics," he says. "Almost there now, Murph! You're going to make it!"

He's right. The hill is evening out, the incline becoming more gradual. The lodge is close enough that even my blotchy vision can make it out up ahead. The possibility of getting safe and warm fills me with a final adrenaline rush, and I straighten my skis the slightest bit to pick up speed.

This is a mistake, as two seconds later, I nearly collide with a line of orange barrels. I've tempted fate enough. I snowplow hard until I come to a stop, then I unclick. I drag the skis to the building and lean them against the wall. "I did it, Mason. Thank you for helping—" I say, but it turns out I'm talking to myself. He's gone.

CHAPTER 15

Now that I'm close to the lodge, it is really dark, with shadows everywhere and just the faintest gray glow off the snow to give me a clue about where the walkway is. I shuffle along at a sloth's pace toward the oasis of illumination at the side doors, careful on my trembling legs. It would be so like me to make it all the way down a death-defying ski run and then trip on a crack in the sidewalk and break my arm.

I've just started wondering whether anyone can see me doing this strange creeping when I hear murmuring, shushing, *giggling.* It puts me on high alert. Other people's giggling always triggers my paranoia, even though, realistically, the odds that some shadowy randos are laughing about me are near zero. The sounds are coming from a pitch-black corner up ahead. The other thing coming from that corner is the pungent skunk of weed, which is probably not a coincidence. Pot smell in an enclosed room makes me gag, but outside it's intriguing. I pause at the door to inhale the scent. I wonder what these ski stoners' lives are like. Is it one party after another? Do they ski all winter and surf all summer, except when they're backpacking around Europe? Then I hear Richard's unmistakable chuckle.

I duck inside, my heart pounding. Those aren't dudes who live on the mountain all season, those are kids from our trip. Wistfulness overwhelms me. If I could see like everyone else, I might be there with them right now, trying weed for the first time with my more mature boyfriend, feeling like I belong to that group through mutual mischief. I shake my head. No. A change in my medical status wouldn't change the fact that Richard is a self-absorbed waste of an Oxford shirt. Mason was so right. Richard is a massive dick.

Inside the lodge, I think about finding one of our chaperones and telling them I need to get to a doctor and find out what is happening with my eyes. But I'm so unbearably tired that the thought of all the explaining, all the words I would have to come up with to communicate my situation, makes me start to tear up again in frustration. Plus, what is a doctor going to say to me if they do examine me? "Oh my gosh, you're right, you do have an emergency, it appears that you are going blind?!" I already fucking know that. And I don't want to hear it again.

Luckily, my room is empty. I strip off my jacket and snow pants and leave them in a drippy pile on the thin carpeting that looks like it's been through decades of drippy piles. I burrow underneath the covers of my bed, arranging the pillows to make my little nest. There aren't enough pillows, so I borrow some from Amanda's bed, just for a few minutes. I stretch my legs out and wiggle my toes through the pinprick sensation of my feet thawing out. There's a strange looseness in my jaw, and the skin across my forehead becomes smooth. Holy crap—I'm calm. This is the first moment in the last twelve hours when I haven't been performing, trying to do the right thing, trying to say the right thing, trying on top of trying. Now everything has crashed and burned. There is nothing left to prove. This afternoon, Richard said my legs got sore because I was fighting the mountain. But it seems like there are mountains in every aspect of my life. And I don't want to fight them anymore.

I'm starting to drift off when I hear the sound of someone punching in the door code. Amanda bursts in and flips on the lights. She jumps, surprised to see me.

"What are you doing in here? Everyone's hanging out," she says.

I feel self-conscious, hoping she doesn't notice that I've stolen her pillows and tucked them under each knee pit.

"I'm toast. My bed has ordered me to hang in."

She frowns. "Are you sure? You're going to waste a night away from parents by going to sleep early?"

It does sound pretty weak when she puts it that way. My instinct is to think that she's trying to make me feel like a loser, but her tone says otherwise. She's just pointing out the obvious.

I shrug. "This is literally the first time I've felt warm all day." This is true, but what's truer is that this is the only place I can think of where the fact that everything appears slightly smudged won't put me in danger of embarrassment or injury.

She puts her hand on her hip, looking like she's trying to decide whether to reach under the blankets and pull me out of bed by my ankles. One thing I'm realizing about Amanda is that she is stubborn.

"Hold on a sec," she says, and disappears back into the hallway.

A minute later, I hear the beeps of the keypad again and Amanda is there holding the necks of two bottles of beer in her left hand. She puts them on the nightstand and starts screwing off the caps.

"Oh, no thanks," I say before she can open the second bottle. "I don't really like beer."

She pauses for a second, then unscrews the second cap anyway. "That's okay. Neither do I. But my therapist says it's important to mark special occasions, you know? So let's toast. To freedom," she says, holding her bottle aloft.

I hold mine up, too, since that appears to be the only option. "To freedom," I say. But I'm not free, I'm trapped. Trapped on a trip with someone who is now my ex, trapped in unfamiliar surroundings while my eyes shut down on me, trapped inside my head with all my secrets. I feel more closed in than when my parents make me stay home playing Trivial Pursuit with them on Christmas Eve.

I still haven't put the bottle to my lips, so Amanda clunks the bottom of her bottle down onto the mouth of mine, making it fizz and overflow. I rush to suck it down before it soaks the bed. She nods and takes a long drink.

"Yep, still gross, but in a good way, you know? Like coffee ice cream."

I want to say, *No, Amanda, I don't freaking know.* But I don't. Instead, I say, "What made you start seeing a therapist?" Probably too private, but she brought it up.

The bubbles from the beer seem to travel all the way down

the length of my body and are now bouncing and tingling in my feet. It's sort of nice.

"Nothing revolutionary," she says. She puts her beer on the table, then kicks off her boots and unzips her fleece. "Just your typical 'parents hate each other, parents get divorce, parents need to feel better about messing up their kids so they put them in therapy' sort of situation."

"I'm sorry."

"Don't be. I like it. The therapy. And the fact that there's no more fighting. I like that, too."

I've never thought of Amanda at home before, with her own life and her own problems. "I'm sort of hiding out tonight," I confess.

"Ooh, from who? What's going on?" Amanda uses the heels of her hands to hoist her butt up onto the dresser, then sits cross-legged next to the beer bottle.

My eyes start swimming even thinking about saying his name out loud. I can't cry about something so stupid when Amanda has just told me her parents got divorced. I wave my hand dismissively as I blink back the tears. "Oh, you know. Richard."

She's silent for a moment, and I can't help but wonder if she's inwardly thrilled. "Wow. You guys seemed so cozy on the bus."

So she *did* absorb more of our canoodling than she let on. Was that really just this morning that I was trying to rub it in Amanda's face how hot and heavy Richard and I were? I gulp a few swallows of beer and try to pretend I'm already in the phase where my fiery wreck of a love life is just a memory, material for a funny story. "Things change," I say.

I can't make out her exact expression. Is she confused? Inwardly laughing at me? Already thinking about sinking her hungry teeth into him? Whatever. I shouldn't care anyway, right? I'm so done with him.

"You can have him," I say before I even realize the words are coming out of my mouth. "I mean, if you want to get with him, it's fine with me. I know you guys are close."

I mean for this to sound mature, like I'm evolved and far removed from petty jealousy and territorial tendencies. Instead, it sounds childish. Like why would dating someone for a few days give me any semblance of ownership? I start to formulate how to dial this ridiculous statement back when Amanda bursts out giggling. Then she downs her beer in big, open-throated gulps. She wipes her mouth with her sleeve.

"You are too funny!" she says, shaking her head. "Me and Richard. Richard and me." She puts up air quotes with her fingers. "Close."

I search her face. "Aren't you?" I ask.

She giggles again as she peels the label off her bottle in skinny strips that curl and waft to the floor like snowflakes. "Strictly geographically speaking, yes, in that we're neighbors, right? We've been hanging around together since we were both in diapers. But he does not live in a romantic part of my brain. Besides, I've seen how he does relationships and I'm not a fan." She looks up at me, apologetic. "No offense."

"None taken," I say. "What do you mean exactly? About how he does relationships?"

"Oh, you know, like someone's filming him. Like he's starring in his own romantic comedy. Just over the top."

She sounds like Mason. I think back to Richard blindfolding me so he could lead me to the ski trip poster down the hall. That was pretty silly.

"God, you must think I'm an idiot," I say.

"What? Oh no! That's not what I meant at all. I'm sure it's exciting when it's coming at you at a hundred miles an hour. I've just seen his whole playbook."

So that's what he has. A playbook. And I was just a girl in a line of girls, the next on the assembly line. How did I think it was something special?

So all this time, Amanda and I haven't been vying for the same guy. We're not in competition. She's not my nemesis. What is she to me, then? I look at her without all my misinterpretations for the first time. I drink my beer. This is going to take some getting used to.

"Boys are gross," I say.

"And love? The grossest," she agrees.

"This beer is putting me to sleep. I'm going to crash."

"Crash away. I'm going to go prowl around a little more," she says. "Suck the marrow out of the night. Is that cool? I'll be quiet when I come in."

"Happy sucking," I say. She snorts. She peeks in the mirror and tucks some blonde hairs that have escaped her braid back behind her ears. Then she stuffs her feet back in her boots and heads out.

I click off the bedside lamp and curl into a ball. "I'm not going to fight the mountain," I mumble out loud. I close my eyes and try to ignore the incessant floaters and flashing that is playing against the back of my eyelids. I can't worry any more today. And I don't. I sleep a sleep that's heavy as a weighted blanket and as black as the bottom of the ocean.

CHAPTER 16

"From what you're telling me, it's very likely macular edema," Dr. Porter says through the phone. It's late the next morning, and I'm back in the lodge lobby, this time on a bench by a massive picture window, holding my phone with one hand while I tear at the fingernails on the other with my teeth. I quit biting my nails in eighth grade after I heard my grandmother ask my mom what she was going to do about my "filthy habit." I kept polish on them for years to remind myself. But now they are naked, and it seems more acceptable to chew on them than to punch random passersby, which is the other option my nervous energy is considering.

Even though she's usually full of bad news, I'm starting to like Dr. Porter. She talks to me like an adult, and gives me the straight scoop instead of sugarcoating stuff or dumbing down her vocabulary. And frankly, it's nice to talk to someone about RP without worrying that they won't understand, or that I'll have to take care of them somehow while they have an emotional breakdown about it.

This is the reason I decided not to call my mom back. If I had told her my vision is rapidly declining and that I almost killed myself night skiing, she would have freaked out. And I didn't want to be responsible for her careening down the highway at eighty miles an hour to come get me, her panic making her driving even worse than mine would be. No thanks. Stuffing me into her minivan wouldn't actually fix anything. It would just make me have to deal with her out-of-control feelings on top of my own.

So instead, I looked up Dr. Porter's number, and was comforted when the off-hours emergency number yielded a familiar voice.

"Edema means swelling, right?" I say. All that time my mom said I was "wasting" watching medical dramas on TV is paying off.

"Exactly," she says. "It's not unheard of for a change in altitude to have this effect on people with RP. Or it could even be as simple as the retina reacting to dehydration." She pauses for a second, maybe debating how much information to give me, then continues. "Even though, in a direct way, RP breaks down the rods in the retina, it also tends to pick up a lot of hitchhikers along the way. Not just edema. Cataracts and cysts are also things we want to keep an eye out for as we move forward." Keep an eye out? Is she doing that on purpose? Aargh.

"Is this"—I wince in anticipation of the answer—"is the edema permanent?"

"Oh! I wouldn't think so," she says. "Usually, vision returns to normal within a few days back at a lower altitude. You should be fine once you come home. If not, there are some eye drops we can try."

It feels like I've been underwater for the last day and I've finally kicked my way up to the surface. If you had told me a few weeks ago that getting back to my regular crappy vision would be something to celebrate, I would have laughed at you, but now it feels like winning the Powerball.

I thank Dr. Porter and hang up. Outside, the morning crowd is hitting its peak, and the line to the chairlift goes right past the window. Groups of girls are taking selfies, their goggles perched perfectly on their soft ski hats. How they can be dressed in such bulky clothes and still look skinny is like alchemy to me. Guys are shouting to each other from different spots in line. I can't make out what they're saying through the glass, but based on what I witnessed yesterday I'm sure they're challenging their fellow adrenaline junkies to black diamond races, talking trash that might be more for the selfie girls than for the person they're talking to. Directly up the blurry hill in front of me, I can just make out a class of little kids flying straight down the bunny slope, unencumbered by any of that annoying fear of death that would slow them down. In fact, *unencumbered* would be my description for everyone but me in the ski universe. Like the only care in the world anyone here has is how many inches of new snow there are. The idea that anyone else could have health problems or relationship problems or certainly dead friend problems seems completely impossible.

The bus isn't leaving until this afternoon so the group can maximize their skiing time. I want to go back to bed, get the rest that eluded me when I woke up at three last night and my brain kept me busy troubleshooting doom-and-gloom scenarios, but we've already checked out, all our bags sitting on a train of luggage carts by the front desk. I land on a caloric solution. I'm going to après-ski, which the internet informed me means socializing, entertainment, and refreshment after a day of skiing, without the skiing. I'm going to "après-nothing."

The café is dead. I slide into a booth and grab a plastic-coated menu from between the salt and pepper shakers. I flip it open and the anticipation drains out of me. I can't read it. The blurs in my vision seem to fall in all the essential spots, the junctures that differentiate an *R* from a *B* from a *5*. I blink and try again, but no matter how my eyes strain to reach around the blurry spots, they move along with the center of my gaze, like a queen stalking a pawn across the chessboard. I close the menu and close my eyes, pinching the bridge of my nose to stave off a burgeoning headache, still not quite believing that I can't do the simplest, most automatic thing in the world.

"Made a decision?" The waiter might be about my age, but his easy smile makes him seem like he's been on this planet longer, enough to get real comfortable. He's got a hint of a Southern accent, which could be why he reminds me of a life-sized version of Woody from *Toy Story*, except with a five o'clock shadow. I like him right away.

"Um, no, actually, I couldn't decide," I lie. "What's your favorite thing on the menu?"

"Without a doubt the loaded tots. They are life-changing. I eat them for breakfast, lunch, and dinner."

This guy is my kind of eater. "I better get them, then. I could use a few changes in my life."

"You got it. Drink?"

"What life-changing beverages do you have?"

"Well, nothing truly transformative, but your meal will take care of that. Might as well get hot chocolate with whipped cream. It's basically its own food group here." He shrugs affably.

"Done and done," I say. "Oh, and two big glasses of water, please."

"Smart." He gives me a little two-fingered salute and saunters off to the kitchen.

Moments later, the waiter returns with a giant pottery mug of steaming hot chocolate.

"Not hitting the slopes this morning?" he asks me as he slides the drink onto the table.

"Nah, I had a pretty unnerving time skiing last night," I say. "I think I'm all set for now."

He nods. "Yeah, I never really bought into that 'get right back on the horse' thing. What about what your gut is saying? I listen to my gut."

"I don't trust the horse," I say. "The horse is very slippery and does not appear to like me."

"Maybe another horse on another day," he says.

"Exactly." I'm glad he gets it.

He pulls a can of Reddi-wip out of the pocket of his apron and artfully sprays a mound of whipped cream into the cup so high it resembles the peak outside the window.

"Tableside service," he announces.

"Wow, that defies the laws of physics," I say.

"There's no such thing as too much whipped cream," he answers. "Now, what would really defy those laws is if you could drink it without getting a white mustache."

"I'm not even going to try to rise to that challenge. Thanks for the hot chocolate."

"No problem. I'm going to grab the waters and those tots. And some more napkins, since you are clearly going to need them."

I take my time over my food, since I have absolutely nowhere else to be. Normally, if I was stuck sitting somewhere by myself, I would read a book or look at my phone, like a semi-normal human. But my retinas—retinae? Shit, I should know the name of my own body parts—have decided those activities are off-limits for now. I have no choice but to watch my cowboy, a cute boy who is not Richard Walker, wipe down the tables and refill the salt shakers, his every movement making it seem like what he's doing is more about fun and less about work. He was probably just being so nice to me to improve his tip, but in the moment he did an excellent job of making it seem like he was enjoying himself. I pretend like I'm considering writing my phone number on the check, as if I've never met myself and don't already know I'm way too much of a scaredy-cat to do something like that. And anyway, a long-distance relationship isn't exactly an option for sad sacks like me with neither a car nor the ability to drive.

Finally, the amount of time I've been sitting in the same place without doing or saying anything gets cringeworthy. I can't read the check, so I put down what I'm sure is entirely too much money just to be safe. I don't write my number.

"Make sure you stop in and visit me next time you come to tame horses," he calls after me.

"I will!" I promise, wishing it were true but also knowing there's no way in hell I'm ever coming skiing again. Not this mountain or any mountain, I guess. I can almost hear the click as the scope of my future tightens even smaller.

I'm the first to board the bus. This is by design so I won't have to choose who to sit with. The tough-as-nails woman behind the wheel looks up from her sandwich to see me tapping on the glass and yanks on the lever to slide the door open. She's clearly a little annoyed that I interrupted her snack. She eases the volume down a few notches on her murder podcast and stares at me. I pause, but then she waves me in.

"C'mon up, you're letting all the heat out." Her voice isn't unfriendly after all, so I climb the stairs.

The warmth inside the bus encircles me like a hug. I go way to the back and settle down in the corner. Maybe I can just lie low all the way home until I get back to the safe tedium of my own room. I close my eyes and drift back to the time a few weeks ago when everything in my life felt much more predictable and within my control. When every day Mason would be smirking at me from across the lunch table. I remember thinking my life was so boring then. Now I would give anything to be that bored.

Soon I hear laughing outside, and I lift up my head to peer out the window at the group of kids gathering. The tinted windows of the bus allow me to see them when they can't see me. Again, ironic. Not surprisingly, I zero in on Richard right away. Even though he's a little fuzzy through my altitude-addled vision, I can still read his body language enough to make my skin crawl. He looks positively jaunty. He and Amanda are standing next to each other, their hands each stuffed inside their pockets, playing some sort of jostling game. She elbows him in the side and then he elbows her, back and forth until one of them gets pushed hard enough to have to take a step to the side. Looks like a dumb excuse to have physical contact. I wonder about the truth of what Amanda said. Maybe she's just in denial about her love for Richard. Or maybe he lusts after her so much he's creating enough chemistry for the two of them. One thing's for sure. He is *not* looking for me.

A bone-chilling wind rushes through the bus as the door is reopened and everyone climbs aboard, bringing a wall of noise with them as their voices bounce around inside the enclosed space. I'm trying and failing to look unconcerned about who will join me at the back of the bus when Jeff's friendly face appears. I'm so happy I could kiss every one of his floppy dark curls.

"There you are," he says. "I've been looking for you, Hatts."

"Here I am. Sit with me!"

Jeff unzips his jacket, pops it into the overhead space, and settles in next to me. It feels like protection, like a Saint Bernard sat down in my row.

"I probably could have convinced Lucia to come if she knew you were gonna be here. Why didn't you tell us?"

I'm not really sure why. After our last conversation about Mason, I've been steering a little clear of the whole group. I guess I'm afraid he'll come up again, which makes it hard to hold the secret that, for some reason, I'm the only one who gets to keep talking to him. Or maybe I was trying to keep the whole Richard situation out of their awareness because on some cellular level I knew how ill-advised it was. "It was very last-minute," I finally say.

This seems to satisfy him. Jeff is not the kind of guy to look for subtext. He takes people at face value.

"So, how'd the snow treat you? I didn't even know you skied."

"I don't," I say.

Just then we hear a high-pitched whistle from the front of the bus, and the shouting subsides. I get up on my knees to see over the seat backs in front of me. It's our chaperone, Mr. Williams, standing next to the driver.

"Attention, minions." That's what he always calls students, like he's an evil mastermind or something. Mr. Williams phrases everything in a weird way, and it's impossible to know whether he's doing it on purpose or not. The awkward contours of teachers' senses of humor never stop fascinating me.

"So it has come to our attention that there was some unauthorized substance use of the green leafy variety among our illustrious group last night, which is not at all what I expected from ambassadors of our Crimson Tigers. And as you of course realize, this is a blatant violation of the Code of Conduct that you all signed in order to participate in any school extracurriculars."

Jeff and I look at each other, and his eyebrows are raised in surprise. He clearly has no notion of what Mr. Williams is referring to, the lucky duck.

"Anyway, I am not going to execute any discipline myself. I am merely the messenger, and will be letting the administration know. But I wanted you all to have something to mull over with your consciences on the long ride home." He leans in and says something to the driver, and she pulls the bus door closed.

"I hope you enjoyed your testing of a zero-tolerance policy. I think you will find that it is not, in fact, just a formality." And with that, he disappears, lowering himself into the front seat. I slide down off my knees, too. I'm just trying to get comfortable in my seat despite all the uncomfortable thoughts in my head when I hear Mr. Williams again.

"Hattie! Come to the front, please."

CHAPTER 17

What?! Why? Has Mr. Williams chosen me for human sacrifice to make a point? I climb over Jeff and drag my feet, which now feel extremely clumsy, down the aisle. Every pair of eyes on the bus is turned up to my face, some with sympathy, others with sheer curiosity. Every pair of eyes, that is, except Richard's. I can't help noticing that he's looking out the window instead of in my direction.

"What's up?" I say when I get to the front, like everything's normal. Mr. Williams doesn't respond, just jerks his thumb toward the door and goes back to his book. I look down the stairwell as the bus driver slides the door back open to see a very appealing five o'clock shadow on a handsome jawline. It's my waiter!

"What are you doing here?" I ask, taken aback by how delighted I sound.

"I thought I'd come home with you. Meet your folks."

That quote from *Alice in Wonderland* suddenly runs through my head, when things get "curiouser and curiouser." "Really?" I squeak out, like the definition of gullible.

He chuckles. "Would be nice, but can't. This place would fall apart without me," he says, sweeping his hand toward the resort building behind him. Then he digs into his pocket and pulls out a familiar purple puffball. "You forgot your hat." He holds it up the stairs toward me.

“Oh, wow. Thanks.” Usually, I hate it that my bad eyesight causes me to constantly leave things behind, but in this particular case, it’s worked out in my favor. “You really didn’t have to do that.” I come down two steps and take the hat from him, then pull it back on my head. I’m still a step up from the ground so our faces are about even. I grin and bite my bottom lip.

“Well, I figured you’d want it. It looks good on you,” he says. He stuffs his hands back into his pockets, and I notice that he doesn’t have a jacket on. He must be freezing. I resist the urge to hug him.

“Let’s get to moving,” Mr. Williams says now. The rest of the bus, which I had temporarily forgotten existed, is waiting on me. I blush.

“Okay, well, thanks again. I appreciate it,” I say as he starts back toward the café.

“No problem. Glad to see that hat back where it belongs,” he calls. It’s clear to me that this boy has never been embarrassed in his whole life, which is one hell of an awesome superpower.

The door slides closed in front of my face. I turn, mumble “Sorry, Mr. Williams,” out of the corner of my mouth, and move back to my seat. By now, even Richard is looking at me. Feeling emboldened by the receipt of a recent hat compliment from a cutie, I return his gaze. I even smirk a little bit, like I’ve got a juicy secret, challenging him to say something. Instead, he exhales through his nose and shakes his head a little, like he’s disappointed in me. I keep my head up, but my smile fades. Somehow it seems like he won that round, too.

As we finally get on the road, the bus is silent. The quiet combined with the rocking motion of the drive works like a sedative, and soon I'm pretty sure everyone but me is asleep. For a while I rerun the conversation with the waiter on a loop in my mind, trying to hold on to the glow I felt when he looked at me, but the torturous energy of Richard's presence four rows in front of me overwhelms anything yummy. I wince whenever I peek over the seat back to see the top of his head still there, unmoving. Is he asleep, too? Or is he aware of my eyes on him? Is he sitting there silently mocking me? Thinking about what an inconvenience I was/am? If I'm being honest with myself, he's probably not thinking about me at all. The pinch of that truth makes me squeeze down lower in my seat. I will myself not to think about Richard the rest of the way home. It's about as effective as saying, "Don't think about elephants."

When my mom picks me up, I avoid all her questions by pleading exhaustion. This is a fact, I am exhausted, but I can talk until sunrise at a sleepover, so I still feel a little guilty. Especially since she looks like she's starving, and any piece of information from me is a big juicy hamburger with extra pickles.

"You could tell me whether you had a good time or a bad time, at least," she says.

"It was all the things," I say unhelpfully.

There's no school on Monday because it's a professional development day for the teachers, so I sleep for fourteen hours. When I finally wake up, I stay under the blankets for most of the afternoon, as I still can't read or study or even look at a screen with my eyes so wonky, and the idea of hanging out or talking to anyone just makes me think about Richard. My surroundings are in a haze, sort of like they're all melted together, and I've got a mishmash of thoughts to match. I go down a music rabbit hole after listening to the *Pitch Perfect* soundtrack, searching for all the weird a cappella covers I can find, which somehow leads me to listening to some super sultry Argentinian tango music. Who knew the accordion could tap into my soul?

My mom has decided I'm sick, probably as much to soothe herself as to take care of me. She doesn't know what to do with brooding, but she knows what to do with sick. She brings me Tylenol and feels my forehead. Sometimes I pretend to be napping when she comes in, and then she dims the lights and turns the music down. At one point, Asha must have called or stopped by, because I find a Post-it on my nightstand in my mom's perfect printing that says, *Call Asha.*

The person I want to talk to is Mason. He saw me on that mountain—he's the only one who could understand. But this isn't a movie; I don't have a magical phone that accesses the afterlife, and I don't know how to reach him. Wanting him in no way leads to getting him. So I call Asha.

She picks up on the first ring, like she's been waiting for me.

"There you are! Hatts, you gotta tell me next time you're going to be gone all weekend. I mean, for Christ's sake, I thought you—" She stops suddenly, and I know she was about to say *died* before she caught herself. "I thought you'd run away," she finishes. Hearing my friend who always says the right thing get caught in a moment of mortal doubt makes my insides feel hollowed out.

"I called you, you didn't answer," I say, almost too weary to get the words out.

"So you leave a message. You text. You know how phones work, right?"

I envision the text I could have sent: *New boy was too thirsty—let me down just like the ghost said he would. Also, now half blind.* Um, no.

"Anyway," she plows ahead, "so I hear you're skiing now? We should get a whole Beaver Bunch ski trip together. Oooh, that would be so fun! Jeff can teach Lucia, you can teach me, and Nolan can— Well, you know Nolan. He'll probably go snowmobiling or something. Maybe over winter break!"

"I can't," I say.

"Hattie, you're not going to be one of those girls who gets a boyfriend and then disappears, are you?"

"I told you, he was never my boyf—" I start, and then stop before I start to cry about how freaking sad that is. Just answer the question. "No, definitely not."

"Okay, good. So why no ski trip?"

"It did not go well."

"Hatts, it was your first time! You just need practice, and—"

"No." I say it too loud. I clear my throat. "No, I mean it was really bad. I'm not cut out for it. I just can't."

"All right, I hear you. Hard pass on skiing. But I've got

another invite for you and I won't take no for an answer. Beaver Bunch hangout at my house on Thursday. My whole family will be out, so we can do whatever we want."

"I'm in. But, Ash, I've got to go." Normally, I love that Asha is a planner because without her and Lucia, the Beaver Bunch would probably never do anything but sit around the lunch table, but today it feels like pressure. Pressure to be normal. No, better than normal. Pressure to be together, sharp, fun. Pressure to be like Asha. "We'll talk about it tomorrow."

There's a beat. Then she says, "Bye, Sweets."

"Bye."

Fortunately, everything changes when I open my eyes Tuesday morning. I almost yell, "Let's go!" but that would be very loud at six thirty a.m. Instead, I wriggle around in my sheets, letting the relief flow into my arms and legs. The weird film over the world has evaporated, and I can see the way I'm used to again. Not perfectly, not even that well, I guess, but regular for me. No random fireworks and fuzzy raindrops, no halos and haze. Just my white metal daybed, my lilac walls that Mom and I painted when I was in third grade, and my flowered curtains that let in most of the gray light of an early winter morning.

I feel like I've been in a cocoon since I got home. During that time, I thought I was grieving about Richard, but considering how much better I feel now, I guess I was mostly scared about not being able to see. And it's better!

For the first time, I let myself think about my diagnosis in a way that isn't all doom wrapped up with a pessimistic bow. So

I can't see perfectly. So I'll need some extra accommodations along the way. But I can see most things right now, the important things, like faces and nature and really good streaming shows. And maybe I'll hold on to that vision even longer than my dad held on to his. Maybe by the time I start to not be able to get around or read, there will be a cure. Maybe I'll volunteer for a clinical trial and I'll help in that cure's discovery! Okay, so it's unlikely I'm going to be freaking Marie Curie, but there's a shift. The cocoon of fear is broken and I am emerging a butterfly. No, nothing that beautiful. More like a moth, plain and dusty but still able to fly.

CHAPTER 18

When Mr. Pinski calls me to his office after third period, I'm not super freaked out the way I would be with any other administrator. Mr. Pinski has only been our principal for a year and a half, but I liked him from the first day.

Before Mr. Pinski, I always felt nervous around someone in his position, like they were a big spider in the garage and I didn't know enough about arachnids to tell if they were poisonous or not. But Mr. Pinski is known to call kids in for "State of the Union" visits, meaning he's going to ask you a gabillion questions that may or may not reveal if you're being bullied or whatever. I figure it's going to be that. When my mother interrogates me, I want to claw my own skin off, like I need to exfoliate her presence. But that's because she's got an emotion or a judgment about every single word that comes out of my mouth. Mr. Pinski usually nods, says, "Tell me more" or, if something is even remotely good, he says, "Outstanding." He doesn't even raise his eyebrows. Very nonthreatening.

I breeze into the office, still celebrating how easy it is to navigate around furniture and through doorways when it doesn't feel like my vision needs to go through the car wash. The office clerk, Ms. Wendy, doesn't look up from the red accordion folder she's flipping through when I appear, just says, "Go on in." The door is ajar, so I pad silently to his desk. I bypass the armchair and perch on the roly-poly stool, enjoying the little game of Don't Fall on Your Ass that it requires. I think it was bought for kids with attention issues, but it seems like the stuff they make for ADHD is actually awesome for everyone. That's why half the girls I know still have fidget key chains hanging on their bags.

Mr. Pinski is looking down at his phone, which gives me a full-frontal view of his baldness. Not his best look. When he presses send on whatever he's typing and raises his attention to me, my intestines start to pretzel. He's looking graver than I've ever seen him. What the fuck?

"Hattie, thanks for coming. I'm having something of a dilemma."

"Sure, of course," I fail to say comfortably or naturally. "What's up?"

"So I think everyone on the ski trip is aware there was a report of marijuana usage on a school-sponsored outing?"

On guard now, I choose my words carefully. "Yeah, Mr. Williams told us on the bus." This is technically true, even though I also witnessed the "usage" in real time. Is that why I'm here? Somehow Mr. Pinski knows that I was there, near the huddle of weed smokers? And now he wants me to point fingers and name names. Part of me would love to revenge tattle on Richard; getting busted might wipe that smug smile off his dumb face. But once it's out of my mouth, I won't be able to take it back. Seems like being a snitch might be something I'd regret. My brain is grinding so much it's hard for me to hear him through all the static.

". . . So it was lucky, in this way, that the role was double cast, so that there's a ready-made substitute," he's saying. "But now it appears it might not be so simple."

Wait, he's talking about the play? Why?

"I'm sorry, Mr. Pinski, can you back up?"

He looks pained, like whatever he just said was hard to spit out in the first place, and now he definitely doesn't want to repeat it. He stands up, comes around the desk, and turns the armchair ninety degrees so he can sit facing me. The wave of dread I feel reminds me of sitting in Dr. Porter's office.

"As I'm sure you recall," he says, even though he seems to know that I'm not recalling much of anything right now, "the Code of Conduct you all signed to be part of extracurriculars at the beginning of the year states that any infraction of the agreement will mean automatic suspension from those activities." This does sound vaguely familiar, although I didn't exactly pore over the conduct paperwork. It was just something you had to sign to do drama, so I signed it.

"And since she was one of the people smoking pot, Amanda won't be allowed to continue as Guenevere."

"Wait, Amanda? Amanda was one of the people smoking pot? I don't think so," I say now, realizing after I blurt it out that I may have revealed too much about what I know if I'm not intending to tell on Richard. Fortunately, Mr. Pinski doesn't pick up on it.

"Yes, yes, she's already confirmed it herself, so it isn't a question. But that's not why I called you here."

"It isn't?" I'm feeling disoriented, like I spun around ten

times in the pool with my eyes closed before a game of Marco Polo. I wish I'd sat in the armchair.

"No, Hattie, you see"—he leans forward, putting his elbows on his knees and lacing his fingers together—"we've also now received an allegation against you."

"I did not smoke pot on the ski trip, Mr. Pinski. I've never smoked anything in my whole life!" I shake my head so hard it hurts my brain.

"That's not the concern, actually," he says, watching me. "We were told you drank alcohol. Did you drink beer on the ski trip, Hattie?"

I stare at him. I know that I did, in fact, drink a beer on the ski trip, but it seemed so trivial at the time, like such a nonevent, it almost feels like I can just take out a pencil and erase that beer from my memory. All this interrogation and pressure over one beer seems excessive. A beer I didn't even ask for, by the way. That I drank to be nice, for fuck's sake. To someone I don't even like, who clearly has had it out for me from the beginning. It doesn't seem right.

I think about lying, about saying no. But if Amanda told him, which is the only possibility I can think of, she could probably prove it. She probably framed me, saving my empty beer bottle and presenting it to the administration as DNA evidence. Even though I know that's ridiculous, that my crap-ass public school definitely does not have a CSI budget, I can't get the image of Amanda holding my bottle with latex-gloved fingers out of my head. A flush of anger hits my face and brings me back to the present. I have to answer. And I have to answer yes, because I've waited too long to make a no remotely buyable.

"Yes, I did," I say, humiliated. "But just one."

Mr. Pinski rubs his jaw like he's been stuck in an airport waiting for a canceled flight for sixteen hours, like everything around him makes him discouraged. Especially me.

"I'm afraid the quantity doesn't make any difference. It's a zero-tolerance policy, after all." He turns his head and his eyes change focus as he looks out the window, and I can tell he's wishing he were somewhere else. I get it. I would like to be on a beach somewhere also.

I can't believe I messed up so majorly without even thinking about it. I can't own the shame; it hurts too much. I want to shake my life like I'm shaking a kaleidoscope until a new picture emerges. Or maybe what I want to shake is Amanda. She tried to convince me to party while I was attempting to go to sleep. She clinked the top of my bottle to make my drink fizz so I'd have to chug it. Was it really all a setup?

"So, what happens now?" I ask.

"Well, we'll have to notify your parents, of course." Of course. My parents are such total rule followers, they don't even keep extra change if a cashier makes a mistake in their favor. They always do the math for the clerk and return the money, even though that usually only serves to annoy the clerk. So breaking the Code of Conduct? Mr. Pinski might as well call them and tell them I burned the school to the ground.

". . . And we'll need to sign you up for the decision-making class that we offer," Mr. Pinski is saying. "As for the play . . . I'm not sure. We were going to have you take over the part for Amanda, but now we may have to cancel the whole thing. I hate to do that, though. That punishes the whole cast." Yeah? Well, maybe some of the cast deserves punishing. Maybe the part that frames people and snitches on them just so they can get more stage time. He sighs. "I have to talk it over with Mr. Price and see if we can figure something out."

This is a lot to take in. I need to get back to the first thing. "Do you think I could tell them? My parents? I'll have them call you tomorrow so you know that they know." The thought of them finding out what a juvenile delinquent their daughter is on this random morning and then having to stew about it all day until I get home is intolerable.

"That's not the normal procedure—" he starts.

"Please, Mr. Pinski? I haven't been in trouble at school before." He's still pressing his lips together. What can I say that would be convincing to an adult? "And . . . and this will allow me to take responsibility."

Yes. Mr. Pinski looks at me, and his eyes soften. "Oh, I don't see why not," he says. "I'll have more information for them tomorrow anyway."

I know this is me getting special treatment, reaping the benefits of my honor roll history, but I don't care. I need all the scale tipping I can get right now.

"Thank you," I say. Then I blurt, "I'm sorry" like a little kid. Mr. Pinski nods kindly, but I'm really talking to myself. *I'm sorry I'm constantly being such a pain in the ass and messing up my life, Hattie. I'm sick of me, too.*

"That's all for now, Hattie. Here's the schedule for that class you'll need." He goes back around his desk, picks up a slip of paper, and hands it to me. "You can go back to—what class are you in now, math?" He looks at his computer screen. "You can go back to math." I hurry out and duck my head past Ms. Wendy, my face burning with the certainty that she knows everything about why I'm there.

The rest of the day passes in a blur. Somehow my automatic pilot systems get me to all the correct classes at all the correct times, but I don't remember what happens in any of those classes, and I skip lunch because the one thing I do know is that I definitely do not want to talk about it. Nonetheless, my mind is filled with questions. What's happening to the other kids who got caught? What is going to happen to the play? What will my parents say? Why are grown-ups always focusing on the wrong things? Behind it all lurks this sneaking suspicion that the universe hates me. After all, how long did it give me to feel good about my eyes before it brought new disaster rolling in? Four hours? What a raw deal.

I'm staring blankly into my locker after the dismissal bell, paralyzed by the mystery of what homework I have and what books I'll need to do it, when I hear a familiar voice greet me. Amanda. I feel like a caged tiger when they finally lift the iron door. I whip around.

"Don't talk to me. Don't even say my name."

Her mouth drops open and then her brow knits together. "What's up, Hattie?"

My hands ball into fists. All the little anxious what-ifs filling my body are more than happy to gel together into a white-hot rage. "Like you don't know. Just walk away before I lose it."

But she doesn't walk away. Why would she listen to me when she's clearly set on controlling everything and everybody? She steps closer to me. "Hattie, is this about the ski trip? It sucks, right? But we're all in trouble. Myself included."

"So what, then? You had to throw me under the bus, too? I was right about you and Richard. I knew something was off. And this is—what? Revenge for the fact that I got the tiniest piece of his attention? Or was it just for kicks?" My voice gets higher and higher. I'm screeching by the end of this rant. Somehow I kept it together in Mr. Pinski's office, but now all that stored-up emotion is rushing out. And here comes the stupid climax. "I hate you so much!" I blubber like a baby.

Suddenly, I'm aware that all other movement and sound in the hallway has stopped. Everyone is watching. I would be embarrassed if I wasn't so pissed off.

Amanda is speechless, her body frozen. I guess she didn't expect a confrontation.

"I knew I couldn't trust you. I knew it!" I try to say it in a lower register. It comes out like blubbering with a side of growl.

That statement seems to bring her alive. "Whoa, wait a minute—"

"And this is what I get for letting my guard down with you for one second. It's not fucking fair!" My hand flails out when I say this and hits the locker door, banging it shut. Pain shoots through my knuckles and up my arm, and my brain decides that this, too, is something Amanda has done to me. It's all her fault, and I can't stand the innocent expression she's trying to pull off for another instant.

"Stop it!" I yell in her face, although even I have lost track of what specifically the "it" is by now. Some of my spit may have flown out of my mouth and touched her skin because she's backing up and wincing. I keep moving forward. I want to unload everything onto her, want to push the uncomfortableness of everything out and dump it on her head.

She's all the way against the wall when someone grabs my shoulder and spins me around. It's Asha, who has materialized next to me. She entwines her arm tightly with mine and drags me down the hallway, scooping up my backpack with her free hand on the way.

"Sorry, Amanda, Hattie will have to continue this—this *mini scene rehearsal* another time. I need her for a sec. Great work, though! Very believable." She bumps the exterior door open with her hip and drags me into the cold, leaving Amanda with her mouth hanging open in the hall.

"My coat is still in my locker," I protest, reclaiming my arm.

"That's what you have to say? You just acted like a fool in there in front of half the school and you're worried about your coat?"

"It's cold."

"What's going on with you lately?" She seems genuinely concerned about me, looking out for me as usual, being a good friend. But I'm too far gone. Her goodness makes me feel ugly.

"What's going on with me? What about you? I already have one overprotective mother, you know, I definitely don't need another." This isn't fair, she just did me a solid back there, but I want her to back the fuck up a bit because I hate that she's watching me unravel.

"Are you going for a world record in picking fights or something?" she says.

"Are you sure I'm the one picking the fight here? You grabbed me, remember? And now you're interrogating me."

"Hattie, seriously. I swear, if I had some ice water, I would pour it over your head. Snap out of it. Take some deep breaths or something."

I'm about to tell her not to patronize me, when she looks back from scanning the pickup line. "Anyway, my mom is here," she says. Her tone softens. "Come home with me. We'll hang, we'll talk, we'll eat enough buttered popcorn to make the world make sense again."

"I don't think I can," I say, my voice still full of misdirected bitterness. If only I could tell her that the person I'm really mad at is myself. Oh, and Amanda. Ha. Can't forget about her. "I have to go home and deal with my parents."

I can see Asha's desire to question me further playing across her face, but she holds back. Instead, she sighs.

"All right, Hatts. I just don't love this for us."

“We’re good,” I say. “Sorry. I was out of line.” I’m trying to emulate her maturity, her calm in the face of chaos. I want us to be good, too.

“You know I love you.”

“I know.” I attempt a casual smile like I’m comfortable.

“Okay, warrior. Try not to eviscerate anyone on the way to the bus.” With that, she turns and walks her long-legged walk over to her mom’s Honda Odyssey with the delicate elegance of royalty as the door automatically slides open to receive her. She is a shining star and I suck. I am a puddle of guilt and regret. I’ve shut her out, hidden all the things that are making me *me* right now away from her. I need to tell her everything. If only I didn’t hate the everything so much.

The key to communicating with my mother is timing. It is unwise to tell her anything when she’s just woken up and tired, or when she’s going to bed and is tired. She’s tired, like, a lot. It’s also not advisable to tell her anything when she’s rushed, busy, or hungry. Or sick. In fact, I’ve found the best time to talk with her is when she’s folding laundry. The rhythm of it seems to calm her, like she’s meditating or something.

I don’t know when the best time is to tell my dad something because I try not to tell him anything. He’s too unpredictable, too rigid, too caught up in his own moods. But my mom seems to have some secret tactics with him, so I tell her all my mistakes and then wait for her to pass them on, like a depressing game of telephone. That’s the other key to my parents. Avoidance.

The first thing I do when I get home is dump the contents of my hamper into the washing machine with a couple of detergent pods and start the cycle. Then I unload the dishwasher and wipe down the kitchen counter, hoping to score some extra points. By the time my mom walks through the door, I've already moved my clothes to the dryer. I put in three dryer sheets, which I know my mom will say is wasteful, but I can't resist the smell. When she hears the dryer singing its little "I'm finished" song, she wanders to the laundry room like a mosquito to a porch light. So predictable.

This is the time I've so carefully planned; I won't get a better opportunity. But I feel like my pink shag carpeting is quicksand. I have to steel myself the way we do at the beginning of the summer when we're jumping in the unheated park pool that's just been filled with freezing water straight from the hose. *They can find out today from you or tomorrow from the principal.*

I lurch forward and careen into my parents' bedroom, where my mom hovers over a mountain of socks and jeans, startling her. She touches her chest to indicate I could have given her a heart attack.

"Where's the fire?" she asks, recovering.

"Mom, they might cancel the play because some kids were caught smoking weed which breaks the behavior code so they can't participate and I broke it too with a beer so you or Dad need to call Mr. Pinski about it in the morning," I say, all in one breath.

"They might cancel the play?" she asks, stuck on the first thing.

"It's being discussed. With Mr. Price," I say.

"What did you do with a beer?" she asks, sort of catching up.

"I drank it," I say, still agitated and jumpy, as if I'm late to an appointment and I don't have time for these trivial facts.

"Oh," she says, perching on the edge of her bed, concern in her eyebrows. She takes a deep breath, slowing my energy. "When?"

"On the ski trip." I'm tracking her expression, hoping she won't cry. "I'm sorry," I say now, feeling present in the room for the first time in the conversation. "It was a mistake."

"Yes," she says. She seems unsure of what to say next. She looks in the laundry basket for the answer, then picks up a T-shirt and starts folding again. "Does your father know?"

I bite my lip. "No. Can you tell him?"

She deflates, immediately appearing older, like she's been folding this particular load of laundry for twenty years. I'm a real shit. First, I break the behavior code, then I make my mom do my dirty work. And she clearly hasn't even recovered from the meeting with Dr. Porter; she looks as dazed as she did last week in Syracuse. I'm a disappointment on so many levels. But I still wait for her answer.

"Of course," she sighs. "I guess we'll discuss what the consequences are after we talk to the principal."

Consequences. What does she mean? My parents have never been big on formal punishments, but this seems right for a first time. I deserve it. Besides, where am I going? I'm apparently no longer in the play, I don't have a boyfriend, and I'm never getting a driver's license, so me and these four walls are probably going to get real comfy with each other.

I've done what I can now, anyway. There's nothing left to do except wait to see what Mr. Pinski says, what my parents say, and what's left of my life after all the adults finish having opinions.

CHAPTER 19

The next morning, I snooze my alarm more times than I can afford, but I can't talk myself into getting out of bed. Yesterday, I jumped out of bed feeling like things were finally getting better, but each day seems to bring some fresh hell. Why should today be any different? But staying in bed all day would invite more trouble. I don't think my mom would buy another random, nonspecific illness that causes me to be bedridden. I have to at least pretend I'm still on track, rather than completely off the rails and requiring additional scrutiny.

I drag myself to the bathroom, brush my teeth and hair, and decide that what I wore as pajamas last night (sweatpants and a long-sleeve V-neck) is low-wrinkle enough to keep on as clothes for the day. The house is silent. I check the clock. I've missed the bus. My dad has already caught his ride to work; my brother is off to school with the neighbor kid. Normally, I would wake my mom up now to drive me. Sometimes, I even miss the bus on purpose because when she takes me we almost always stop at Burger King to get a Croissan'wich and hash browns. But today, I'd prefer to walk. I put on the eighty-six layers required to be outside for more than five minutes at this time of year.

My boots crunch the frost on the sidewalk, and my body immediately sets its internal GPS toward school as my mind starts to wander. Mason's house is 0.3 miles away from mine (we measured it once), so we ended up walking this route together dozens of times when we both ran late. Well, walk is a euphemism for what we did. It was more of a stumble spin on the way to school, me giving him a little shove when he said something snarky, him overreacting and pratfalling to the ground, then jumping back up and air boxing a 360-degree circle around me until I pushed him again. Needless to say, school would be over by the time we got there if we kept that up the whole way, so at some point in every walk we'd race. It was always neck and neck, and we kept a running tally of our victories, adding them to the totals from Ping-Pong games in his garage. I had been down 23-24 when he died. Guess I'm the loser for eternity.

It's just starting to crystallize that since Mason was taller than me, faster than me, and head and shoulders above me in Ping-Pong ability, he might have been keeping it close intentionally, when Mason falls into step next to me.

"You're a bad girl," he says in the way that makes *bad* sound very, very good. "Naughty."

"So are you just stalking me twenty-four seven or is God sending you, like, mobile alerts on everything that's happening to me when you're not around?" I say this as if I'm teasing him, but I'm really curious.

"Maybe both," he says without missing a beat. He starts to whistle, seeming to rub it in that any further information he might have about the existence of God is on a need-to-know basis and I definitely don't. I decide to press. He didn't show up on this sidewalk to *not* talk to me, after all.

"I may be naughty, but you could still do a friend a solid. I mean, I would think there'd be a few perks to knowing someone from the afterlife, like maybe I could get a heads-up on trouble barreling my way. No? No warnings? Nothing?"

"No, not nothing. I told you about human aspartame. You didn't exactly sprint away from him after that."

"Well, I did *ski* away from him, eventually."

"Eventually. Which brings me to my next point. Did you already forget about who got you down that mountain? Guess your afterlife connection isn't as withholding as you say."

He's trying to be provoking, but he's just too darn cute about it for me to be annoyed. More than that, he's right. After that night in the snow it's physically impossible for me to feel irritated with him. I'm glad he's back, even if his conversation can make me feel like I'm spinning around in circles. I attempt to rise to the level of his banter. "*I* got me down the mountain. You were just some sort of ethereal cheerleader. You might as well have been shaking pom-poms in a pleated skirt."

"I do have the legs for it," he says, considering his own legs. "And it won't work."

"What won't work?"

"You know. That thing you do."

"What thing I do?"

"Make like it's you against the world. Put people in your life on the opposite side of a wall." He goes from whistling to humming. He's so proud of himself. Thinks he knows me inside and out.

"As usual, you are making zero sense. Me? Me put people on

the other side? Dude, that's you." I hike my backpack up on my shoulder as I pause at an intersection for a passing car, making eye contact with the driver. Nothing to see here, just two kids headed to school. One of them may or may not be dead. You probably can't see him anyway, so forget I said anything.

"Guilty as charged."

"That's it?" I step off the curb and cross the street. The crisp air and brisk walk, and, let's be honest, conversing with a ghost, have filled me with energy. I want to tussle with him, to push all his buttons and have him push mine, or I might have to start running to release this extra agitation. "No, no, you don't get off that easy. I know you're thinking shit about me at a million bytes per second. Give me your full analysis."

Mason kicks pebbles ahead of us, his hands in his pockets. "Did you know that I was scheduled for surgery next month? Guess it's canceled now. The surgeon probably gets a free day to golf."

The 180-degree in tone of this admission takes me so off guard that I stop walking. I look at him sharply. "You were?"

"They were going to take out a piece of my brain," he says, then adds with a slightly Austrian accent, "They ver going to experiment on zee mind!"

"Oh, damn. To stop the seizures?"

Mason snorted. "I mean, that's what they said, but who knows? Every time they switched a medication, or added a medication, that's what they said. And every time, I felt like I was losing options but keeping the seizures. My mom would say things like, 'So you can't go on roller coasters. So what? Lots of people don't like roller coasters.' Which is true. But *I* like roller coasters. I never got to choose. I had no control. I was always trying to forget it, but my life became more about seizures than anything else. And after surgery? They said this wouldn't happen, but what if the seizures were at the center of who I was? What if I woke up an entirely different person?"

This is the most I have heard Mason say about himself at one time in my entire life. I realize I'm holding my breath for fear that any sound from me will interrupt his train of thought. As much as I loved how funny he was the entire time I knew him, I always craved that he would be serious like this with me. It feels closer.

Unexpectedly, he laughs. "I mean, that was my take until I croaked. Now I know better. Now I know what zero control really looks like. Exhibit A." He gestures to himself while turning slowly, like he's the grand prize on a game show.

"But couldn't you have told your parents? If you didn't want the surgery? They wouldn't have made you go through with it, would they?"

"I mean, if I didn't give a shit about them, then yeah, sure, I could have told them. But my parents, my mom especially, needed to *do* something. They didn't want to feel powerless, either. Doesn't matter now, right?" He paused, then said, "I don't know if she's free from all that with me gone or if she feels more helpless than ever."

"Oh, Mason." I wince. I've spent our conversations thinking

far more about how his death has affected me, and far less about how it's affecting him.

"Forget it," he says, his voice harder now. "I'm just envious of you, is all."

"Envious of me?" Crazy talk.

"Yeah, you. You think you don't, but you've got power. A lot. You just ignore it most of the time."

"Power to fuck up, you mean? I'm fully aware."

"Hey, don't knock fucking up. Fucking up is everything. It's exciting." He regains his swagger. "Especially when you do it, Murph. Your fucking up is epic, it's multilayered, it's breathtaking. Speaking of which, let's talk more about how I saved your freezing ass."

It's times like these when I wish Mason's arm wasn't just mist and shadow, so I could give it a good shove. Or a really long hug.

CHAPTER 20

I arrive at school and am almost to my locker when I freeze. Richard is striding toward me with purpose. Shit. I don't want to deal with him and am fully regretting the decision to make today my own personal pajama day. I look around for an easy escape, but there's none. Then a tiny little piece of hope buzzes in my chest. Maybe he's coming to apologize. Maybe he's going to say that just like me, altitude has an adverse effect on him, except in his case, it makes him a douchebag—clinically speaking, of course. And now he's back to normal and oh so very sorry and won't I please consider forgiving him or he doesn't know how he'll face himself in the mirror?

But when he gets within speaking distance, his eyes are dead and distant. "I'm gathering everyone up. Cast and crew meeting, onstage, five minutes." I nod and he marches off, still a douchebag at sea level.

Inside the auditorium, most kids are already gathered, sitting cross-legged onstage. I see Asha and sit down next to her. I rest my head on her shoulder for a second to show her I come in peace and I'm not feeling explosive. She pulls her earbuds out of her ears and tucks them in their little charging case, then zips that into the inner pocket of her jacket. She lost the first set of earbuds she got for her birthday almost immediately, and had to use a whole lot of hours of minimum wage earnings scooping ice cream to buy a new pair. Not surprisingly, she takes conspicuous care of these. Once they are secure, she puts her arm around my shoulders and gives me a squeeze, accepting my peaceful offering with an olive branch of her own.

"So, give me all your intel before this meeting starts," she says.

"What do you mean?"

"This is about behavior code violations on the ski trip, right? Jeff said there was a four-twenty party? So, who are we talking about?"

I assumed she already knew more than this after my fight with Amanda in the hall, but I guess she witnessed less than I thought. Either that or misunderstood it. I struggle with how to frame what happened. It's even harder to tell Asha I was part of all this trouble than it was to tell my parents. As much as I want to, I can't quite shake the feeling that my stupid mistakes will make her disappointed in me. This is the problem with being friends with someone you look up to.

"Um, I don't know much more about the weed than you do," I start, which is technically true but still feels dishonest. "But I did see Richard—"

"Oh, shit! Richard?" she whispers so loudly I wince. "Weird. He seems like the kind of guy who wouldn't be comfortable losing control, like, *at all*. Did it bother you? Is that why you guys aren't all flirtastic over here?"

Before I can answer, Mr. Price walks in. He stands in the center aisle and looks up at us all, his fingertips pressing together in a tent.

"All right, lambs, first of all, I want to say that I am not mad." He says this in a way that lets us clearly know how very, very mad he actually is, and how lucky we are that he is a saint, because otherwise all the guilty parties would be skewered and slowly turned over an open fire. "I've been in extensive talks with Mr. Pinski, trying to find a compromise that would honor the behavior code but also not needlessly punish those of you who have been pouring your hearts and spirits into this show and have done nothing wrong. And I think we have found a solution."

Wow, he is laying the shame on thick. As I prepare for sentencing, I glance at Richard to see what his face looks like when he actually feels regret, but it's completely impassive, as if he has no idea what Price is talking about. No wonder he gets the lead in all the shows. He has more practice acting than the rest of us. He never stops.

"We are going to cancel the matinee. It had the fewest ticket sales anyway, so hopefully we can notify all our loyal patrons and get them moved to the Friday or Saturday evening performance. Also, we are canceling the cast party, as we do not feel that a school-sponsored celebration of the group is appropriate at this time." This announcement sparks groans. Mr. Price carefully smooths each one of his eyebrows while he waits for the sounds to stop. "Lastly, we are canceling the final dress rehearsal. You can all thank me later for instituting my multiple dress rehearsal policy, so that you aren't utterly unprepared. All I ask in return is that you bloody well kill it this weekend. Dismissed."

As we shuffle out without the normal horsing around, it

sinks in how much I'm dodging a bullet. My Saturday night show lives! I still get to do it. I would feel guilty that Amanda was getting the brunt of the punishment by losing a show if she wasn't the one who got me in trouble in the first place.

Speak of the rat. She's suddenly right next to me. She opens her mouth.

"No," I say, holding up my hand to block her face from my line of sight. "No no no no no no no." I repeat it until Amanda drops back. Asha, though, stays in step with me.

"So many questions," she says. "Do I dare ask?"

"Probably not. It's petty and dumb and not worth rehashing." I'm not proud of a single piece of that story.

Asha steps in front of me and turns around so we're facing. "Let me be clear. I know friends sometimes grow apart and that's a normal part of life and all that, but I don't plan on doing that with you, okay?"

"Okay."

"I mean it," she says. "You need to let me in."

And here we are again. I hate the fact that trying to avoid all my super uncomfortable thoughts and feelings is making Asha think I'm trying to avoid *her*. It's enough already. "Does that offer to eat popcorn with me until I'm sane again still stand?" I say.

"Abso-fucking-lutely," she says. She looks lighter, like I just took a backpack full of rocks off her shoulders. "See you after last bell." She blows me a kiss and ducks into her French class.

Okay, good. I start mentally preparing myself. I'll bite the bullet and tell her about the beer. How harshly can she judge me, really, when half the cast just got caught smoking pot? And I'll tell her what happened with Richard. That will take some time, because knowing Asha, I'll probably also have to talk her out of going on some crazy crusade of justice where she hunts him down and verbally eviscerates him in public. As much as I'd enjoy watching Asha annihilate Richard, I don't need that kind of attention on my failed fling. Plus, I should be able to fight my own battles if I want to, although at this point with Richard, I really don't. I want as little to do with him as possible.

What about the RP? I need to tell her that, too. It's hard to explain, though. I failed miserably when I tried to tell Richard on the mountain. I don't know where to start. I envision her shaking her head, maybe thinking I'm exaggerating or overreacting because she knows me well enough to know that those are bad habits of mine. Then she'll say, "Maybe you just need new contacts." She wouldn't really say something so dismissive, of course she wouldn't, but I can't think of what she could possibly say that would make it an iota better.

Turns out, I don't get to find out what either of us will or won't be able to say, because when I get to my locker after school and pull out my phone, there's a voice text from my dad: *Let's talk after school.* It's consequences time.

I text Asha a quick *got to cancel—parents' orders. Rain check?* to which she immediately responds *as long as I def see you tomorrow night at my house.* Yes, ma'am. I head straight home. When I get there, Dad is waiting for me at the kitchen table, hands spread out on the cool surface. Usually, he has the radio on, but not now. Now he's just sitting.

"Hi, Dad." He doesn't respond, just presses his lips together and nods slightly. I sit, completely unnerved.

"Am I grounded?" I blurt. I don't know why, since my parents have never grounded me before. Usually, when my dad is mad at me, he just gives me the silent treatment for a few days. I hate it, but at least it's predictable. This new "let's talk" strategy has me off-balance. I hope he doesn't say he's disappointed in me. I don't think I could take it.

"What? That's not something we– I don't think so. Did your mother say that?"

"No, I just– She said that you were going to discuss next steps after you talked with Mr. Pinski."

"Well, it sounds like the school has already taken care of that. Don't you have some decision-making group you have to go to now? What's it called?"

"Hold on." I pull the form with the rotating schedule out of my backpack and look at the bold type. "Better Bets," I say.

"Wow. Okay." He rubs the crease at the bridge of his nose. "So you'll do that, then."

"Yes, of course." Is that it? I tentatively stand up.

"One thing, though. This Better Bets is during school?"

"Yeah. It's a different period every week."

"I don't want you missing calculus."

I look back at the schedule. "It's going to fall during calculus at least twice."

"I don't want you missing calculus. You can't understand the new concepts presented if you're not there."

"Dad, um, you want me to *skip* behavior code class?" It seems crazy to break the rules of a class about breaking rules. "It doesn't seem like that will go over very well."

My dad sets his jaw. "Well, if anyone gives you a hard time about it, tell them they can give me a call. I'll handle it."

"Okay, Dad." I let out a little cough. "Thanks."

"Our word is our bond, Hattie. Try to remember that in future. It's all we have."

I wander up to my room, befuddled. He almost seemed more irritated with the school than with me. I can't explain that, but it's a relief to be on the same team for a change. If he wants to have my back, I'll take it.

CHAPTER 21

When Asha answers the door, I can only see her face. She's dressed all in black and it's pitch-dark behind her.

"Good, you're here, you're here!" She air-kisses me on both sides. "We've been waiting for you to start."

"Start what?" I step into the hall. "Why is it so dark in here?"

"Here, take my arm." Asha doesn't know my official diagnosis, but she's so freaking perceptive that she's been clued in to my sucky night vision for a while now. Sometimes she seems to anticipate how well I'm going to be able to see in a situation better than I do. "Two steps down here."

"Is the power out or something?"

"I'm just creating a mood." We turn the corner into the den and my stomach drops. There are tea lights on every surface, and cushions set up around the coffee table. In the center of the table sits a Ouija board, the glass orb of the pointer thingy flashing the reflection of wavering candlelight. "Ta-da!"

"Asha, I thought we talked about this. How we weren't going to do it." My armpits have started sweating like I've sprung a leak or something, so I strip my sweater off over my head before my T-shirt underneath gets visibly wet.

"I know, you said, but everyone else was into it. Come on, I promise it's not going to be creepy. We're going to do good vibes only. I think it'll be cathartic for everybody." She leaves me standing by the cushions, and opens one of the French doors to the backyard. The rest of the group's voices come streaming in with the cold air.

"Guys! Come in! Hatts is here and I want to get started."

Lucia appears in the room almost immediately, pausing on the mat by the door to pluck at her shirt. "My gem of a boyfriend just stuffed half a snowman down my back," she says. "I swear, he's lucky he's so cute."

"Aw, thanks, babe," Jeff says, coming in behind her. "I think you're cute, too, even when you're a little moist." He grins, kicks off his hiking boots, and plops down on a cushion. "Now come be cute over here."

"Hey, Hatts," says Nolan, coming up and giving me a lazy side hug. "How goes it? Where do you want to sit?"

"I don't. I don't want to sit." My voice sounds a little panicky. How do I stop them from taking Mason and changing him into some character from a cheesy horror movie? "Asha, can't we just hang out? We can make popcorn, find something bingeworthy—"

"Sure. After. Let's do this first."

"But we agreed—"

"Actually, just you agreed. With yourself. The rest of us voted after you left and it was a unanimous yes for séance. We've got a lot of questions that only Mason can answer." Her voice is breezy, but her words cut through me.

"Don't you want to at least try it?" asks Lucia, with so much hope in her eyes I hesitate. Am I being selfish, just trying to keep him all to myself? No, he's not some generic ghost of the occult, he's our friend.

"I'm sorry, L, but I don't. It seems, I don't know, disrespectful," I say. Then I try another tack. "Besides, I doubt it'll work."

Asha takes a deep breath. She's looking at me like she can't decide whether to forget the whole thing or tie me to a chair and stuff a sock in my mouth. She settles on a third option. "Look, Hatts, if you don't want to join us, you don't have to. It's probably only going to take like fifteen minutes anyway. So make yourself a snack, hang in my room, whatever you want. But I did some research today, and there's supposed to be only positive energy when you start so you don't bring in negative spirits. I already burned all the incense. Therefore, anyone staying in this room has to be all in."

I don't want any of this to happen, but it looks like I'm not going to be the tiniest bit successful at stopping it. Having smart, successful friends with "perseverance" and "follow-through" means they also have a lot of "bullheaded stubbornness."

Maybe I will escape upstairs so I don't have to think about this anymore. "I guess I'll be in your room, then," I say, and I shuffle toward the door.

"Aw, and miss all the fun?" Mason's voice. I whip around. He's sitting on the last empty cushion, the one that was supposed to be for me.

"Did you change your mind?" asks Lucia, seeing me turn.

"Yeah, you can sit on my lap if you want," says Mason helpfully. No one else bats an eyelash.

I open my mouth and close it. It seems fake to pretend Mason isn't here, but what would my friends do if I started talking to thin air? Would Asha think I was mocking her? I sit on the arm of the couch, a couple of feet back from the coffee table. I don't want to leave Mason here without me.

"Actually, maybe I'll just watch," I say. Asha shoots me a look. "With positive energy."

Nodding, Asha takes Lucia's hand on one side and Nolan's hand on the other. Then Lucia grabs Jeff's hand. After a beat of chortling about it to show how masculine they are, Nolan and Jeff grab hands, closing Mason out of the circle. He pouts at me.

Asha closes her eyes. The rest of the circle does the same, and suddenly, all the smirking is gone. "Tonight we are here to contact a friend on the other side. We call upon Mason Leary to come and talk with us." Mason touches his own chest in faux shock as if they've just announced he won an Oscar. Asha seems to be thinking of what to say next. She tilts her head slightly. "You are welcome here. Cross over and keep us company."

Mason scans the circle, eyebrows raised, as if he is just as curious as everyone else about what will happen next.

"Are you with us, Mason?" Asha asks, opening her eyes. "We need some sort of sign." She drops Lucia's and Nolan's hands and rests two fingers on top of the Ouija board indicator, and the others do the same. It starts to wiggle.

I look at Mason, and he holds his hands out innocently. "I'm not doing anything, I swear. It must be Elvis. Or Marie Antoinette. Or Jack the Ripper."

The indicator slides to *YES* and Lucia gasps.

I find that I have abandoned the arm of the couch and have come to hover directly behind Lucia out of sheer nervousness. Now, since Mason doesn't seem to be suffering under any Ouija-related magic, I finally relent and sit on the cushion next to him. I put my fingers lightly on the indicator and so does he. Even though our bodies and hands are close, there's no warmth coming from him. If anything, it feels cooler on his side.

"Mason, can you tell us if you are okay?" Asha asks.

Mason laughs. "Huh, where is the 'that's always been debatable' option?" The indicator wanders the board for a moment, then slides back to *YES*. "Still not doing it," Mason says to me. I wonder who is. Is it Asha? Or just the collective subconsciousness of the whole group wanting to make things nice and peachy?

"How can we see you?" Asha asks now.

This is not a yes-or-no question. The indicator seems to get that immediately and careens into the alphabet. After roaming for a few seconds, it stops on *A*. Asha takes her hand away and writes the letter on a small pad she's placed on the table. *S* comes up next. Then *K*.

"Ask! That's a whole word!" Lucia says, amazed. "But ask what?"

As if to answer her, the piece shifts again. *H*, a shudder, then *A* again.

Suddenly, I know what the Ouija board is going to say. I look at Mason. He looks like he's enjoying himself far too much. He's clearly stifling a laugh. No, don't turn this on me, Mason! Don't put my name down in black and white!

I feel the pointer moving toward the *T* so I try to steer it to the *R* instead. Maybe I can make it spell *ASK HARDER* without the rest of the Beaver Bunch noticing that I'm influencing it.

But a stronger force is pushing back against me. The indicator seems to be quivering with pressure. I'm losing ground. I give it one more hard push, and at the same time the resistance disappears, so the pointer goes flying off the table and skitters across the floor, coming to rest somewhere under a large armoire.

"Oops," Mason says.

"Whoa," Jeff and Nolan say simultaneously, then immediately start cracking up. Nolan grabs a throw blanket off the couch, puts it over his head, and starts staggering around making a series of ghostly *oooooohs*.

But Asha is not amused. "Hattie! What the hell?" She picks up her pad and slams it back down on the table in frustration.

"I didn't do anything. I mean, I didn't mean to do anything," I say, glancing around for support. But Jeff and Nolan are too busy horsing around. Jeff is holding the blanket over Nolan's head so he can't get out, and Lucia looks like she's trying to decide whether to intervene and scold her boyfriend or let him wallow in his immaturity.

"Yeah, Hattie doesn't know her own strength. Her default

setting is beast mode," Mason offers, as if Asha can hear him.

"I said you could sit out. You didn't have to go and ruin everything!" Asha says, like I'm a toddler.

This pisses me off. "Give me fucking break, Ash," I say, standing up. "You can't convince me that a smart girl like you actually thought this would be productive. It's a dumb gimmick that screams trashy reality show. Which is why I told you it was a bad idea. Mason would never–"

"Don't tell me what Mason would do!" she yells. Holy shit, she's actually yelling. The boys drop the blanket and Lucia covers her mouth. "You don't know what Mason would do, because Mason is dead!"

The force of her emotion has me dumbstruck. I look at Mason and I can tell he's just as shocked. He shakes his head, like it's all his fault. It makes me feel guilty, too, guilty for not getting what she was going through and why she wanted to do this séance so badly. I want to tell her that he's here, right now, feeling for her, but before I can think of a way, she speaks again. Her voice is hard and bitter. "You're not the only one who lost a friend, you know. I did, too. And so did everyone else here. We're all grieving. Just because you not-so-secretly wanted to get into his pants doesn't mean you get special rights to him."

"Oh, snap!" Mason says, perking up.

"What?!" I squeak, my lungs struggling to breathe. "I didn't want to get into his pants."

"Sure. Of course not. And I suppose Richard isn't your little consolation prize, either. Your rebound for a romance that never even happened."

"What the hell does Richard have to do with any of this?"

She suddenly looks exhausted with all of it. "Forget it. It's none of my business. You want to cope by pushing us away and losing yourself to some tool, you should be allowed to do that. Because everyone grieves differently. But stop acting like you're the only one grieving."

This conversation has gotten away from me at light speed. I feel disoriented. I barely recognize Asha like this, and none of her accusations seem fair.

"Maybe I should just go," I say finally, at a loss.

"Maybe you should." She stands up and I'm taken aback when I realize she's still going to lead me back through the dark maze of rooms. I flinch and pull my elbow away.

"Can't you just turn the lights on?" I ask.

Without a word, she walks toward the door and flips the switch, flooding the room with harsh fluorescents. I squint in the glare, then I'm out the door.

I don't dare to look back.

CHAPTER 22

It's the night of the performance, and I'm standing in the hallway listening to the overture and trying to breathe away the jitters when Richard slides up next to me. "Look, I'm a professional, and I know you'll be one, too." He puts out his hand like he's selling me a car. "Let's concentrate on the craft."

God, *craft*? How did I ever find him sexy? That's one thing Asha was right about. He is a full-fledged tool.

The fact that he's so transformed in my mind is tragic, my passion obliterated like a snail shell smushed on the sidewalk. Tragic, but also useful. When I watched Amanda and Richard do the first performance last night, the obvious fun they were having with each other made my nose wrinkle like I was smelling a fart. That was not surprising. What *was* surprising was how their good chemistry actually seemed to hurt the portrayal. It was so light and smooth, it didn't fit the intensity of the character dynamics at all. So I'm sort of glad for the hard feelings tonight, for his coldness, for my disgust. Maybe that'll be what makes everything real.

"Craft is my middle name," I say. Get ready to rumble, dick.

The first few scenes go great, but suddenly it's déjà vu. Here I am again, rushing offstage into total darkness for a lightning-quick change that I'm not equipped to manage alone. Too late, I realize my error. My whole solution was wrapped up in Richard not being an asshole, and I have forgotten to come up with a plan B. Richard isn't here. Of course he's not. How could I think I could still rely on him to help me out with a little stage logistics when he basically left me to die in the snow? He's a professional, my ass.

My mind is racing as I try to troubleshoot the possibilities. I could start shouting for help, but the audience will hear me for sure. I need a quiet way to get help.

Mason. Maybe Mason, if it's really an emergency, can help guide me. He helped me down that mountain. He could get me to the props table. But how to summon him? I couldn't do it on demand at the ski resort, so what could I do differently now? What are the common denominators of all the times he's shown up? One thing is that I'm usually feeling raw, vulnerable, and just generally like a total fuckup, so maybe that will work to my advantage now. I start picturing his face. Mason. Mason. Mason. A couple of seconds tick by. How long can I wait? I'd really hate to do another awkward square dance during an actual performance.

I squint into the backstage void. "Help me, Mason," I whisper, and to my utter surprise and joy I feel two hands on my shoulders, steering me to the table. My tunics are quickly exchanged and then the garlands are placed across my outstretched palms and I am led back over to the edge of the lit stage. It all happens so fast that I actually have to stand and wait for my cue, in awe that Mason has touched me, and that his hands felt so warm and real, so alive.

"Go get 'em," the owner of the hands says now, and I realize that I haven't been helped by Mason at all, but by a girl. Amanda. It's seriously demented that I think it would be less strange to be helped by a bona fide ghost than by her, but demented is getting to be my specialty.

Intermission comes without any more close calls, and I head to the band room/makeshift greenroom to relax for a few minutes.

But relaxing is out of the question. The only person wearing street clothes in a sea of tunics and draping gowns, Amanda draws my eye immediately. And she sees me. I'm going to have to say something to her, something that acknowledges that she helped me out despite the fact that I almost physically assaulted her the other day, and possibly also explain why I was busy whispering a dead guy's name. I wonder what an etiquette book would suggest for that scenario. As I approach, I have to push the idea out of my head that this, too, is some sort of trap. *Rise above*, I tell myself. *For your own sanity.*

"Thanks for your help out there," I say, my voice husky with the effort to sound casual.

"No problem. It's going great so far, don't you think?" she says. I nod, but she's already turned away to help a freshman girl unlace her corset. Last night, when I came to the performance Amanda was starring in, I stayed in the audience during intermission. It didn't even occur to me to come back to the dressing room to help people change. I hate that this makes Amanda seem nicer than me. Am I the only one who sees the trick, that she's the absolute worst?

As if on cue, she says, "I didn't tell on you, you know."

I wave my hand. "I don't want to talk about it." I can't start arguing about the evidence of her betrayal now. I still have Act Two to do in about five minutes, and I don't want to have to redo my hair and my makeup after I tear her delicate flesh from her bones.

She grabs my hand and looks into my eyes hard. "Hattie, I'm serious. Honestly, I didn't even know why you were so mad at me at first. I mean, can you imagine me giving you a beer and then snitching on you for drinking it? I would never."

Of course I can imagine it. That's pretty much all I've been imagining for the last several days. "You were the only one who even knew," I say, pulling my hand away and shrugging at the obviousness of this "case closed" investigation.

She looks guilty then. *See, I fucking knew it!* Let the flesh-tearing begin.

"That's true. I did tell someone. But not to snitch! I was just talking about our night. I never thought you would get in trouble over it."

Just talking? On what planet is that an excuse? "Sure," I say. This is exactly how I didn't want to feel in the middle of the show. Worked up and childish. "'Cause you and Mr. Pinski regularly do lunch to spill tea and—what—swap recipes?"

"Oh my gosh, Hattie, you're so extra sometimes! I told Richard, okay? I just told Richard. That's all."

His name makes me jump. He's probably in the room right now, and if he hears me talking about him, it'll be total humiliation. I scan the kids sitting around us. No Richard. Even still, I walk over to a practice room and wave Amanda inside, shutting the door behind us.

What she said is starting to sink in. "So wait, *Richard* told on me?"

Amanda looks uncomfortable. If she wouldn't tell on me to the school, she probably doesn't want to tell on Richard to me, either. A piano takes up three-quarters of this tiny room and she starts tapping two adjacent keys back and forth, like she's playing the suspense music in a horror movie. Then she stops. "He said he was just trying to protect me." She sighs and shrugs. "'Cause I was already caught smoking with everybody else. He thought if you were implicated, too, we'd both get to keep our parts. Which is basically what ended up happening. But I swear I didn't know anything about it until it was already done." She's been looking at the floor, grinding the toe of her boot into the carpet, but now she looks at me again. "Just don't hate me, okay? I like you. I want to be friends," she says, then with a hint of smile adds, "Or at the very least not have you attack me in the halls."

The stage manager, Sofi, opens the door a crack and pokes her head in. "Places, ladies, places," she says, then hustles on.

My mind is swimming. For some reason, I keep misreading Amanda. But she didn't betray me. She likes me. She likes me enough to tolerate a lot of bad behavior from me and still want to be my friend. Enough to be honest with me right now. I really hate hating someone. It means walking around ready for battle all the time, and every time I see the target of my hate, adrenaline shoots to every nerve ending and my mouth goes dry. I would love to stop doing that, and start liking her instead. But letting go of a feeling that I've been gripping so tightly is giving me a weird sensation, like I'm falling.

I step through the doorway and then look back at her. *Say something to make her feel better. She deserves it.* "I'm putting my claws away, I promise," I say.

"Thank you," she says, chuckling. "Have a good second act."

I do. I have a great second act. Partially because Richard and I are obviously competing, one-upping each other. We're so "professional and focused on the craft" it's like we're maniacs. I wish someone was keeping score because this is clearly an act-off. Every push of intensity on his part amps me up, too, and vice versa. This is the time in the play when Guenevere has fallen in love with Lancelot and cheats on Arthur. Richard always transmits the torment of the situation well, but this time his performance is also filled with total disgust for me—I mean, for Guenevere, and her unethical behavior. His noble dignity is condescending. It lights a fire in me. I need to show how Guenevere had no other choice, that fate was driving her into Lancelot's arms and it was impossible to resist. I sing "I Loved You Once in Silence" with so much passion that Carter actually looks taken aback at first, like he might be a little afraid of me. But the level of power is contagious, and soon we're both swept up in it. We're just supposed to hug at the end, but this time, we somehow both fall to our knees together, overcome. The song gets a huge round of applause. It's so freaking fun.

After the curtain call, the hallway is a crush of people, everyone talking and shouting congratulations to each other. My mind feels wiped clean, blank, and my body feels lighter, like I'm half helium balloon. Amanda appears next to me. "Bravo," she says, smiling. "Some of us are going to Friendly's for ice cream. You coming?"

"Ooh, yes. Let me just find the fam and tell them."

I locate them waiting on the edge of the throng of audience members loitering in the hallway. Both my parents are beaming, and my brother is excitedly shaking a big bouquet of flowers toward me.

"These are for you!" he crows as soon as I get to them. He thrusts the stems into my hands. "Break a leg!"

He's being so darn cute I don't correct him on when it's the right time to say that. It's refreshing to see all three of them looking happy at the same time. All four of us, I realize suddenly.

"Thanks, Nate," I say, making a big show of burying my nose in the blooms and inhaling deeply. "These are beautiful!"

"You were wonderful," my mom says at the same time as my dad says, "Poise and presence. Real star quality." It's so like him to be over the top. I wonder for a millisecond what it's even like to go to a play and not be able to see it, like you're listening to an album in the dark.

"Thanks. Some of the cast are going to Friendly's. Can I go?"

"Of course, hun," my mom says. "Do you have enough money?"

"Yeah, I'm good."

"Oh, here, take this anyway." She presses two twenties in my hand. Whoa. Free money and no curfew reminder? I should be in a play more often.

The Friendly's is mostly empty, so us theater kids feel entitled to take over. We spread out over half a dozen booths, which is good because Richard ends up at the opposite end from me. I briefly wonder how long my brain is going to constantly keep track of his location in relation to mine, like some hormonal GPS. *Ignore him. No, more than that. Forget about him.*

Amanda and I slide into a booth at the other end of the group from Richard. I note how unusual it is for her to be so far away from him, and I wonder if she's feeling torn. I didn't really get her take on whether she thinks he betrayed her trust or saved her skin. I study her, but she doesn't look conflicted, just ready for sugar.

My favorite thing about Friendly's is that there's basically a whole page on the ice cream menu of stuff with peanut butter in it. Peanut butter cups, peanut butter sauce, Reese's Pieces, peanut butter shell coating. The only thing I like more than chocolate is peanut butter. Asha's favorite is the strawberry shortcake sundae, which, to me, is a missed opportunity. Why get fruit when you can have a peanut butter explosion?

Asha arrives in the next carload of kids and ends up stuffed into our booth, too, directly across the table from me. We haven't spoken since the failed séance, and the distance between us is getting more excruciating by the second. I try to catch her eye, but she studiously avoids looking at me. At a loss, I turn and start chatting with Amanda. I laugh a little too loudly. If that makes Asha a tiny bit jealous, maybe that wouldn't be the worst thing in the world.

I probably should apologize to her, but I can't frame in my mind how that would even look. I didn't say anything I didn't mean at her house and she knows it. And what about what she said to me? Maybe I'm the one who should be receiving an apology. But are apologies something Asha even does? Ultimately, I would rather just skip ahead to the part where we've already made up. The messiness in between there and here feels like an ocean, and I'm wearing cinder blocks of shame on each ankle.

Ignore it. Pretend to have fun. Our cast parties always turn into boy versus girl duet battles, and since the official cast party got canceled, we do it here. We go completely over the top, the cheesier the better. The antidote to the cringiness of singing show tunes in a restaurant is to totally embrace it. As usual, we start with *Grease* and end with a goofball song from *High School Musical 2*. I watch Amanda effortlessly harmonize. At least I can now feel the freedom of being able to enjoy it instead of hate her for it. At least I'm not mad at *everyone* here.

The orders hit the tables and the singing stops, the clinking of spoons against glass making the most sound now.

Asha has been looking at her phone every thirty seconds since she sat down. Now she says to the table, "This was fun, y'all. Congrats, everybody. I've got to go."

"Go where?" I can't help asking. I had been hoping we'd get to talk before the night was over, which can't happen if she leaves now. At least I've broken the seal with my intrusive question.

"A house," she says, perfectly neutral. "I'm just trying something out," she adds, as if that clarifies anything.

"Something or someone?" I ask.

"Nothing wrong with a little practice date."

"But it's like eleven. Isn't that a little late to start something?" I say. Why am I being her mother right now?

"Exactly. If it's going to be a practice date, I want it to be short. Only an hour until curfew. Okay?" she says, making it clear she doesn't care whether it is or not.

"Okay," I say helplessly. I may have surrendered any say I ever had in her life.

I go home with Amanda and end up sleeping over. After midnight, when I'm lying on the foldout chair in Amanda's room in the dark, I can't stop thinking about how Asha talked to me at the Friendly's, like I was someone whose name she couldn't remember. Asha and I have never really been on the outs before. Which is pretty amazing, considering I've been friends with her for years and years.

The day we met at orientation before middle school started, I noticed her the minute I walked up to the sign-in table. Intense concentration was coming off her in waves. I remember thinking, *How hard is it to write your name on a sheet?* but then I leaned over to see what she was doing. She had a name tag sticker in front of her and a fine-line Sharpie in her hand. *Asha* was already inked across the middle in perfect block letters, but what was taking all her focus was the drawing she was working on around her name, which was a handful of tiny but incredibly realistic sharks.

"That's amazing," I gasped without thinking.

She looked up with an open face and pushed her hair back over her shoulder. "I'm wholly obsessed with sharks right now. And lions. Wolves. Pretty much all the apex predators."

"I thought you were going to say you were obsessed with art," I said. "You could put that in a frame and hang it on the wall." I didn't know then that Asha was good at everything she tried, but that would become clear in a matter of weeks.

"Thanks," she said, drawing a final dorsal fin. Then she peeled the sticker off the backing and placed in on her right thigh instead of over her heart, which at the time I thought was a real rebel move.

"I like octopuses," I said. I immediately felt dumb about it–it made me sound like a first grader–but Asha just nodded like that was a good choice.

"Which grade school are you from?" she asked.

"Fillmore. You?"

"Revere. So glad to be out. It smelled like diapers there. Clean diapers, but still."

"Haha. Wow, that's really specific." I'd never really thought about what my elementary school smelled like. I guess mostly chalk and that weird odor books get when the paper is old. "What does this school smell like?"

She closed her eyes and took a deep breath through her nose. "Dry-erase markers and sawdust."

I was enjoying this game. "What do *you* smell like?"

This time she didn't have to inhale. She struck a pose. "Like magic. And you?"

I pulled the front of my shirt up to my nose. "Mmmm, better than magic. I smell like"—I took another whiff—"Cheeto Puffs."

She threw back her head and cackled loudly enough to startle several parents nearby. "You're funny," she said.

I drank in the sound and then blushed when I realized how much I was smiling. Looking down, I grabbed a name tag and scrawled my name, but before I could put it on, my mom came up and tried to get me to put on a sweatshirt because the air-conditioning was blasting. I fought her off. When I turned around, Asha had drawn a delicate octopus wrapping its tentacles around my name, gathering up the *H* on one side and the *E* on the other like it was giving the letters a hug.

"Ooh, it's so cute. I love it," I said. I suddenly wanted to put the sticker on my right thigh, too, but I didn't want to be a copycat. I settled for slapping it on my right sleeve above the elbow.

"We should probably sit," she said. I nodded, and we moved toward where the chairs were set up. Some friends from Fillmore waved at me and I headed toward them. I thought she was behind me, but when I turned around, she wasn't there. After the presentation, I saw her on the other side, sitting with friends of her own. They weren't in chairs but were sitting cross-legged on the floor along the wall, which again, seemed cooler than anything I would do. I felt a rush of disappointment that we hadn't talked more, and completely irrational jealousy of the strangers she was with.

But after the orientation, Asha found me again as I was walking to the parking lot with my parents. She introduced herself to them without a hint of shyness, and asked my mom to put Asha's mom's number into her phone. Then Asha squeezed my hand. "Call me when you get your schedule so we can see if we have any classes together."

"Okay, I will," I said, and I did, and that was that. I've always felt lucky to have her, although I've also always wondered what she saw in me that first day. I still feel the urge to try to deserve her. And I've spent the last few weeks utterly failing. I hope it's not too late to fix it.

CHAPTER 23

Amanda is driving me home the next morning when I remember something I've been trying very hard to forget. It's my birthday today. My sixteenth birthday. The first day I could officially get a driver's license if I wasn't cursed with shitty genes. What a stupid day.

"Today's my birthday," I say out loud because I can't help myself. When I was little, we would go out to dinner on my birthday and I would get to pick the restaurant. I picked Red Lobster every year for nine years in a row. I wonder if some Cheddar Bay Biscuits would make me feel better right now.

"Shut up," Amanda says.

"No, I'm serious."

"For realsies? It's your actual birthday?! Why didn't you tell me before?"

"It's not a big deal. I didn't really want to celebrate this year."

"HAPPY BIRTHDAY!!"

She looks at me and grins, pulling over onto the shoulder, wheels spinning a little on the gravel. She picks up the keys from the center console, spins them on her finger, then holds them out to me.

"Wanna drive?"

What?

"I can't," I say. Then, pushing back the whole truth, "I mean,

I don't have my permit yet or anything. And you're not exactly adult supervision."

"Technicalities. Anyway, who's going to tell on you," she says, sweeping her hand toward the endless snowy fields, "the cows?"

She's right. There's no one for miles. We've got so much roadway to ourselves, it's like we're in a car commercial. I look at the keys.

"For chrissake, birthday girl. Live a little." She pops her door open and jumps out. A second later, she opens mine and offers to help me up, like we're on a date in a black-and-white movie. I find myself giggling.

"You're so freaking weird," I say, taking her hand.

She settles into my spot. "Thank you. Now hurry up; it's cold."

I walk around the car, my legs feeling a little wobbly, my breath coming in quick, visible puffs. Is this fear or excitement? Is there even any difference? These days, good and bad are all mixed up together, like pain is the main ingredient of pleasure somehow, and vice versa. Would the show last night have felt like such a success if it hadn't almost been canceled? For that matter, would Amanda seem like such a supercharged friend right now if I hadn't been putting her on the top of my enemy list for months? Well, if I'm scared, that's probably a good thing; it'll up my focus. Let's do this.

I press the ignition, and the engine thrums through the seat in a way that it doesn't when I am a passenger, like it's connected to my nervous system. I shift the car into drive, my foot still on the brake. Then, stupidly, I go to flick on the turn signal, even though we're alone in the hills. Instead, the wipers spring to life with a squeal that makes us both jump.

"Oops," I say. I move the arm back to its starting position and the wipers settle.

"Do you want to adjust your mirrors or something?" Amanda says to me with a smirk. I can't tell whether her joke is that I'm being too careful or not careful enough, so I try to laugh it off while glancing at the mirrors.

"I think we're good," I say.

I press evenly on the gas, and I'm driving. I'm driving! It's the easiest thing in the world. It feels so much easier than all the pretend driving I've done in my life, easier than bumper cars, easier than go-karts, and way easier than any simulated, video game version of driving. The lane is wide, and the double yellow line at the center of the road is solid and supportive, like the railing on a staircase.

It's so natural and intuitive that I start to feel angry. Why would anyone think I couldn't do this? How fucking stupid do they think I am? An orangutan could do this! I speed up, so that as we crest each rolling hill, the next descent feels a little like a roller coaster, like we left our stomachs at the top. I'm dominating.

"How about some music?" I say.

"DJ Amandazing is here and fierce!" Amanda rolls through the channels, pauses at the "garage band" station, and cranks it. Heavy bass shakes the windshield in its frame. I touch the brakes to ease us around a bend, then give it gas to pick up speed again. The sun's feeble winter rays manage to break through the wall of clouds, and it looks as though someone dropped a warm filter over the entire landscape, like maybe Mother Nature wants to wish me happy birthday, too. I start to feel good.

"Amandazing? Did you just make that up right now?" I ask.

"Um, yes?"

"Oh no, no you didn't. You've been waiting months to use that!" I look over at her for a moment, and she's covering her face with her hands, a silent laugh shaking her body. I've caught her. I start laughing, too. "You've probably been doodling that name in glitter pen all over your diary."

In mock outrage, she takes one of her mittens out of her lap and starts slapping my arm with it. "OMG, I don't have a diary," she says, snorting. "And I definitely don't have a fucking glitter pen!" She hits me once more for good measure.

I hold up my right hand to block the surprisingly strong sting of the wet fabric. "Hey! Hey, I'm driving here! You don't want me to scratch your precious baby, now, do you?"

"That's right, you better concentrate. More focus, less roasting, before my mitten gets a mind of its own."

I pull a pretend zipper closed across my mouth. Then I unzip a tad and mutter out of the right side of my lips. "It's not my fault you had Amandazing business cards printed." I grin. This is fun.

Amanda collapses against her door, fake exhausted. "I give up. I'm a complete fraud. Do your worst."

I pat her hand. "Aw, you know I say it all with love." We both take a big inhale at the same time, recovering from our giddy fit.

What happens next probably only takes five seconds, but those seconds stretch out like the sticky hands you get as arcade prizes, where there seems to be no limit to how long they can get without snapping. I am pushing the gas pedal, almost flooring it, to get the tiny sports car up the steep hill. Then we're at the top, and the sideways sunlight glances off the windshield. The glare fills my vision with a bright yellow blur. I grab the edge of the visor above me and flip it down hard, blinking, and with each blink, starburst fireworks flash in front of my eyes. I refocus, and everything is fine. Then it happens. I don't know where he came from or what he's doing, but there's suddenly a person.

A person stands in the road in front of me, and it's too late to swerve out of the way. My hands leave the wheel and shield my face, my body acting reflexively, unwilling to watch what happens next, to watch us run over a human being. I slam on the brakes, and Amanda's scream fills the car. She grabs the wheel, steadying it as we skid to a stop. The industrial smell of burning rubber is immediate. I'm half gasping, half crying. I can't get any oxygen into my lungs. Is this what hyperventilating feels like? I mouth the words *paper bag* but no sounds come out. I might die of suffocation right here, which would be a relief. Amanda grabs my arm and gives me a shake.

"What the hell? What was that?" she yells at me, pissed. Like I don't already know I've done something unforgivable. Fatal.

I shake my head again and again, wishing myself back in

time so hard I might snap my wincing muscles. "Do you see them? Are they dead?" I finally manage, hoarse.

"What?" she says, easing the gearshift into park from the passenger seat and pressing the ignition button off. She opens the door and stands up, pulling her hiked-up skirt back down over her tights and smoothing her sweater. She doesn't look behind us. I can't look, either.

"Can you call 911?" I want to get out of the car, too, but my right foot is still smashing down the brake pedal while my other leg has gone completely numb.

She laughs then, a little bitterly, but she actually laughs. "Why, because you're completely mental?"

Why the hell would she ask why? I can't say why. It's too awful. "Amanda, can you just go look?"

"Look at what?"

"At the guy!"

"What guy?"

Oh my gosh, she didn't see him? She doesn't know? No, no, I can't possibly tell her that I just ran over someone with her car, that she was just witness to a murder, no, not a murder, what do they call it, what will they charge me with before I go to jail for the rest of my life—

Wait. Wait a minute. "Why did you scream just now?" I ask.

"Uh, 'cause you took your hands off the wheel, closed your eyes, and slammed on the brakes? Hello! I realize you don't have your license, but it's supposed to be hands on ten and two, baby, ten and two. And eyes on the road. Duh."

Finally, all the adrenaline I'm pumping starts to work for me. The door flies open and I lurch out of the car, sprinting back up the hill. Dark skid marks attest to the scene of the crime. But where is the victim?

I spin around, bewildered. What the—?

All at once the truth becomes clear, and I start spinning again, this time laughing like a complete maniac. A "get out of jail free" card from the worst fuckup I ever made. Only I didn't really make it. My eyes played a trick on me, and all I can think now is, *Thank you, universe.*

Time to do some damage control with Amanda. "I am so sorry, lady. I thought I saw something in the road. Is the car okay? Are you okay?"

Amanda looks a little less mad now. She shrugs. "Yeah, I'm fine." Then she leans over the hood of the car and says to it, "How are you, my baby? You gonna be all right?" She looks at me and grins. "I think her tires are a little sore, but she'll survive. You just scared her there."

"I scared me, too! I'm really sorry. I shouldn't have been driving."

Walking around the car toward the driver's side, Amanda pats my head on the way. "I forgive you. But only because it's your birthday."

We climb back in, Amanda driving and me on the passenger side where I belong. As I pull the door closed, a voice in the back seat makes me jump out of my skin all over again. "You didn't tell me it was your birthday today! Happy birthday!"

Instantly, I know. The person I suddenly saw, the person I ran over, wasn't a person at all. It was actually just a snarky, always-has-to-be-right, pain-in-the-ass ghost.

"Happy birthday to you, happy birthday to you," Mason is singing full volume in the back seat, and being dead has done nothing to change the fact that he is completely tone deaf. "Happy BIRTHday, Hattie Murpheeeee—"

"Oh, eff me," I let slip out.

Amanda says, "Seriously, it's okay," in response, but it's hard to hear because Mason is crowing the last line of the birthday song with way too much enthusiasm.

"Thanks for understanding, Amanda," I say, shooting a glare toward the back seat. "It's just—I don't know why—my head is splitting all of a sudden."

"Maybe that's why you thought you saw something. My sister gets these migraines and they totally affect her vision." Amanda flips down the visor on my side of the windshield for me.

"Do you think that's what happened, Murphy?" Mason asks, feigning innocence. "Are you getting a migraine?"

I'm already furious with Mason for scaring the crap out of me, so I have no patience left for him now. All I can do, though, is try to ignore him. I can't carry two conversations simultaneously.

"Yeah, migraines sound tough," I say.

"Anyway, once you get your license, I'm sure you'll be more relaxed," Amanda continues.

"Why don't you tell her what really happened?" Mason leans forward so he's wedged between our two seats, looking back and forth between us like he's at a tennis match.

"And once you're relaxed, the rest of it becomes almost automatic," she says.

"Tell her what happened," Mason says again.

"So do you think you'll get your license right away or are you going to wait awhile?"

"You should probably tell her the truth."

"Shut up!" I snap at Mason. My head is spinning.

Amanda lets out a little gasp and puts one hand to her mouth. Mason pushes back and slumps against the back seat.

"Oh, shit, Amanda. I wasn't telling you to shut up," I say.

"You weren't? Then who were you telling?"

Oh my God. How to explain this? I sigh. "I guess I'm talking to myself."

"But you weren't even saying anything."

"My brain is, though. My brain is full of things I don't want to hear."

Amanda's eyes leave the road for a second to glance at me. "Like what?"

"Like—" I pause, trying to drill down to the core of it all. "Like do you ever just look at your parents and think, 'No matter what, I just don't want to be like them'?"

"Only like every day. You know my mom threw a plate at my dad once? An actual dinner plate. She shattered it against the wall like she was the villain on a daytime soap opera or something."

"And then, even while you're thinking about how different

you want to be, the transformation is already happening. You can feel yourself morphing, becoming more and more like them in all these inescapable ways."

"And then you're trapped."

"Exactly."

"Powerless."

"Yeah." My eyes start to well up with tears. I let them fall. "I'm glad you get it."

"Are you kidding? My parents are forever in a sweat about money, about saving every cent, and guess what? Now I am physically incapable of buying something at the mall unless it's on sale." Amanda shakes her head as if she's a lost cause. I feel so connected to her I want to hug her sweet face.

"Yeah, so, the whole situation makes me feel pretty fucking crazy sometimes," I say.

"Now we're getting somewhere," Mason says from the back. I guess he can't help himself.

I turn toward the car door, and as quietly but seriously as I can, I say, "Please, just go."

Amanda laughs. "Girl, the light is red! I'm gonna go ahead and wait. I think we've had enough vehicular excitement for today."

"You are so right, Amanda. Right, and also an excellent driver. Dare I say an Amandazing driver?"

"Thank you!" she says, then chuckles. "I guess I'm not like my mom in that way."

"Oh, snap, mom burn," I say as I check the back seat. Mason is finally gone.

CHAPTER 24

That night, my parents insist on taking me out to dinner. The thought of being in a car again today makes my stomach feel like it's trying to French braid itself, so I pick Pontillo's Pizza because we can walk there. Nate is thrilled; it's his favorite. I sit, detached, half listening to him try to convert my parents into fans of his favorite YouTuber while he waves a piece of cheesy garlic bread around for emphasis. It all feels so innocent and sweet that it makes me sleepy. I suddenly have an overwhelming desire to go to bed.

Once I'm finally in my room, though, I can't sleep after all. I start thinking again about this morning in the car. Why the hell would Mason do something like that? Was that supposed to be some kind of practical joke? How could anyone think that was remotely funny?

I need to talk to him—alone this time. I start playing top ten pop drivel to bait Mason into showing up, but it doesn't work. I can't sit still anymore. I throw my door open, pound down the stairs, and head out the back door. It's almost ten p.m., but it's also my birthday, so all my mom says is, "Take your coat!" I don't even do that.

Near the line of evergreens that mark the back boundary of our property is a big old oak tree with a swing. I used to spend hours on the swing, going higher and higher until I felt like I was flying, enjoying the way it let me think about nothing at all. But I haven't even been in the backyard since the summer. I feel about a hundred years older now.

I sit on the swing and kick back hard to get going. I'm determined to swing until my mind is blank. But it might be awhile. I keep thinking about what a mean trick that was from someone who's supposed to be my friend. The wind is icy as I soar through the air, and I regret not taking a coat like my mom said, but I can't bear to go back inside to the brightness and dry artificial heat. It's claustrophobic.

So. Mason *was* my friend, but this isn't really Mason we're talking about anymore. We're talking about the ghost of Mason, which might mean all friend bets are off. Maybe his soul isn't his own anymore. If he's in some version of hell, he could even be like a demon now or something. Not that I think he deserved to go to hell, but that's based on the rules I know, rules that were basically just made up by living people. Who knows what the real rules are.

Oh man. I've been thinking he was appearing to help me, but maybe he's doomed to torment me. I have felt sort of tormented by him lately. To care this much and then be trying to navigate his unpredictability, his mysteriousness, his total inaccessibility, is near impossible. Even as I'm thinking it, it doesn't sit right, but fuck, it does seem like I've been entirely too trusting about this whole situation.

Just then, I hear the snap of twigs. I drag the heels of my

boots through the crust of ice-covered snow to stop myself from swinging.

"Finally," I say. Time to find out what side he's really on.

"Oh, my apologies, did we have a date? I must have neglected to put it in my calendar."

"Don't. Don't be cutesy. It's not funny. *You're* not funny." I want to unleash some major scorned-woman fury on him, but the lump in my throat threatens to ruin my attack.

"So you don't like my sense of humor. That's fine. You don't need to look so depressed about it," he says.

I get up off the swing and walk a few steps toward the woods, turning my back to him so I can brush away the angry tears that are gathering.

He catches it. "Hey, okay, I'm sorry, what's going on?"

"Why the hell did you do that to me?" I don't really want an answer. I just want him to know how bad it hurt.

"What's that now?"

"You made me think I had run over a real live person! Do you know how scared I was? That was too brutal. Too mean. Even for you."

His voice is overly calm. "I don't want to fight with you about this, I really don't, but I feel like I should point out that you were the one doing the running over. I was just standing there."

"Standing right in my blind spot!"

"Your blind spot directly in front of you?"

"Yes! It was the sun! And I was just coming over the hill, and . . . and . . ." Why is the truth so hard to say? Why does it get caught in the back of my mouth like a too-big spoonful of peanut butter?

"And I can't see!" I finally splutter.

He takes my place on the swing. "I know."

"No, I mean I really can't see. And not just the stars. Like I wouldn't be able to find my way back to the house right now if the yard lights weren't on. Like I'm going to end up entirely blind, same as my dad. My retinas are rotting as we speak."

"I know," he repeats.

"What do you mean you know? I sure as hell never told you. What, did Saint Peter or Mary Magdalene or some other heaven-type character grab one of those stone tablets and chisel in 'BTW, Hattie has a genetic retinal disease' right under 'Thou shalt not covet thy neighbor's wife'?"

"Ha. Not exactly. Just, when you could see me, and no one else could, I knew that your eyes were different."

"You mean bad."

"In some ways, I guess, but definitely not all."

Suddenly, an idea pops into my mind. "Wait, so if I took you into my living room now, do you think my dad could totally see you? His eyes are even more different." The thought makes me nervous, but there's also hope mixed in. Maybe seeing a ghost would jolt my dad out of his denial-based personality.

He shakes his head. "No, I think there's more ingredients in this recipe." He chuckles. "Clearly, the fact that you're obsessed with me has something to do with it."

He's so freaking consistent.

"Well, if I was obsessed with you before, you cured me of that with your 'what's it feel like to be a murderer' prank." He's not getting out of this that easy.

"Oh, so tricky Dick can stop right in front of you to test your skiing ability but I can't stop in front of you to test your driving ability?"

"Wow, stalk much? And I didn't like it when he did that, either, by the way." I hug myself, rubbing my arms to warm them up.

"Yes, I could totally tell that when you had him stick his tongue in your ear as a punishment."

"God, could we just get off of Richard already?"

"Gladly. Back to the driving. What's your takeaway from that, by the way?" God, he goes from serious to snarky and back again in dizzying fashion.

"You mean, besides that you're an asshole?"

"Do you think you'll drive again?" he persists.

Oh. Fuck me. "No," I say. "Never."

"Well, that's something, right? Now you know. I mean, if someone had given me a trial run on taking the boat out that night, who knows where I'd be now." He pushes off with his feet and starts to swing, pumping his legs to get some height.

All the anger I have left drains out of me. He did it as a wake-up call. To protect me from me, from my own tendency to make disastrous decisions. "I was right," I say, half to myself.

"About what?" he asks as he swoops past me.

"About why you're here. That you were sent here to help me. That you're like my guardian angel."

At the word *angel*, Mason jumps off the swing, and he's so far from the ground my chest clenches in fear. *Relax, Hattie*, I remind myself. *People who are dead can't break their leg.*

Sure enough, he jumps up from where he landed and casually brushes snow off his pants. "Is that what you've been thinking?" he asks.

There's an energy in his voice that makes me think he's about to tease me, but then I realize he's genuinely curious.

"Yeah, I guess. Aren't you?"

"Beats me. Lately I've been thinking I was here for another reason," he says.

"Another reason like what?" I push. I don't want any more cryptic, riddle-like responses from Mason. I want answers.

"I don't know. Sometimes I think it's a punishment and sometimes I think it's a reward."

"Those are two very different things."

"What can I say? The afterlife is complicated." Mason sits in the swing again and twists it around and around until it won't get any tighter. Then he lets go, spinning, his head back.

The word *punishment* makes me think about hell again. I really hope he's not condemned to flames and fire when he's not with me. "Like, how are you punished? And why?"

He staggers off the swing now, dizzy, and collapses back in the snow. He is incapable of sitting still tonight. Is it because this conversation is torture for him? I try to be patient. I wait.

"Well," he finally says, "you know how at church they always say that suicide is this terrible sin?"

"Suicide?" The word tastes like acid in my mouth.

"Calm down, Murphy. I didn't die by suicide. Don't go all psychotherapist on me. I just think, you know, I didn't take my own life, but I didn't really save it, either. Could be a half-terrible sin."

"And how are you being punished?"

"Like life is taunting me. It's all a big tease. The things I wanted, the things I miss. Almost living it, but not quite. It's excruciating." He picks up an ice chunk and chucks it.

"But then how can you sometimes think it's a reward? What happens then?"

He laughs now, softly, and his voice cracks a little when he says, "Strangely enough, it's sort of the same thing. Except sometimes I really like how excruciatingly sweet almost living can be."

"Wait. What do you mean?"

But instead of explaining, he disappears. The trees groan in the wind and I turn my head toward the sound for a second, and when I look back, he's gone. No matter how many "come to Jesus" moments we have, one thing is unchangeable. Mason is an enigma.

CHAPTER 25

I always used to think that the universe handed out the bad stuff sort of evenly, so if nothing bad had happened to you for a while you should probably prepare for disaster. This meant that when I was happy, it was hard to not brace for the other shoe to drop. And vice versa. If life dealt you a couple of catastrophes, then in my mind it should take a break for a while, give you some recovery time, focus on passing out crises to a bunch of other people. But that was before my friend died, I found out I was going blind, I almost froze to death, and I got caught doing something illegal. *And* I almost killed somebody, or it felt that way at least. So no, life doesn't give you a break. But could that also mean that sometimes you get to be happy without it triggering a universal alarm that you need a takedown? That would be refreshing.

I hesitate outside room 38, having just excused myself from Spanish class, following the instructions on the little slip of paper Mr. Pinksi gave me. What am I afraid of anyway? It's just a class, a stupid class, and all the kids in there have fucked up, too, so they can't even judge me without being hypocrites.

Okay, so go then. I swing the door open with such force it flies out of my hands and bangs against the wall inside. I flinch. The group gathered looks at me. The only adult speaks.

"Nothing like making an entrance." It's Ms. Clark, the Global

Studies teacher, which is weird because I thought a program like this would be taught by the nurse or the school counselor or something. I guess they didn't want to be here, either. Maybe Ms. Clark violated the school behavior code, too.

"Hi, sorry about that," I say, closing the door as quietly as I can.

"Not at all. I forgot you were joining us, Hattie. Go ahead and grab two placards."

I grab the signs from the table next to her and sit in the closest chair. Everyone else has their placards in their lap, so I do the same. There are four boys in the group and one girl, and none of them are from the play or the ski trip. I guess there must be quite a few sections of delinquent class. I'm relieved. Misery might love company, but humiliation loves anonymity.

That being said, I vaguely recognize these boys as seniors, and they make me feel immature right away because they all have some sort of facial hair: two with goatees, one a full beard, and the other a mustache that I'm guessing is meant to be ironic because he looks like he's spent his entire life perfecting being bored. He's also so tall that even though he's sitting opposite me in the circle, one of his feet is hooked around the leg of my chair. I have to keep my feet tucked way to the right to avoid resting my foot on his, which I'm going to be absolutely sure not to do.

The girl next to me is Ellory Fiske, her long brown curtain bangs completely hiding her eyes as usual. Ellory has been in various classes of mine since seventh grade, but I have no memory of ever hearing her speak, and I doubt today will be any different.

"Okay, you find a fifty-dollar bill lying on the sidewalk. You pick it up and put it in your pocket. Then you see a woman searching for something on the sidewalk. You avoid her and hurry away." Ms. Clark looks up from her paper, her lips pressed together, eyebrows raised in a sort of prejudgment look.

I flip my placards over. They say "okay" and "not okay." Wow, they've really put us in morality preschool. No wonder Mustache is bored. We all hold up our "not okay" signs, and Ms. Clark moves on with about a hundred more of these unrealistic scenarios. I use a tiny sliver of my brain to hold up the correct card every time she pauses, and the rest trying to figure out what the other kids in the group did to get stuck in here. They're probably doing the same to me.

I'm marveling at how a clock can tick so loudly while at the same time seem to not advance at all when I hear the door open behind me. The Better Bets class perks up in their chairs. Even Mustache pulls his foot back and lets his eyes focus. I turn.

It's Asha.

"Line at the ladies'," she says by way of explanation. "What'd I miss? Wheel of Addiction? Responsibility charades?" She strolls around the circle and sits next to Mustache. Now she notices me for the first time. "Hey, Hattie," she says, sounding formal but not unkind.

"Hey," I say back. What is she doing here? What could my super-perfectly-put-together friend possibly have done wrong?

And how could any mere mortal grown-up have caught her at it? I hate how many secrets seem to exist between us. I cock my head at her, question marks filling the air around me, but the answers will have to wait.

There's no denying that the class is a lot more interesting now that Asha is here. She cracks jokes about each hypothetical situation in such a charming way that even Ms. Clark is chuckling. But Mustache is the most charmed of all. He hasn't stopped smiling since she sat down next to him.

The bell rings, signaling both the end of class and the end of the school day. This is it. I can't take it anymore. I need to fix this thing with Asha, and I don't even care if it's humiliating. I wait for her in the hallway. When she emerges, Mustache is right behind her with his hand on the small of her back.

"Lincoln, Hattie, Hattie, Lincoln," she says by way of introduction, and I notice a hint of a flush on her face. It dawns on me that this must be the first-date guy from the other night.

"Hey," we say to each other.

"Meet you in a few? By the vending machine?" she says to him.

"You got it," he says, enclosing a few stray hairs of hers between his fingers and placing them gently back behind her shoulder. "Hattie." He nods to me then and ambles down the hall.

As she turns to me, my words start tumbling out. "Let me start before you say anything. I know I've been pretty MIA lately and I know I've been weird—well, more weird than usual. I suck. And I know I said I was fine when I really wasn't fine. But I promise I'm all done running away, and I'm done attacking. I miss you. And I'm really sorry."

She looks at me for a second, unsure.

This is killing me. Mason's assertion that I pit myself against the world is ringing in my ears. I can feel the cold draft between Asha and me, our intimate friendship frayed with estrangement at the edges, and I know that I am the perpetrator. That my fear of being judged and rejected has become a self-fulfilling prophecy, so I've been pushing away before I get pushed. "Please, Asha. Accept my apology. I promise I'll make it worth it, 'cause I'm going to spill all my guts out about every stupid thing I've thought or done in the last month. I'll overshare so hard you'll wish I'd shut up already."

She smiles a little then and holds her hands up. "All right, all right, you're forgiven. Jeez."

"Okay, good, because I want to hear all about you, too. Let's start with this new boy—"

"Hold on. You're not the only one who needs to apologize."

"Nope. Not necessary."

"Yes it the fuck is." Asha takes a deep breath. "I was way harsh the other night, and I'm really sorry. And I shouldn't have said that shit about you and Mason. That was beyond rude. It's just—well, you know how you two were."

"What do you mean?"

"I mean, I knew that there was something between you. A bond. Separate from the rest of us. And I swear, it never really bothered me. Like, at all. I wasn't envious of it until after he died. Now that he's gone, though, everything feels like a missed opportunity. And you . . . you always got him. Knew him better."

I did? I never for a nanosecond thought Asha would be envious of me for any reason, much less for something that I didn't even realize I had. But if I did in fact have some sort of special status with Mason, maybe that's the source of the pain porridge I'm currently stewing in. But what's hitting me most right now is how uncertain she looks, how vulnerable and human and *like me*, and I just want to bear-hug her until it hurts. So I do.

"I love you, lady," I say into her hair. "I'm here for you, too, okay? I don't want you to just be there for me. It should go both ways."

"Okay," she says, hugging me back. Then she untangles herself from my grip. "Now let me go before you make me cry. Jesus, you're a harder hugger than Lincoln."

"Ah yes, the boy who looks like he wrestles bears in his free time. Spill. I'm assuming he's the practice date." We begin walking toward the stairs. She smiles, her eyes lighting up.

"We're doing a bit more than practice dates now. And he's helplessly in love with me," she says as she pushes open the fire door to the stairwell. We let it close behind us and then sit on the wide windowsill that borders the landing, pulling our knees up to our chests so there's room for both of us.

"Of course he is. How did this start? Why does he look like he's about thirty-five? And what the hell got you thrown into Better Bets class?"

"I might ask you the same question."

"I asked you first."

She untucks the lock of hair he straightened and rolls it gently between her fingers like she's trying to pick up any hint of him that was left there. "About three weeks ago up at the college, most likely testosterone levels, destruction of property."

Whoa, too much information. Or not enough. Or in the wrong order. "Wait, at the college? I thought he went here. Exactly how old is this hairy man?"

"Relax, he's a senior here. You remember when we had that pupil-free day? I think you were on the ski trip."

"Yes, of course." The ski trip I didn't tell you about. Where a lot of other shit happened that I didn't tell you about. Because I'm a big old shame bunny.

"Yeah, so my paranoid parents didn't want me home alone all day—I swear my mom is afraid some pedophile is going to jump right out of my computer monitor if she's not in the next room."

"Ugh."

"So whatever, they took me with them to the college, there was an exhibit at the gallery they thought I'd like. After I went through the exhibit I stopped at an animal rights rally happening on the quad, got some material about slaughterhouses. And Lincoln was there. He'd driven there specifically for the rally. He's a vegetarian, too, so we have that in common. Actually, he's a vegan. He's been trying to convert me, but no mac and cheese? I might have to see him naked first."

The fact that she's talking about a boy having the potential to influence any of her decisions surprises me. Asha always talks about boys like they're one step above zombies—largely brain-dead but a possible threat if you don't keep the upper hand.

"Sounds like that 'helplessly in love' thing might be a smidge mutual," I say.

"So far so good, I guess," she says. "What about you? I got the distinct impression there was trouble in paradise."

"Turns out he was not such a great guy."

"Oh, that sucks, Hatts. I was afraid of that."

"What tipped you off?"

"I don't know, he seems a little, um, lacking in authenticity."

"Oh my gosh, that's exactly what Mason"—I catch myself just in time—"would have said."

"You think?"

"He would have called Richard human aspartame."

Asha barks out a laugh and shakes her head. "You see? Special bond. That sounds exactly like him." We're both quiet for a minute, and I can almost hear Mason's voice in my mind. Asha must be thinking something similar, because when I look at her, her eyes are shining with unshed tears. Then she says, "All right, well, I've gotta go catch up with Lincoln." She stands, straightening several bracelets that have gotten tangled at her wrist, and throws the strap of her bag over her head.

"Wait," I say, wanting to hold on to the connection that I let lapse, desperate to keep the conversation going. "You didn't tell me how you got pinned with destruction of property."

She laughs again, and the sound is so contagious, I laugh, too, before I even know what we're laughing at. "We snuck into the cafeteria kitchen and threw out all the pork products. The hot dogs, the deli ham, everything."

I gasp. "You did not."

She nods. "We did. Did you know that pigs are smarter than chimpanzees? They can play video games, for fuck's sake! We should eat some of the bros in our grade before we eat pork."

Only Asha could end up breaking the behavior code while maintaining the moral high ground. I grin. "Well, that explains why there's been no BLTuesdays at lunch recently," I say. "And the other part of the 'we' was Lincoln?"

"We are coconspirators," she says, rolling the word around in her mouth like it's delicious. "Poor kid, he insisted we make a statement. He painted 'Who's the pig now?' on the fridge in red paint, but then he tracked paint all the way to his locker. I confessed in solidarity."

"Very loyal of you." I nod.

She pauses now, looking at me. "So is that what was twisting you into an emotional pretzel? Richard's slithery behavior? Or Mason?"

Yes on both counts. Plus . . . "There's something else."

"What is it?" I can almost feel the trademark Chawla intensity bubble forming around us as her eyes hold mine.

Where to begin? "I'm defective."

The criticism breaks her intent gaze. "What?" she asks, incredulous.

"They didn't make me right in the factory."

Asha puts her hands on her hips. "Hattie, speak English. What the hell are you talking about?"

Spitting it out is the only way. "My mom made me go to the doctor and they ran a million tests and it turns out I have the same thing as my dad and am now slowly, inevitably going blind."

The admission sits like a stone on the window ledge between us. A stone that I would love to pick up and hurl through the window. What's going to happen now? I steel myself for all the questions she'll undoubtedly have, the confusion about what exactly that means and what there is to be done.

But there's no interrogation. Asha touches my arm. "That's brutal," she finally says.

"Yeah."

"And having watched your dad going through it, knowing exactly what you're in for . . ."

"Makes it worse," I finish.

"Well, so we'll handle it. One day at a time." I notice the "we" in there and I almost cry from the comfort. She's got her intensity face on. I can feel her energy encircling me. "Shit, I can't believe you've been holding this on your own. How are you feeling?"

"Honestly, right now I'm just feeling relieved to have told someone. And to have it, you know, be you."

"I'm glad you told me." Then she grins. "No wonder you've been assaulting people in the hallways."

I groan. "Yeah, I guess I haven't been coping the best."

She waves my guilt away. "Totally normal and understandable."

"Well, you better go catch up with your partner in crime," I say.

"Nah, I'm here with you. He'll wait. Let's talk through this."

I love her. "Thanks, Ash, but I think I'm tapped. I've got to get used to this 'being vulnerable' thing in small chunks."

She cocks her head. "You sure?"

I nod.

"All right. To be continued," she says, giving me a quick hug, then opening the fire door.

"But Asha?"

"Hmm?"

"Want to sleep over? If you can get away, of course, from all the mustache kissing." I am sort of curious to know what it feels like to kiss a mustache. Another thing we can talk about when she comes over.

Now the smile on her face is open and easy, and I can tell we're back in sync. "Yeah, sounds good."

Phew.

I get home to an empty house. Good. I need some time to think, not talk. I drop my stuff by the front door and head straight into the pantry for a sugar fix. Mom has recently stocked it with healthy crap like chips made out of chickpeas and quinoa and little bags of snack mix that look deceptively full of fun surprises but are really mostly dried cranberries. I can't find a single cookie. I give up on the dessert shelf and rummage in the back of the baking box. Score. I bring a whole king-sized bag of M&M's upstairs with me.

The late afternoon sky is so gloomy that it's already pretty dark in my room, so I turn on the twinkle lights I've strung along the top of the wall. I feel like over the last few days I've been gathering experiences the way you would fill up a laundry basket. My brain is a big wadded-up jumble. I need to shake everything out and fold it into piles.

So I'm definitely in trouble, but unlike how I usually feel when I've done something wrong, spikes of shame aren't stabbing me in my rib cage. I should have said hard pass to a beer on a school-organized field trip, to be sure, but it feels more like a mistake than a crime, like maybe I don't need to keep beating myself up about it. Especially since my parents aren't laying on the disapproval particularly thick. And the fact that I don't have to hide it from Asha is the best part. I'm going to check "behavior code violation" off my list of things to keep sweating.

My convo with Asha makes me feel like I've entered an anti-gravity chamber. I am lighter, floatier. What the hell did I think would be better about keeping her at arm's length, about hiding things from her? It seems my hands are mimicking the organizing happening in my mind, because without really thinking about it, I've poured out a pile of M&M's and sorted them by color. Now I eat all the brown ones, just to get my least favorite color out of the way, and line the others up like a rainbow.

They've probably done scientific studies somewhere about chocolate and dopamine and concentration, because chocolate helps me think, no doubt. It all started with Richard; I knew that Asha didn't really approve of Richard. And neither did Mason. I need to start seeing things the way they do. Shit—*understanding* things the way they do. I hate that I use metaphorical vision words all the time.

And it wasn't just the pheromones that clouded my judgment, either, because I also misjudged Amanda. Like, by a lot. So someone I thought was amazing was actually a douche and someone I thought was a supervillain was actually just trying to be my friend. Who else am I getting wrong? Am I getting *myself* wrong? Am I worse than I think, or better? Why are human beings so freaking confusing?

I've even been getting a ghost wrong. I thought Mason was being mean when he materialized in front of the car, but he was trying to keep me safe. I can't be too mad at myself for misunderstanding that one, though. His method was pretty rough. Rough, but effective.

He was so calm when I told him about the RP. It didn't seem to change his view of me at all. Same with Asha. I guess people aren't as into perfection as I think. Maybe that's *my* problem.

The red M&M's are all gone now, too. Coming up here without a big glass of milk was a tactical error. I'm in chocolate overdose mode, so I scoop up the rest of my rainbow and dump it back in the bag. Except for the greens. The greens I put in a little pile next to my alarm clock on my nightstand, for later.

As I pad downstairs to hide the depleted bag back in the baking box, I think again about my last conversation with Mason, about why he's here. He thinks I'm wrong, but if he's not here to help me, then what's my part in all this? Why keep haunting me or whatever? I think about Richard and Amanda and Asha. Not everything's about you, Hattie.

Wait. Maybe that's it. It seems glaringly obvious in retrospect, but what if *I'm* supposed to help *him*? He said that the "almost living" part was the punishment, that it felt excruciating. Yep. Makes total sense to me. I know how painful being powerless is on a wide variety of levels. But maybe I could give him some power by acting on his behalf, by doing something that he would do himself if he had a moment to be fully alive again. I'm not sure what exactly he would do, but I have an idea where to start.

CHAPTER 26

For the second time in a day I'm standing outside a door with my stomach twisting about what's on the other side. Below all that, though, there's a little nugget of calm. This is the right thing. I ring the bell.

The porch light comes on and Mrs. Leary appears. Her makeup is perfect, her expression blank and inscrutable. "Hattie. Come on in, quick, it's freezing out here."

Well, she didn't slam the door in my face, so we're already winning. She takes my coat and hangs it on a row of hooks screwed into the wall. Mason's favorite baseball cap is hanging on the far hook. I half expect it to burst into flames from my sheer awareness of it.

"Thanks, Mrs. Leary," I say.

"Hattie, I think I've told you. Please call me Cat," she says, wiping her hands on her pants. Does she think my coat has germs?

"Is Mr. Leary here?" I ask, glancing in the living room. At least he likes me.

"No, he has choir tonight." She puts her hands in her pockets and cocks her head, waiting, lips pressed together.

I should have brought food or flowers or something; that would have justified my awkward appearance. Instead, I fib. "Sorry, Cat. I was just walking in the neighborhood, and I realized I hadn't come by and, well, I probably should have already, which is my bad." On my way here, I thought I could help her find some peace, somehow, for Mason's sake. Let her know that Mason is okay. But how can I possibly do that when she's looking at me like I'm here to sell her something? Why should she believe anything I say? I thought the words would come to me and I would know what to say, but her stiffness is so unsettling.

She seems to finally accept that I'm not just going to turn around and run away. "Well, what can I get you? Hot chocolate? It's just the instant kind with the mini marshmallows, but it's good in a pinch . . ." She leads me through the hallway and into the kitchen, where I cough to cover a gasp.

Mason is sitting on the counter.

"Um, what?" I say, distracted. I haven't seen him since Asha said we had a "special bond," and now it's all I can think about.

"Cocoa or Coke Zero?" Mrs. Leary asks again.

"Nothing, thanks. I can't stay that long," I say.

"Well, this should be interesting," Mason says, while at the exact same time Mrs. Leary says something about a glass of water.

My mouth feels like sandpaper. "Sounds great. Thanks," I manage to get out. As Mrs. Leary busies herself with the ice dispenser, I try to catch Mason's eye, but he's looking at her. I want to explain to him why I'm here, but of course I can't say anything without it seeming completely insane to his mom. He finally looks up, and I smile as if to say, *Just relax, I've got this.* But do I?

Mrs. Leary puts the glass on the counter in front of me and

starts unloading the dishwasher. "So how are your parents?" she asks, filling her hands with butter knives and dropping them in a drawer.

"All good."

"And your brother? Is he, what, in second grade now?"

"Third," I say, like the sparkling conversationalist that I am.

"Christ, is she going to ask you how you're enjoying your classes next? Why does she always talk about nothing?" Mason jumps down off the counter and paces behind me.

He's right. Breaking through small talk feels as rude as smashing a full-length mirror at Mrs. Leary's feet, but there's no other way.

"Mrs. Leary—" I say finally.

"Cat," she corrects me.

"Cat—" Just dive headlong. "I know I've never exactly been your favorite person, but—"

"Hattie, what a thing to say!" She closes a cabinet a little too hard and turns to me. "Why on earth would you say that?"

"Uh," I start, finding it difficult to swallow. *Because you do things like yell "What a thing to say!" at me?* Nope. Can't say that. "I don't know. I just always got the feeling that maybe you didn't like me very much." I think about when my brother was little and one of us would try to be firm with him about bedtime, and he would cry in his adorable baby voice, "You spoke to me in a harsh tone!" That's what Mrs. Leary has. Chronic harsh tone.

Mrs. Leary sighs heavily and rubs her eyelids just under her brows. "No, no, no. It's not that I don't like you." She tosses her hands out helplessly and looks around, like the magic words to make me disappear might be written somewhere on the kitchen ceiling. "I may have felt, and this really wasn't fair to you, but in any case I felt, a bit, that you might not have always been the best thing for Mason. In terms of his happiness."

"Mom!" Mason says sharply.

I feel like someone stuck a vacuum tube down my throat and sucked all the air out of my lungs. "Why?"

Mason interrupts. "You know, I was trying to let you do you here, Murph, but I think this is maybe headed in the wrong direction. This isn't good for either of you." He's buzzing around me now, trying to usher me back into the hall. But I'm rooted to the spot.

"Why?" I say again.

"There didn't seem to be parity in your relationship. It wasn't even," she clarifies, as if I don't what the word *parity* means. "As his mother, I wanted him to be able to get out there, grow, maybe find a nice girlfriend, to have the full high school experience. And now—" She stops, choked on the obvious.

Before I know what I'm doing, I touch her arm. My mind is whirling with what she's saying. She thought I was keeping him from getting a girlfriend? How exactly? But in the eye of that mental storm, I know she's wrong about at least one thing.

"Cat, there's nothing I can do to make any of that better now. But if you're talking about our relationship, all I can tell you is that Mason was and is very important to me. I cared about him. A lot. More than a lot."

She smiles then and nods. The air between us relaxes; the only one who still seems tense is Mason. Then Mrs. Leary seems to remember something. "Wait here," she says, and disappears into the darkened hallway.

While she's gone, I turn to Mason. "Parity?" I whisper.

He blushes—*and now you've seen a ghost blush, Hattie, check that off your bucket list*—but then just shrugs. "You know how moms are," he says. "Always overthinking."

Cat reappears, and in her hand is the unmistakable neon of a pile of Post-its. My sloth facts. "Are these yours? Lucia said she thought they might be."

I take the pile and look at the one on top: *A sloth can hold its breath for 40 minutes.* I was so excited when I found that fact during an internet deep dive on sloths. It had been getting harder and harder to find more things about sloths that were true but would still elicit a "Holy shit!" out of Mason. But this one . . . He must have held this piece of paper, must've read the words, was undoubtedly impressed, and all the while some part of him was thinking about *me*. The stack of Post-its practically vibrates with his energy.

Instead of responding, I go into the hallway, reach into my coat pocket, and pull out an identical pile of neon paper. It is suddenly essential that Mason's mom get to feel part of what I'm feeling, that connection to a specific moment when he was alive that we can linger in.

"Here are Mason's. I think you should have them," I say, handing her the facts written in his tiny, slanted printing.

"Oh," she says, taking them carefully like they're a rare first edition. "Thank you." She presses them into her palm, and I know she gets it. I wonder if she can sense, somehow, how closely Mason is hovering next to us right now.

"I feel like if Mason were here, he'd want to tell you something," I say. I look at him.

"You were a good mom," he whispers.

"You were a good mom to him," I say.

"It's not your fault."

"It's not your fault," I repeat, breathless.

Cat nods and smiles again, and when she closes her eyes for a moment, I notice how tired she looks.

"It's not your fault," I say again. She opens her eyes and cups my chin in her hand, like she's drinking in my face. "You're sweet to come," she says, and leads me back to the door. "He thought the world of you." I put on my coat and she fixes my collar, seeming to linger on being able to do the tiniest bit of mothering.

As I head down the front steps and turn onto the sidewalk, I'm not sure I did what I set out to do, but I guess as long as I don't feel like I've ruined everything, that's an improvement. I feel her standing at the picture window, watching me, and I turn to wave. But when I do, it's Mason, hand pressed against the window toward me, and for a moment it feels like the only thing separating us is a piece of glass.

CHAPTER 27

I step through our front door, keeping my hand on the storm door so that as the spring contracts it doesn't slam closed. My dad hates that slamming sound. He's gotten a lot more sensitive to loud noises since he lost his sight. Last month, he sent my brother to his room in the middle of dinner for laughing too loud.

I hear my dad now, washing his hands in the powder room. I know it's him and not my mom because it's pitch-dark in there—he doesn't turn on lights anymore. I think of all the things Mason must have wanted to say to his mom but didn't when he had the chance. Maybe I should give it another shot.

"Hey, Dad."

"Hi there, Henrietta." He shuffles his way into the living room and we sit, him in his big chair and me on the rug.

"Where's Mom?" I ask.

"She's picking up Nate from a friend's. They'll be back shortly. What do you need?"

"Nothing, just curious." I pause. "Hey, I didn't ask before, is Dr. Porter your eye doctor, too?"

"No."

"But isn't she the best in the state?"

"That seems to be the consensus."

"So why don't you go to her, too?"

He inhales through his nose like he's doing an anger management technique. "Until there's a cure, I don't really see the point of the drive." His face is darkening. I can tell I'm losing him. This isn't what he wants to talk about, like ever. But instead of switching the subject, I talk faster.

"Well, Dr. Porter said there was a lot of promising research, clinical trials and studies and stuff. There's injections and tiny robots—a lot of possibilities that are, like, straight out of a sci-fi series."

He clears his throat. "To be clear," he says, "the medical field has been saying that a cure was about five years away for a very long time, twenty years at least. And the initial treatments won't really be cures—they'll just stop your eyesight from getting worse. That's an important step, and could be really significant for you. But unfortunately"—he shrugs—"won't have much of an impact on me."

"I get all that, but what about just going to see her to be ready for when something breaks? You know, stay in the loop."

They say that the eyes are the window to the soul, which really blows, because it means that when you have a blind dad there's no way in. I want to look hard into his eyes, to tell him without words that we're in this together, that I want to be close, or at least closer. But his eyes are a dead end, and the rest of the muscles on his face have built a wall.

"You seem to be quite the expert all of a sudden," he says, and there's a meanness in his voice that I usually only hear when he's criticizing a politician on TV. It feels like shame.

"What, me? No, not at all. I've just been thinking about it a lot since I went to see her. I don't know."

"No. You don't." A stony silence follows. There's nowhere to go from here. My shoulders hunch as the tendons on my neck twist into little knots. The air in the room is suffocating, and all I want now is to go back in time three minutes and not have this conversation. I stand up.

"Okay, Dad. Sorry I said anything." I say it because it's true, but it comes out sounding sarcastic.

I'm halfway up the stairs when he says, "Hattie. Wait."

I turn to see him in the doorway. He holds his hand out, palm up. I come back down and put my hand in his.

"I didn't mean to speak sharply." He wants to smooth this blip over. Conflict is not tolerated with my dad. The unwritten rule is that if you can't resolve it immediately, you're at least supposed to pretend it's resolved. Fake it till you make it, or just fake it indefinitely.

But faking isn't possible for me anymore. There doesn't seem like much left to lose. I pull my hand away.

"You did, Dad. Which sort of sucks when I'm trying to help." He starts to say something else, probably about me being disrespectful, but I talk over him. "We should help each other. I've got it, too, remember. So you should be helping me. Not lecturing me. Helping me not be scared. Helping me deal. Because you know what it's like. And because you—you gave it to me."

That last sentence pierces him. He takes a step back, then runs his hand along the wall until he feels the banister. He eases himself down to sit on the stairs and rubs his chin hard enough to make it red. Oh, shit, is he going to start crying?

"I didn't mean that, Dad," I say, backtracking, panicked. "It isn't your fault. There's nothing you can do about it. I shouldn't have said that."

"No, Hattie. It's all right. And I am so sorry that you've inherited this from me. It's difficult to even think about. And if I could cure one of us, I would choose you without hesitation. You know that, don't you?"

"Yes."

"I have deep regrets that I can't set an example for you. I can't be the resource you need. Don't do what I've done, Hattie. You're young, you have so much more potential. You can take this on and still excel, I know you can."

"Oof. No pressure," I say, but my shoulders relax. It's a relief to at least hear him say something that's not stilted.

"No pressure," he agrees, as if I wasn't being sarcastic. "I've been too rigid, for a long time really, maybe always, but not you. That's something you haven't inherited from me. For me—when my eyes started getting bad, it was like Pandora's box. I didn't know how to think about it, to reflect on it, without it drowning out everything else. It was all or nothing. So I tried to put it out of my mind as much as possible. I had to manage to still get up and go to work every day."

I hadn't thought about that. That despite the world disappearing, he still figured out how to keep doing his job and getting a paycheck. The difficulty of that hits me like a blast of cold air.

"Look, Hattie, I know you're scared. I would take it away if I could. But I think I'm going to learn a lot from you. I'm so proud of you."

"Thanks, Dad." I am not proud of me, so I can't quite take that in. But I'm glad that we're talking, finally. It feels like I've been waiting sixteen years for him to talk to me.

Even the silence feels better now. I move to sit next to him on the stairs, our arms touching. We sit there in the almost darkness for a minute or two, slightly swaying back and forth, listening to the quiet of the house. He's not a big strong authority figure right now. He's just a person, a powerless little boy, even. For years, I've blamed him for not getting me, for not even trying to. But what have I been doing? Arguing with him about nearly every aspect of what's been happening to him, service dog or cane, the reason he was destined to be blind in the first place, and on and on and on. Bringing up stuff that was painful to him. He doesn't get me? Sure, okay. But I haven't gotten him for a long time.

"Mason has been coming to visit me," I say suddenly.

"In your dreams?"

"No, like, for real. While I'm awake. Like a legit ghost." I hold my breath, waiting to see if he goes straight to the phone and dials 911.

"He's been visiting me, too."

I jump up. "What?! He has?!"

My dad smiles then, shakes his head. "No. I was just kidding."

"Dad!" I guess he's not too concerned, if he's able to joke around. Which is pretty wild. I plunge ahead.

"For some reason, I feel like it's RP related. Like the parts of my eyes that don't work right are picking up other things. You think that's possible?"

"Anything's possible, Hattie." He rubs his face again, less hard this time. "Is it scary?"

"No, I like it." I think about the day I was driving. "Most of the time, anyway. You don't think I'm crazy?"

"Hattie, I went to Catholic school for twelve years. Our teachers gave us prayer cards to pray to our own personal guardian angels. And there's the Holy Ghost, the very core of the trinity. These things are essential for people of faith, and I think it's primarily because they provide comfort. So if you can find something akin to that, I think that's great."

"You know I don't believe in God, though, right, Dad?"

A playful expression crosses his face. "Henrietta, perhaps you can give your father a small reprieve and save your 'I'm an atheist' announcement for another day. Would that be all right?"

I laugh. "Sure, Dad."

"Much appreciated. And no, I don't think you're crazy."

Even though I don't believe in them, I get his point about angels. I had kind of forgotten that people believe in things that can't be explained all the time.

My mom and brother are on the porch now, my mom jingling her keys out of her purse. I stand up and put my hand on my dad's shoulder. "Okay, Dad. Thanks for the talk."

“Of course. And Hattie?”

“Yeah, Dad?” I say as I head up the stairs.

“I’ll see Dr. Porter if you want me to.”

“Okay. We can go together if you want.” That might make being in the Holding Cell of Pathetic Blobs a little less pathetic.

“Great.”

He said he was proud of me. But for what, exactly?

If I were going to be proud of me, and I’m not saying that I am, but if I were, it would be for continuing to exist. I’ve had to say goodbye to the life I thought I was going to have. But I’m still here. Still brushing my teeth and tying my shoelaces and going to class. I keep thinking I’m a different person now. But really, I’m still just me. Or maybe I am different, but not worse. I still don’t buy Dad’s bit about how we need an untreatable disease to keep us humble, otherwise we’d be too superior for the world to even handle us, but maybe there’s a way that RP is making me think more. About what I want, what I appreciate, what’s important to me. Honestly, maybe that’s what Dad meant in the first place.

CHAPTER 28

Later that night, Mason's voice breaks through the recording on Spanish verb tenses I'm listening to for homework. "I've been thinking about what you asked me before. About why." *Hattie escuchaba a español cuando Mason interrumpió*, I think as I pull off my headphones.

"Why what?"

"Why I didn't wear the life jacket."

Oh, that why. "It's not your fault. I hope you don't think I implied that. It's nobody's fault," I say.

"It's a legit question. If I had worn it instead of tossing it onto the dock, I would still be a red-blooded, breathing, human person. There's no erasing that."

I don't argue. Instead, I say, "I don't usually get blessed with so much Mason in such a short period of time."

"What can I say? Your visit to the old homestead got me all energized."

I wait, then say, "And did you figure it out? About the life jacket?"

He sighs. "I didn't take anything seriously. When I did, the whole world seemed like it was in all caps. Too real, you know? It made me feel like my skin was on fire. I had to always sort of look away from myself. Like I was too busy or distracted to even notice I was alive. Now I can't look away."

"I get that." It sounds like a mash-up of my dad and me. Like we're all Goldilocks and the porridge is life. Sometimes it's too real and sometimes it's not real enough and we're all trying to find just the right amount.

"You do?"

"Existing is hard." I prop myself up on my elbow. "Which reminds me. I know you said you weren't here to help me. But I thought maybe you're here so I can help you. That's why I went to your house. So what do you think? Did talking to your mom do anything helpful? What else can I do?"

"Nothing. You don't need to do anything, Murph. I mean, yeah, I liked what you said to my mom before. But all the reasons are overlapping now."

"What do you mean?"

He's quiet for a long time. Then: "Like I said. I didn't take anything seriously. And that was including you. No, wait, that's not right. I didn't take how I felt about you seriously."

My heart is suddenly pounding. "How you felt about me?"

So quietly I can barely make it out, he says, "How I *feel* about you."

It's hard to pull in enough air to get out the question with all the butterflies bouncing around my chest. "How *do* you feel about me?"

He clears his throat. "You know, all the things."

"Like what things exactly?" I feel like I'm torturing him a little bit, but I can't help it. I need to know.

"I was pretty into you, okay?" he says, pushing the words out.

Then he snorts. "I mean, apparently I was so into you that even my mom was clocking it." Mason's face darkens. "But I never did anything about it. Not a single thing. And why? 'Cause I might look stupid? You might say no?" He's combing his hands through his hair. "Doing nothing was the same as a no anyway. And now I can't do anything. What a waste. What a waste of air I fucking was—am—was."

Mason Leary was into me. Mrs. Leary tried to tell me when I was in her kitchen, but it was too easy to rationalize away as coming from an out-of-touch adult. But now he's here in front of me, telling me himself. It's real. The amount of dopamine or adrenaline or endorphins or whatever that floods through me finally drives home that I was also into him. I think about us sitting together on the picnic table in the campground, watching the sun come up, huddled close. God, I was so fucking into him.

"But you're forgetting something," I say.

He shakes his head. "What?" he says, like a stubborn child about to be corrected by a parent.

"Look, if you messed it up, so did I. I'm just as big a chicken as you. I did nothing, too." My brain is catching up with the reality of it all the way a big file loads in chunks after you open it on your laptop. I pretended it wasn't there, but part of me always knew he liked me. My mom said way back in fourth grade that when boys tease you, it's usually because they like you. At the time, that idea just confirmed my general sense that boys were the absolute worst, because why would you be anything but kind to someone you liked, and who, theoretically, you wanted to like you? On the other hand, there was no denying that Mason knew how to push my buttons, because he always paid attention to what I said. He listened to me. He knew me like maybe no one else did.

It had scared me. It was too scary to be with someone who could really see me, who would make me be myself all the time. Mason paid such close attention that sometimes I felt like an insect in the science museum, pinned to a mat in a display case for examination. Twenty-four hours a day being myself seemed too hard then. And what if I had been able to do it? If I had let him in, given in to my heart utterly and totally, and then it went wrong? I would have fallen to pieces. But maybe it would have been the opposite. Maybe it would have been joy.

"No, I did worse than nothing," I add now. "I kept space between us. I wish I hadn't. More than anything." The urge to bury my face in his chest is overpowering; I see now all the times he opened a romantic door for me to walk through and I stayed safely back on my side of the threshold. Like last spring, before the cotillion dance, when he kept saying I should ask him, but he did it so casually that I thought maybe it was a setup to prank me, and I was too scared to call his bluff. Or last Valentine's Day, when he sent me a carnation through the dance team's flower sale and I convinced myself he did it purely as a friend. I clench and unclench my hands over and over to release some of the helplessness that surges with the memory of each moment that I let slip through my fingers.

"Me too," he says, his voice gravelly.

"I wish I could go back."

"Why did you have to be so infuriatingly irresistible, Hattie?" He sits down next to me on the bed, and I try to stop my brain so that I can just feel him there, close to me. My eyes fill up and tears start to stream down my face.

"Do something for me," he says.

"Anything."

"Look up."

"What? Why?"

He snorts. "Jeez, you just said anything." I wipe my cheeks off and tilt my chin up to see my lumpy cottage-cheese-like ceiling.

"Okay, I'm looking up. For you."

Suddenly, the lights go out and now I see nothing.

"Whoa, what are you doing? I told you I can't see in the dark."

Then I feel his words right next to my ear, and he whispers hoarsely, "Look."

Is he teasing me? I strain my eyes. Then a jolt runs through me, a delicious electricity that feels like my bloodstream is coursing with sparks. When it settles, suddenly I can see the sky. Not just the sky. The stars. Galaxies upon galaxies of them. Points of light, some bright and piercing, some hazy and dim, in varying shades of white, yellow, even orange. Each is nothing special on its own, but there are so many, clustering in swirls and waves, arranged in ways that seem organized and random all at once. It's infinity. And every point is twinkling, flickering in an almost imperceptible movement that makes the whole sky alive.

"Wow wow wow," I say.

"Everyone should see the stars at least once," he says.

Suddenly, I know that this is the last visit, that I won't see him again. The unending spirals I see are countless opportunities extending out forever, most of which will never be followed, like the relationship we never got to have, the love we never experienced. It's alongside every other possibility that has existed or will exist. All together, mixing in an expanding universe.

"I'll always love you, Mason. No matter what," I say.

"Oh, Murph. Thank you," he says.

I open my eyes, and he's gone. And so is the little pile of green M&M's I saved for him.

CHAPTER 29

The heat hasn't even kicked on yet when I head down to the kitchen on Saturday morning to get some protein in me before this 5K. I'm surprised to find my mom sitting at the island, holding her coffee mug in both hands, letting the steam rise into her face. This is highly unusual. My mom is *not* a morning person.

"You're up early," I say. "Everything okay?"

She sighs and smiles at the same time. "I couldn't sleep. Couldn't stop my wheels from turning."

I open the fridge and grab a string cheese, pulling the plastic back like I'm peeling a banana. I'm feeling more charitable toward my mom than usual. It's nice to have another person awake when it's this early. "Listen," I say. "I know that Nate seems like a hopeless case now, but you really don't need to lie awake worrying about him. Research shows that people can grow out of the 'extreme doofus' phase with the proper correction." This is a joke because she and I both know that Nate is the one person in this house she doesn't seem to worry about.

"Hey now, not fair teasing your brother when he's not here to defend himself," she says automatically. Then she focuses in on my face, pained, and I immediately know what she's thinking.

Escaping her look, I open the pantry door. I tear open a packet of chai powder and shake it into a mug, fill the kettle, and put it on a burner. Then I turn back to her. "Seriously, Mom, I know you're stressed that I'm going to end up like Dad, but honestly? He's got a pretty good life, if you think about it. Good job, good wife, good son, *gorgeous* daughter." I wink at her, trying to lighten her mood. "He could do a lot worse."

"Mm, I don't know if you noticed, but he's also pretty depressed."

That's true. Can't argue with that. But does she want us all to be depressed with him? I go and get a spoon out of the drawer and stand next to the kettle, willing it to whistle through the silence. It resists, punishing me for watching it.

She seems to read my mind in return. "Forget I said anything," she says, running her hands through her hair, "I don't want you to worry about him. It's not a child's job to worry about their parents."

Why do parents always say shit like this? Stuff that puts them on one side and kids on the other? It's so binary, so black and white and . . . totally unrealistic.

"Look, the fact is I do worry about Dad sometimes, Mom, and I don't think that's so terrible. He's a person, and I'm a person, and people worry about each other. But I'm not worried about him right now. You know why? Because I think this depression is temporary. Like maybe even now he's starting to come out of it."

"I hope that's true." She pauses. "It's one of those hard things in life—loving someone who's struggling, and you can't really help. All you can do is just keep on loving them. You know how much I love your dad, right?"

"Of course I know, Mom." Not the worst thing in the world to hear her say it every once in a while, though.

"And what about you?" she says, and I can hear the exhaustion. "How are you going to handle the progression? You always take things so *hard*, Hattie. You're so *sensitive*. I worry about you heading down the same path."

The kettle finally comes to my rescue. I pour the hot water in and stir. When I speak again, new thoughts are taking hold.

"The RP is not a choice. I'm stuck with it. But what I do while having RP *is* a choice. A choice that is one hundred percent mine." Ever since I got my diagnosis, everything has felt like it was happening *to* me, like I was out of options. But that's not true, really. I mean . . . "Yes, some things are out of my control. I can't drive no matter how much I want to. But I still have options." How I move through the world in general will have limitations. But there's still an infinite number of decision points, as many as there were stars in the sky last night. The thought of all that possibility fills my lungs. I take a sip of the chai and smile. Do I want to be an actor? Maybe I won't be able to navigate backstage in a theater, but I could do Shakespeare in the Park in the bright summer sun. Or I could do commercials. Or movies! And if I go totally blind? I put my mug down and spread my fingers out on the cold granite countertop. I can't remember the last time I saw a blind character in a play or a movie. So where is the choice there? I know right away what Mason would say to that. "Well, Murph, maybe you'll just have to fucking write the play yourself." Write the play myself. That last thought causes a thrill to shiver through me.

My mom is listening, waiting for me to say something else. Is she getting it? She's really not that different from Mrs. Leary. Even though I'm alive and breathing and standing right in front of her, she's holding all this weight, taking all the responsibility for everything that's ever happened to me in the past and will happen to me in the future.

I sit kitty-corner to her and almost chuckle. Here she is labeling me as sensitive when she takes everything at least as hard as I do. "Mom, I know it's tough for you whenever you feel like I'm on my own or being independent or whatever. But I also know you know that it's good for me deep down."

"Of course. I know you need to individuate. I've read the books!" She laughs. "It's so important," she says more softly.

"Yeah, except what I think you don't think about is that it's good for you, too."

"Well, you'll always be my baby," she says, like it's a reflex.

"That's not what I mean. I mean, you don't have to be scared for me. I'm going to be okay. I really am. And if I'm not okay sometimes, well, that will be okay, too. It'll be good." Her hands are folded on the table and I put my hands on top of them, feeling calm in how sure I am about what I just said.

She takes one hand out from under mine and sandwiches my hands in hers. "How did I get such a smart, mature daughter?"

I stand up and toss my hair behind my shoulders, playful. "Who knows?" I tease. "But keep working at it and maybe one day you'll deserve it."

She raises an eyebrow. "You're going to mock me and in the next breath—what?—ask me for a ride?"

I laugh and kiss the top of her head. "Exactly."

"I know this 5K is in honor of Mason, but he would never approve of anything that started at eight a.m. on a Saturday," Jeff says when he arrives at the makeshift booth we've constructed at the end of Main Street. Two dowels are duct-taped on each side to hold up a butcher paper banner announcing, RUN FOR EPILEPSY AWARENESS! and then, in smaller font underneath, CHECK IN HERE.

"It's not my fault. That's what time races *start*," Lucia says, unfazed as ever by Jeff's razzing. "Also, you're complaining to the wrong people. Asha, Hattie, and I have been here since six thirty setting up."

This reminder that I've been working in the freezing cold for an hour causes me to pull my hat farther down over my ears. "At least running will make us warm." I smile as I hand the tablet to two more runners to sign in and then give them their race numbers, taking off my mittens for the fiftieth time in twenty minutes to pick out eight tiny safety pins from the box so they can pin their bibs to their chests.

Across the street, Asha has her own card table for her speakers, which are pointed directly at us. Once again, she has managed to get out of joining the rest of us lemmings in the prescribed activity by providing the musical accompaniment for said event. Normally, I would watch her in awe, wondering what it must feel like to call your own shots all the time, but if

I've learned anything recently, it's that other people's lives aren't as simple or as perfect as they look.

With her headphones over one ear, she transitions to some Lil Nas X, and a few of the runners waiting behind the starting line start to bounce in time to the beat. I catch her eye and jerk my thumb up toward the sky, and she turns the volume up a couple of notches. I show my approval by doing some of my nerdiest dance moves. The lawn mower dance, the sprinkler dance, all the classics.

As she covers her mouth to stifle her laughter at me, Lincoln sneaks up behind her and puts his hands over her eyes. She strokes the hands, seeming to know who they belong to, and then turns toward him, disappearing into his bear hug. It must be refreshing for Asha, to feel small and delicate next to Lincoln, when often she's the tallest one in class. They are so freaking cute. I never would have picked him for her. I add that to my continually unspooling list of evidence that I have been stupid about people.

There's another guy next to Lincoln, but it's not one of his usual crew. He has a kind smile and the kind of lean muscles that wear a fitted shirt really well. His face looks familiar—do I know him? Then it comes to me. It's my cowboy waiter from the ski resort! What is he doing here?

As if my eyes are shooting laser beams across the street, he seems to feel my stare and looks up. He waves at me, then saunters over in a way I imagine only Southerners can do.

"Hey there, how's your horse wrangling these days?" he says.

It takes me a second to figure out what he's referring to. When I do, I feel a flush of pleasure at the fact that our conversation made enough of an impression for him to remember that detail.

"I've tangled with some pretty wild stallions, actually," I reply. I mean that to be a clever metaphor, but instantly realize it maybe sounds like I've been fooling around with a bunch of guys. I shift gears. "What are you doing here? And did you bring loaded Tater Tots with you?"

"Ha! I wish. I haven't even seen a Tater Tot for about a month. Which is nice—I was starting to have nightmares that I was being swept out to sea on a tidal wave of Tater Tot grease."

"Well, guess it's lucky you're here then. This town is entirely landlocked. Not one Tater Tot tidal wave on the books."

"Good to know. I've got to get educated on my new home."

I swallow. "You moved here?"

He nods. "Two weeks ago. Snowcap Mountain was just a temporary stop on the highway of life. I'll be starting at the high school after Christmas break."

I feel a momentary panic. "As . . . a . . . teacher?"

"What? Oh no, ma'am. I'm a senior."

"Right, of course. Um, welcome, then. I thought maybe you were done with high school." I mean seriously, what brand of growth hormones are they putting in boys' cereal these days?

"It's the facial hair." He's right; that and his impeccable manners had me confused. "I turned seventeen on Halloween."

"A Halloween baby? That's cool. You must have the best birthday parties."

He grins. "I'll be sure to invite you to the next one and then you can tell me how it ranks." Is this flirting? I bite my lip.

Some more runners walk up behind him, and he moves to the side to let them approach the table. After he watches me do my "mittens off–four safety pins–mittens on" routine a few times, he starts counting out the pins for me, since his fingers are bare.

"So, speaking of facial hair," I say, "how do you know Lincoln?"

"We just met yesterday. I had a job interview at that restaurant down the street–the Hollywood?–and Lincoln was on shift. Anyway, he told me this was happening, so I thought I'd come support."

Of course, that would be just like my cowboy to make friends so easily. I flush deeper at the realization that my brain thinks of him as "my" anything. It's a good thing that it's cold outside, otherwise my red cheeks would be a dead giveaway of how happy all my nerve endings are to see him.

"Did you get the job?"

"I start Thursday."

"Well, see if you can get them to put Tater Tots on the menu."

"Only if you promise to come in and order them from me."

There's that charge of pleasure again. "It's a deal. I'm Hattie, by the way."

"Jay," he says, enveloping my mittened hand in both his bare ones. "Want to run-slash-walk together, Hattie?"

"Yeah, sure." It's not until I turn to ask Lucia if she thinks she can handle the last few stragglers on her own that I realize she's been staring at us, open-mouthed and eyes all twinkly, for some time. She answers my question before I can ask it.

"Go, go, go!" she says, practically shoving me away from the table. "I'll finish up here. Nice to meet you, by the way, Jay. I'm sorry my rude friend didn't introduce us. I'm Lucia."

"That's Lucia," I echo. "Lucia, Jay. Jay, Lucia."

Jay actually touches his hat in Lucia's direction, which could not be more cowboy, even though it's a White Sox baseball cap. "Thanks for sparing her."

"No problem. You two kids have fun," she replies, ever the maternal type. Part of me wishes she could play it a little cooler and not seem so obviously excited for this match, but most of me is glad she's seeing this. Whatever happens now, it won't be a secret from the Beaver Bunch.

As we walk over to the starting line, a parking curb I don't see catches my right toe and I almost go flying. Jay grabs my elbow and pulls me back up. "You okay there, Hattie?" he asks, his eyes smiling.

"Yes, thanks," I say, and then, I don't know why, I keep talking. "I have poor peripheral vision from a genetic eye disease." Awkward, yes. Positively cringy. But ultimately, just true.

The expression in his eyes goes from teasing to one of concern. Not like he's worried about me, exactly. More like he's paying very close attention.

"Well, all right. Stick close to me during this race then, just in case."

In this moment, there's nothing I'd like more.

Jeff and Lincoln both join us at the back of the pack to wait for the start. Amanda shows up, and I introduce her to Jay, aware of how much easier it is to be around her and a boy I like when I'm not jealous of her. Then I pull her aside.

"Hey, I've been meaning to ask you. Do you think you could give me the number of that therapist you see?"

"Of course! She's the best. Is everything okay?" she asks, cocking her head.

"Absolutely. Just, you know, dealing with life."

"I hear that," she says, squeezing my arm.

The gun goes off and we run. Normally, it would be hard for me not to race for time, to try to get a personal best or pick off runners in front of me. But today, that seems wonderfully pointless. We all jog along, laughing and talking, each burst of giggles making a cloud of steam in front of us.

Soon we're outside town, the houses dropping away and leaving cow pastures and patches of trees in their place. We turn onto a road with a sloping hill and my pulse pounds a little harder. This is where I drove. In front of me, I see the dark slashes of the skid marks from that day angling off the road. It makes me a little dizzy.

"Want to walk?" Jay has slowed and is looking at me closely in that way of his again.

I shake my head slightly and speed up, trying to run away from the feeling. Suddenly, Mason is up ahead, standing on the side of the road just like before, except this time he's waving a banner like a bona fide race supporter.

I sprint toward him, not really sure what I'm going to do when I get there.

But it's a false alarm. When I get close, I see it's not Mason with a banner at all, it's the flag to mark a turn in our course, to tell us which way to go.

So I hug the turn, brushing past the flag, my feet light on the pavement. And I realize—it doesn't matter anymore whether Mason was ever really appearing in my peripheral vision in the first place, or if I was only imagining it because it hurt too much not to. Either way, I had additional time with him that no one else got, like a bonus round. I snort to myself. What I got with Mason, what I had to get in order to not totally implode, was an extra-long goodbye. That's very uncharacteristic of me, or at least the old me. And I wouldn't trade it, because getting real with him made me dig into all the ways I'm broken. They actually aren't so terrible. There's nothing I need to pretend doesn't exist.

I've accidentally put space between me and the group, but now Jay is catching up with me again; I hear his even breath coming up on my right.

"Whoa, you really know how to turn on the gas," he says, matching my footsteps.

Laughing, I slow down so I can take breaks from looking at the road to look up at his face. His cheeks are flushed and full of life, and his eyebrows are raised as if he's anticipating something fun. His face is loaded with fascinating details: a small scar on his right temple, the arch of his hairline. And of course, his dimples. I make a mental note to stare at him more after the race.

"I tend to get carried away," I say.

"Then let's do that," he says.

"If you think you can handle it."

"C'mon, Firecracker."

We both accelerate. On the downslope, the wind is at our backs, pushing us forward. It makes it feel easy, like I'm weightless, like I can just be. The universe definitely does not hate me today.

Maybe it never did.

ACKNOWLEDGMENTS

Jennifer March Soloway, nothing has made me believe in the idea of "meant to be" more than meeting you at the Big Sur Children's Writing Workshop. I think back often to how I basically got the zoomies when I saw you on that last morning because I knew you were about to change my life. I won the agent lottery with you and am still a bit in awe as to how I got so lucky. Your editorial instincts, your emotional support, your optimism combined with sharpened business savvy, and your delightful way of being authentic and hilarious while sharing gems of wisdom are just a few of the qualities I have reaped the benefit of while working with you. Thank you so much. Onward!

Maya Marlette, from our very first conversation I knew that you really *got* Hattie, and by extension, me! You infused every note you gave with a deep understanding of the heart of this book, and taking your notes was easy because they always felt like the exact right thing to do. You elevated the story tenfold. Plus, reading in the margins to see all the places where you laughed at my jokes fed me more than any food. Thank you so much for all the enthusiasm, expertise, sensitivity, and intuition that you brought to this work.

And thank you to everyone at Scholastic for giving such attention to detail, for polishing this book until it shone. I'm so darn proud of it now, and that is partly because of all of you.

Rombutan, I'm so thankful for your gorgeous cover art. It is such a *vibe.* I have yet to look at the cover without getting tears in my eyes.

Colleen and Meghann, you are my rocks. My writing rocks. My lovely, intelligent, loyal writing rocks. Thank you for all your creative help, and for keeping the gremlins of imposter syndrome from creeping in and wreaking havoc.

Thank you to all the teachers and writers of the UCLA Extension Writers' Program, especially Mark Sarvas, and my fellow Novel Revision students: Brigid, Katie, Krista, and Shannon. What a wonderful little instant writing community we made!

I also owe SCBWI a debt of gratitude for providing me with my training wheels when I was still figuring out what kind of writer I wanted to be. Especially the Los Angeles chapter. Y'all work so hard, and your joy in your work is apparent.

Thank you to my mom, dad, and brother, Nick. You have always made sure that I know how proud you are of me, and I'm here for it!

Cooper and Lucy, the fact of the matter is that I probably would never have started writing for the under-eighteen crowd if I hadn't had two amazing examples of that crowd in my house to inspire me. You have always had utter faith in me, and your genuine excitement about each progressive stage of this process has increased my own. I am so touched by how proudly you introduce me to your friends now as your mom: "She's a writer." I guess I really am, huh?

Chad, thanks for pushing me to celebrate each and every writing win. Christy, Kelly, Lesley, thanks for always asking for updates and being ready to celebrate each win as boisterously as if it was your own. You are the definition of excellent friends.

Aaron, your unwavering championing of "author me" is everything. You held the torch of taking me seriously until I was strong enough to hold it myself, and for that I am forever grateful. Thanks for being ready to pitch jokes at our impromptu morning brainstorming sessions in the family room, for bringing in your "scissors skills" when I needed to start cutting, and for letting me see you cry when you were reading my first draft. You are the bestest husband.

And finally, thank you to the Foundation Fighting Blindness. Your unflagging efforts to fund research and explore emerging treatments for retinal diseases are a beacon of hope for people like me and my family. Hopefully, more people will join you in the effort as a result of this book, and soon people with conditions like Hattie's will only exist on shelves of fiction.

ABOUT THE AUTHOR

Photo credit: Theo & Juliet

Kate Korsh has been a public school teacher as well as a licensed marriage and family therapist for teens. Kate has retinitis pigmentosa, and though she still has her driver's license, her night blindness requires her to keep a vampire's schedule in reverse and be parked at home before sunset. She is the author of the chapter book series Oona Bramblegoop's Sideways Magic. She lives in Los Angeles with her husband and two children.